ENTHUSIASTIC ACCLAIM FOR A CRIME FICTION
GIANT—*NEW YORK TIMES* BESTSELLING
GRAND MASTER

TONY HILLERMAN

"An amazing writer. . . . Hillerman's mysteries are
a lesson in how to make the form irresistible
storytelling."
Albuquerque Journal

"Hillerman's stories never grow old. Like myths,
they keep evolving with the telling."
New York Times Book Review

"All of Tony Hillerman's Navajo
Tribal Police novels have been brilliant."
USA Today

"What he communicates better than almost any
other suspense writer is a different sense of time,
a different sense of connection to nature,
a different way of being."
Ft. Worth Star-Telegram

"Hillerman transcends the mystery genre."
Washington Post Book World

"Hillerman's novels are like no others."
San Diego Union-Tribune

"His Leaphorn/Chee series is one of the most
original and influential in modern crime fiction."
Portland Sunday Oregonian

"We couldn't do better for a true voice of the West."
Denver Rocky Mountain News

A THIEF OF TIME

A THIEF OF TIME

A Leaphorn and Chee Novel

TONY HILLERMAN

HARPER

NEW YORK • LONDON • TORONTO • SYDNEY

HARPER

A hardcover edition of this book was originally published in 1988 by Harper & Row, Publishers.

FIRST HARPER PREMIUM PAPERBACK PRINTING JUNE 2009.
FIRST HARPERTORCH PAPERBACK PRINTING DECEMBER 2000.
FIRST HARPER PAPERBACKS EDITION PUBLISHED JANUARY 1990; REISSUED JULY 2019.

Library of Congress Cataloging-in-Publication Data has been applied for.

ISBN 978-0-06-289548-6 (pbk.)

19 20 21 22 23   LSC   10 9 8 7 6 5 4 3 2 1

With special thanks to Dan Murphy of the U.S. Park Service for pointing me to the ruins down the San Juan River, to Charley and Susan De-Lorme and the other river lovers of Wild River Expeditions, to Kenneth Tsosie of White Horse Lake, to Ernie Bulow, and to the Tom and Jan Vaughn family of Chaco Culture National Historical Park. All characters in this book are imaginary. True, Drayton and Noi Vaughn actually do make the sixty-mile bus ride to school each morning but they are even classier in real life than the fictitious counterparts found herein.

This story is dedicated to Steven Lovato,
firstborn son of Larry and Mary Lovato.
May he always go with beauty
all around him.

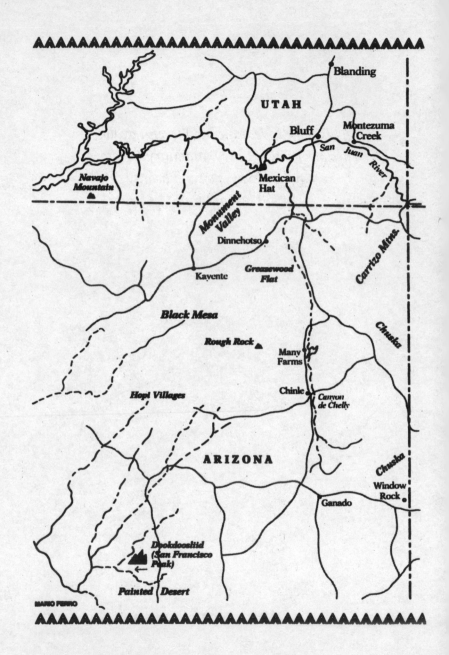

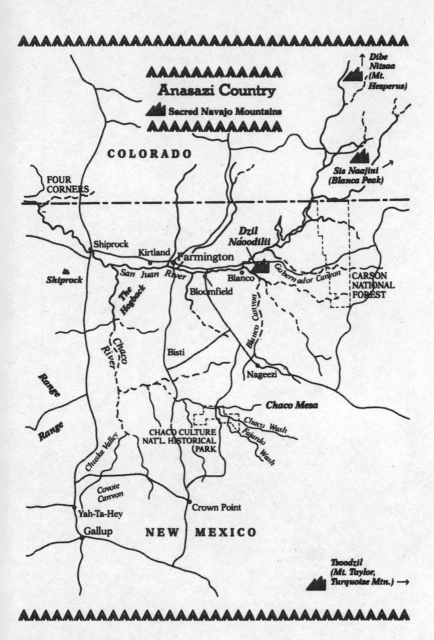

AAAAAAAAAAAAAAAAAAAAAAAAAAAAAAAAAAAAA

AAAAAAAAAAAA
Anasazi Country
▲▲▲ Sacred Navajo Mountains
AAAAAAAAAAAA

↑ *Dibe Nitsaa (Mt. Hesperus)*

COLORADO

Sis Naajini (Blanca Peak)

FOUR CORNERS

Shiprock   Kirtland   Farmington
Shiprock   *Dzil Náoodilii*
                          Blanco
San Juan River   *Gobernador Canyon*
                   Bloomfield   **CARSON NATIONAL FOREST**
The Hogback
                                    Blanco Canyon
Chaco River   Bisti

                                      Nageezi

Range
                          Chaco Mesa
Range   *Chaco Wash*
                  CHACO CULTURE   *Fajardo Wash*
Chuska Valley   **NAT'L HISTORICAL PARK**

Coyote Canyon
Yah-Ta-Hey   Crown Point
Gallup   **NEW   MEXICO**

Tsoodzil (Mt. Taylor, Turquoise Mtn.) →

AAAAAAAAAAAAAAAAAAAAAAAAAAAAAAAAAAAA

AUTHOR'S NOTE: While most of the places in this volume are real, Many Ruins Canyon has had its name changed and its location tinkered with to protect its unvandalized cliff ruins.

A THIEF OF TIME

ONE

THE MOON HAD RISEN just above the cliff behind her. Out on the packed sand of the wash bottom the shadow of the walker made a strange elongated shape. Sometimes it suggested a heron, sometimes one of those stick-figure forms of an Anasazi pictograph. An animated pictograph, its arms moving rhythmically as the moon shadow drifted across the sand. Sometimes, when the goat trail bent and put the walker's profile against the moon, the shadow became Kokopelli himself. The backpack formed the spirit's grotesque hump, the walking stick Kokopelli's crooked flute. Seen from above, the shadow would have made a Navajo believe that the great *yei* northern clans called Watersprinkler had taken visible form. If an Anasazi had risen from his thousand-year grave in the trash heap under the cliff ruins here, he would have seen the Humpbacked Flute Player, the rowdy god of fertility of his lost people. But the shadow was only the shape of Dr. Eleanor Friedman-Bernal blocking out the light of an October moon.

Dr. Friedman-Bernal rested now, sitting on a convenient rock, removing her backpack, rubbing her shoulders, letting the cold, high desert air evaporate the sweat that had soaked her shirt, reconsidering a long day.

No one could have seen her. Of course, they had seen her driving away from Chaco. The children were up in the gray dawn to catch their school bus. And the children would chat about it to their parents. In that tiny, isolated Park Service society of a dozen adults and two children, everyone knew everything about everybody. There was absolutely no possibility of privacy. But she had done everything right. She had made the rounds of the permanent housing and checked with everyone on the digging team. She was driving into Farmington, she'd said. She'd collected the outgoing mail to be dropped off at the Blanco Trading Post. She had jotted down the list of supplies people needed. She'd told Maxie she had the Chaco fever—needed to get away, see a movie, have a restaurant dinner, smell exhaust fumes, hear a different set of voices, make phone calls back to civilization on a telephone that would actually work. She would spend a night where she could hear the sounds of civilization, something besides the endless Chaco silence. Maxie was sympathetic. If Maxie suspected anything, she suspected Dr. Eleanor Friedman-Bernal was meeting Lehman. That would have been fine with Eleanor Friedman-Bernal.

The handle of the folding shovel she had strapped to her pack was pressing against her back. She stopped, shifted the weight, and adjusted the pack straps. Somewhere in the darkness up the canyon she could hear the odd screeching call of a saw-whet owl, hunting nocturnal rodents. She glanced at her watch: 10:11, changing to 10:12 as she watched. Time enough.

No one had seen her in Bluff. She was sure of that. She had called from Shiprock, just to make doubly sure that no one was using Bo Arnold's old house out on the highway. No one had answered. The house was dark when she'd arrived, and she'd left it that way, finding the key under the flower box where Bo always left it. She'd done her borrowing carefully, disturbing nothing. When she put it back, Bo would never guess it had been missing. Not that it would matter. Bo was a biologist, scraping out a living as a part-timer with the Bureau of Land Management while he finished his dissertation on desert lichens, or whatever it was he was studying. He hadn't given a damn about anything else when she'd known him at Madison, and he didn't now.

She yawned, stretched, reached for her backpack, decided to rest a moment longer. She'd been up about nineteen hours. She had maybe two more to go before she reached the site. Then she'd roll out the sleeping bag and not get out of it until she was rested. No hurry now. She thought about Lehman. Big. Ugly. Smart. Gray. Sexy. Lehman was coming. She'd wine him and dine him and show him what she had. And he would have to be impressed. He'd have to agree she'd proved her case. That wasn't necessary for publication—his approval. But for some reason, it was necessary to her. And that irrationality made her think of Maxie. Maxie and Elliot.

She smiled, and rubbed her face. It was quiet here, just a few insects making their nocturnal sounds. Windless. The cold air settling into the canyon. She shivered, picked up the backpack, and struggled into it. A coyote was barking somewhere over on Comb Wash far behind her. She could hear another across the wash, very distant, yipping in celebration of the moonlight. She walked rapidly up the packed sand, lifting her legs high to stretch them, not thinking of what she would do tonight. She had thought long enough of that. Perhaps too long. Instead she thought of Maxie and Elliot. Brains, both. But nuts. The Blueblood and the Poorjane. The Man Who Could Do Anything obsessed by the woman who said nothing he did counted. Poor Elliot! He could never win.

A flash of lightning on the eastern horizon— much too distant to hear the thunder and the wrong direction to threaten any rain. A last gasp of summer, she thought. The moon was higher now, its light muting the colors of the canyon into shades of gray. Her thermal underwear and the walking kept her body warm but her hands were like ice. She studied them. No hands for a lady. Nails blunt and broken. The skin tough, scarred, callused. Anthropology skin, they'd called it when she was an undergraduate. The skin of people who are always out under the sun, work-ing in the dirt. It had always bothered her mother, as everything about her bothered her mother. Becoming an anthropologist instead of a doctor, and then not marrying a doctor. Marrying a Puerto Rican archaeologist who was not even Jewish. And then losing him to another woman. "Wear gloves," her mother had said. "For heaven's sake, Ellie, you have hands like a dirt farmer."

And a face like a dirt farmer too, she'd thought.

The canyon was just as she remembered from the summer she had helped map and catalog its sites. A great place for pictographs. Just ahead, just beyond the cottonwoods on the sheer sandstone wall where the canyon bottom bent, was a gallery of them. The baseball gallery, they called it, because of the great shaman figure that someone had thought resembled a cartoon version of an umpire.

The moon lit only part of the wall, and the slanting light made it difficult to see, but she stopped to inspect it. In this light, the tapered, huge-shouldered shape of the mystic Anasazi shaman lost its color and became merely a dark form. Above it a clutter of shapes danced, stick figures, abstractions: the inevitable Kokopelli, his humped shape bent, his flute pointed almost at the ground; a heron flying; a heron standing; the zigzag band of pigment representing a snake. Then she noticed the horse.

It stood well to the left of the great baseball shaman, mostly in moon shadow. A Navajo addition, obviously, since the Anasazi had vanished three hundred years before the Spanish came on their steeds. It was a stylized horse, with a barrel body and straight legs, but without the typical Navajo tendency to build beauty into everything they attempted. The rider seemed to be a Kokopelli—Watersprinkler, the Navajos called him. At least the rider seemed to be blowing a flute. Had this addition been there before? She couldn't remember. Such Navajo additions weren't uncommon. But this one puzzled her.

Then she noticed, at each of three feet of the animal, a tiny prone figure. Three. Each with the little circle representing the head separated from the body. Each with one leg cut away.

Sick. And they hadn't been here four years ago. These she would have remembered.

For the first time Eleanor Friedman-Bernal became aware of the darkness, the silence, her total isolation. She had dropped her backpack while she rested. Now she picked it up, put an arm through the carry strap, changed her mind. She unzipped a side pocket and extracted the pistol. It was a .25 caliber automatic. The salesman had shown her how to load it, how the safety worked, how to hold it. He had told her it was accurate, easy to use, and made in Belgium. He had not told her that it took an unusual ammunition that one always had to hunt for. She had never tried it out in Madison. There never seemed to be a place to shoot it safely. But when she came to New Mexico, the first day when there was enough wind to blow away the sound, she'd driven out into the emptiness on the road toward Crownpoint and practiced with it. She had fired it at rocks, and deadwood, and shadows on the sand, until it felt natural and comfortable and she was hitting things, or getting close enough. When she used up most of the box of cartridges, she found the sporting goods store in Farmington didn't have them. And neither did the big place in Albuquerque, and finally she had ordered them out of a catalog. Now she had seventeen bullets left in the new box. She had brought six of them with her. A full magazine. The pistol felt cold in her hand, cold and hard and reassuring.

She dropped it into the pocket of her jacket. As she regained the sandy bottom of the wash and walked up it, she was conscious of the heaviness against her hip. The coyotes were closer, two of them somewhere above her, on the mesa beyond the clifftops. Sometimes the night breeze gusted enough to make its sounds in the brush along the bottom, rattling the leaves on the Russian olives and whispering through the fronds of the tamarisks. Usually it was still. Runoff from the summer monsoons had filled pools along the rocky bottom. Most of these were nearly dry now, but she could hear frogs, and crickets, and insects she couldn't identify. Something made a clicking sound in the darkness where dead tumbleweed had collected against the cliff, and from somewhere ahead she heard what sounded like a whistle. A night bird?

The canyon wound under the cliff and out of the moonlight. She turned on her flash. No risk of anyone seeing it. And that turned her thoughts to how far the nearest human would be. Not far as the bird flies—perhaps fifteen or twenty miles as the crow flew. But no easy way in. No roads across the landscape of almost solid stone, and no reason to build roads. No reason for the Anasazi to come here, for that matter, except to escape something that was hunting them. None that the anthropologists could think of—not even the cultural anthropologists with their notorious talents for forming theories without evidence. But come they had. And with them came her artist. Leaving Chaco Canyon behind her. Coming here to create more of her pots and to die.

From where Dr. Friedman-Bernal was walking she could see one of their ruins low on the cliff wall to her right. Had it been daylight, she remembered, she could have seen two more in the huge amphitheater alcove on the cliff to her left. But now the alcove was black with shadow—looking a little like a great gaping mouth.

She heard squeaking. Bats. She'd noticed a few just after sundown. Here they swarmed, fluttering over places where runoff had filled potholes and potholes had bred insects. They flashed past her face, just over her hair. Watching them, Ellie Friedman-Bernal didn't watch where she was walking. A rock turned under her foot, and she lost her balance.

The backpack cost her enough of her usual

grace to make the fall hard and clumsy. She broke it with her right hand, hip, and elbow and found herself sprawled on the stream bottom, hurt, shocked, and shaken.

The elbow was most painful. It had scraped over the sandstone, tearing her shirt and leaving an abrasion that, when she touched it, stained her finger with blood. Then her bruised hip got her attention, but it was numb now and would punish her later. It was only when she scrambled back to her feet that she noticed the cut across the palm of her hand. She examined it in the light of her flash, made a sympathetic clicking sound, and then sat down to deal with it.

She picked out a bit of the gravel imbedded in the heel of her hand, rinsed the cut from her canteen, and bandaged it with a handkerchief, using left hand and teeth to tighten the knot. And then she continued up the wash, more careful now, leaving the bats behind, following a turn back into the full moonlight and then another into the shadows. Here she climbed onto a low alluvial ledge beside the dry streambed and dumped her pack. It was a familiar place. She and Eduardo Bernal had pitched a tent here five summers ago when they were graduate students, lovers, and part of the site-mapping team. Eddie Bernal. Tough little Ed. Fun while it lasted. But not much fun for long. Soon, surely before Christmas, she would drop the hyphen. Ed would hardly notice. A sigh of relief, perhaps. End of that brief phase when he'd thought one woman would be enough.

She removed a rock, some sticks, smoothed the ground with the edge of her boot sole, dug out and softened an area where her hips would be, and then rolled out the sleeping bag. She chose the place where she had lain with Eddie. Why? Partly defiance, partly sentiment, partly because it was simply the most comfortable spot. Tomorrow would be hard work and the cuts on her palm would make digging difficult and probably painful. But she wasn't ready for sleep yet. Too much tension. Too much uneasiness.

Standing here beside the sleeping bag, out of the moonlight, more stars were visible. She checked the autumn constellations, found the polestar, got her directions exactly right. Then she stared across the wash into the darkness that hid what she and Eddie had called Chicken Condo. In the narrow stone alcove, Anasazi families had built a two-story dwelling probably big enough for thirty people. Above it, in another alcove so hidden that they wouldn't have noticed it had Eddie not wondered where an evening bat flight was coming from, the Anasazi had built a little stone fort reachable only by a precarious set of hand- and footholds. It was around the lower dwelling that Eleanor Friedman-Bernal first had found the peculiar potsherds. If her memory didn't fool her. It was there, when it was light enough tomorrow, that she would dig. In violation of Navajo law, of federal law, and of professional ethics. If her memory only had not fooled her. And now she had more evidence than just her memory.

She couldn't wait until daylight. Not now. Not this near. Her flashlight would be enough to check.

Her memory had been excellent. It took her unerringly and without a misstep on an easy climb up the talus slope and along the natural pathway to the rim. There she paused and turned her light onto the cliff. The petroglyphs were exactly as she had stored them in her mind. The spiral that might represent the *sipapu* from which humans had emerged from the womb of Mother Earth, the line of dots that might represent the clan's migrations, the wide-shouldered forms that the ethnographers believed represented kachina spirits. There, too, cut through the dark desert varnish into the face of the cliff, was the shape Eddie had called Big Chief looking out from behind a red-stained shield, and a figure that seemed to have a man's body but the feet and head of a heron. It was one of her two favorites, because it seemed so totally unexplainable even by the cultural anthropologists—who could explain anything. The other was another version of Kokopelli.

Wherever you found him—and you found him everywhere these vanished people carved, and painted, their spirits into the cliffs of the Southwest—Kokopelli looked about the same. His humpbacked figure was supported by stick legs. Stick arms held a straight line to his tiny round head, making him seem to be playing a clarinet. The flute might be pointed down, or ahead. Otherwise there was little variation in how he was depicted. Except here. Here Kokopelli was lying on his back, flute pointed skyward. "At last," Eddie had said. "You have found Kokopelli's home. This is where he sleeps."

But Eleanor Friedman-Bernal hardly glanced at Kokopelli now. The Chicken Condo was just around the corner. That was what had drawn her.

The first things her eyes picked up when the beam of her flash lit the total darkness of the alcove were flecks of white where nothing white should be. She let the flash roam over the broken walls, reflect from the black surface of the seepfed pool below them. Then she moved the beam back to that incongruous reflection. It was exactly what she had feared.

Bones. Bones scattered everywhere.

"Oh, shit!" said Eleanor Friedman-Bernal, who almost never used expletives. "Shit! Shit! Shit!"

Someone had been digging. Someone had been looting. A pot hunter. A Thief of Time. Someone had gotten here first.

She focused on the nearest white. A human shoulder bone. A child's. It lay atop a pile of loose earth just outside a place where the wall had fallen. The excavation was in the hump of earth that had been this community's trash heap. The common place for burials, and the first place experienced pot hunters dug. But the hole here was small. She felt better. Perhaps not much damage had been done. The digging looked fresh. Perhaps what she was hunting would still be here. She explored with the flash, looking for other signs of digging. She found none.

Nor was there any sign of looting elsewhere. She shined the light into the single hole dug in the midden pile. It reflected off stones, a scattering of potsherds mixed with earth and what seemed to be more human bones—part of a foot, she thought, and a vertebra. Beside the pit, on a slab of sandstone, four lower jaws had been placed in a neat row—three adult, one not much beyond infancy. She frowned at the arrangement, raised her eyebrows. Considered. Looked around her again. It hadn't rained—at least no rain had blown into this sheltered place—since this digging had been done. But then when had it rained? Not for weeks at Chaco. But Chaco was almost two hundred miles east and south.

The night was still. Behind her, she heard the odd piping of the little frogs that seemed to thrive in this canyon wherever water collected. Leopard frogs, Eddie had called them. And she heard the whistle again. The night bird. Closer now. A half-dozen notes. She frowned. A bird? What else could it be? She had seen at least three kinds of lizards on her way from the river—a whiptail, and a big collared lizard, and another she couldn't identify. They were nocturnal. Did they make some sort of mating whistle?

At the pool, her flashlight reflected scores of tiny points of light—the eyes of frogs. She stood watching them as they hopped, panicked by her huge presence, toward the safety of the black water. Then she frowned. Something was strange.

Not six feet from where she stood, one of them had fallen back in midhop. Then she noticed another one, a half-dozen others. She squatted on her heels beside the frog, inspecting it. And then another, and another, and another.

They were tethered. A whitish thread—perhaps a yucca fiber—had been tied around a back leg of each of these tiny black-green frogs and then to a twig stuck into the damp earth.

Eleanor Friedman-Bernal leaped to her feet,

flashed the light frantically around the pool. Now she could see the scores of panicked frogs making those odd leaps that ended when a tether jerked them back to earth. For seconds her mind struggled to process this crazy, unnatural, irrational information. Who would . . . ? It would have to be a human act. It could have no sane purpose. When? How long could these frogs live just out of reach of the saving water? It was insane.

Just then she heard the whistle again. Just behind her. Not a night bird. No sort of reptile. It was a melody the Beatles had made popular. "Hey, Jude," the words began. But Eleanor didn't recognize it. She was too terrified by the humped shape that was coming out of the moonlight into this pool of darkness.

TWO

"**ELEANOR FRIEDMAN HYPHEN BERNAL.**" Thatcher spaced the words, pronouncing them evenly. "I'm uneasy about women who hyphenate their names."

Lieutenant Joe Leaphorn didn't respond. Had he ever met a hyphenated woman? Not that he could remember. But the custom seemed sensible to him. Not as odd as Thatcher's discomfort with it. Leaphorn's mother, Leaphorn's aunts, all of the women he could think of among his maternal Red Forehead clan, would have resisted the idea of submerging their name or family identity in that of a husband. Leaphorn considered mentioning that, and didn't feel up to it. He'd been tired when Thatcher had picked him up at Navajo Tribal Police headquarters. Now he had added approximately 120 miles of driving to that fatigue.

From Window Rock through Yah-Ta-Hey, to Crownpoint, to those final twenty jarring dirt miles to the Chaco Culture National Historical Park. Leaphorn's inclination had been to turn down the invitation to come along. But Thatcher had asked him as a favor.

"First job as a cop since they trained me," Thatcher had said. "May need some advice." It wasn't that, of course. Thatcher was a confident man and Leaphorn understood why Thatcher had called him. It was the kindness of an old friend who wanted to help. And the alternative to going would be to sit on the bed in the silent room and finish sorting through what was left of Emma's things—deciding what to do with them.

"Sure," Leaphorn had said. "Be a nice ride."

Now they were in the Chaco visitors' center, sitting on the hard chairs, waiting for the right person to talk to. From the bulletin board, a face stared out at them through dark sunglasses. A THIEF OF TIME, the legend above it said. POT HUNT-ERS DESTROY AMERICA'S PAST.

"Appropriate," Thatcher said, nodding toward the poster, "but the picture should be a crowd scene. Cowboys, and county commissioners, and schoolteachers and pipeline workers, and everybody big enough to handle a shovel." He glanced at Leaphorn, looking for a response, and sighed.

"That road," he said. "I've been driving it thirty

years now and it never gets any better." He glanced at Leaphorn again.

"Yeah," Leaphorn said. Thatcher had called them ceramic chugholes. "Never gets wet enough to soften 'em up," he'd said. "Rains, the bumps just get greasy." Not quite true. Leaphorn remembered a night a lifetime ago when he was young, a patrolman working out of the Crownpoint subagency. Melting snow had made the Chaco chugholes wet enough to soften the ceramic. His patrol car had sunk into the sucking, bottomless caliche mud. He'd radioed Crownpoint but the dispatcher had no help to send him. So he'd walked two hours to the R.D. Ranch headquarters. He'd been a newlywed then, worried that Emma would be worried about him. A hand at the ranch had put chains on a four-wheel-drive pickup and pulled him out. Nothing had changed since then. Except the roads were a lifetime older. Except Emma was dead.

Thatcher had said something else. He had been looking at him, expecting some response, when he should have been watching the ruts.

Leaphorn had nodded.

"You weren't listening. I asked you why you decided to quit."

Leaphorn had said nothing for a while. "Just tired."

Thatcher had shaken his head. "You're going to miss it."

"No, you get older. Or wiser. You realize it doesn't really make any difference."

"Emma was a wonderful woman," Thatcher had told him. "This won't bring her back."

"No, it won't."

"She were alive, she'd say: 'Joe, don't quit.' She'd say, 'You can't quit living.' I've heard her say things just like that."

"Probably," Leaphorn had said. "But I just don't want to do it anymore."

"Okay," Thatcher drove awhile. "Change the subject. I think women who have hyphenated names like that are going to be rich. Old-money rich. Hard to work with. Stereotyping, but it's the way my mind works."

Then Leaphorn had been saved from thinking of something to say to that by an unusually jarring chughole. Now he was saved from thinking about it again. A medium-sized man wearing a neatly pressed U.S. Park Service uniform emerged from the doorway marked PERSONNEL ONLY. He walked into the field of slanting autumn sunlight streaming through the windows of the visitors' center. He looked at them curiously.

"I'm Bob Luna," he said. "This is about Ellie?"

Thatcher extracted a leather folder from his

jacket and showed Luna a Bureau of Land Management law enforcement badge. "L. D. Thatcher," he said. "And this is Lieutenant Leaphorn. Navajo Tribal Police. Need to talk to Ms. Friedman-Bernal." He pulled an envelope from his jacket pocket. "Have a search warrant here to take a look at her place."

Luna's expression was puzzled. At first glance he had looked surprisingly young to Leaphorn to be superintendent of such an important park—his round, good-humored face would be perpetually boyish. Now, in the sunlight, the networks of lines around his eyes and at the corners of his mouth were visible. The sun and aridity of the Colorado Plateau acts quickly on the skin of whites, but it takes time to deepen the furrows. Luna was older than he looked.

"Talk to her?" Luna said. "You mean she's here? She's come back?"

Now it was Thatcher's turn to be surprised. "Doesn't she work here?"

"But she's missing," Luna said. "Isn't that what you're here about? We reported it a week ago. More like two weeks."

"Missing?" Thatcher said. "Whadaya mean missing?"

Luna's face had become slightly flushed. He opened his mouth. Closed it. Inhaled. Young as he looked, Luna was superintendent of this park, which meant he had a lot of experience being patient with people.

"Week ago last Wednesday. . . . That would be twelve days ago, we called in and reported Ellie missing. She was supposed to be back the previous Monday. She hadn't showed up. Hadn't called. She'd gone into Farmington for the weekend. She had an appointment Monday evening, back out here, and hadn't showed up for that. Had another appointment Wednesday. Hadn't been here for that, either. Totally out of character. Something must have happened to her and that's what we reported."

"She's not here?" Thatcher said. He tapped the envelope with the search warrant in it against the palm of his hand.

"Who'd you call?" Leaphorn asked, surprised at himself even as he heard himself asking the question. This was none of his business. It was nothing he cared about. He was here only because Thatcher had wanted him to come. Had wheedled until it was easier, if you didn't care anyway, to come than not to come. He hadn't intended to butt in. But this floundering around was irritating.

"The sheriff," Luna said.

"Which one?" Leaphorn asked. Part of the park was in McKinley County, part in San Juan.

"San Juan County," Luna said. "At Farmington. Anyway, nobody came out. So we called again last Friday. When you showed up, I thought you'd come out to start looking into it."

"I guess we are now," Leaphorn said. "More or less."

"We have a complaint about her," Thatcher said. "Or rather an allegation. But very detailed, very specific. About violations of the Antiquities Preservation Protection Act."

"Dr. Friedman?" Luna said. "Dr. Friedman a pot hunter?" He grinned. The grin almost became a chuckle, but Luna suppressed it. "I think we better go see Maxie Davis," he said.

Luna did the talking as he drove them up the road along Chaco Wash. Thatcher sat beside him, apparently listening. Leaphorn looked out the window, at the late afternoon light on the broken sandstone surface of the Chaco cliffs, at the gray-silver tufts of grama grass on the talus slope, at the long shadow of Fajada Butte stretching across the valley. What will I do tonight, when I am back in Window Rock? What will I do tomorrow? What will I do when this winter has come? And when it has gone? What will I ever do again?

Maxie is Eleanor Friedman's neighbor, Luna was saying. Next apartment in the housing units for temporary personnel. And both were part of the contract archaeology team. Helping decide which of the more than a thousand Anasazi sites in Luna's jurisdiction were significant, dating them roughly, completing an inventory, deciding which should be preserved for exploration in the distant future when scientists had new methods to see through time.

"And they're friends," Luna said. "They go way back. Went to school together. Work together now. All that. It was Maxie who called the sheriff." Today Maxie Davis was working at BC129, which was the cataloging number assigned to an unexcavated Anasazi site. Unfortunately, Luna said, BC129 was on the wrong side of Chaco Mesa—over by Escavada Wash at the end of a very rocky road.

"BC129?" Thatcher asked.

"BC129," Luna repeated. "Just a tag to keep track of it. Too many places out here to dream up names for them."

BC129 was near the rim of the mesa, a low mound that overlooked the Chaco Valley. A woman, her short dark hair tucked under a cap, stood waist-deep in a trench watching. Luna parked his van beside an old green pickup. Even at this distance Leaphorn could see the woman was beautiful. It was not just the beauty of youth and health, it was something unique and remarkable. Leaphorn had seen such beauty in Emma, nineteen then, and walking across the campus at

Arizona State University. It was rare and valuable. A young Navajo man, his face shaded by the broad brim of a black felt hat, was sitting on the remains of a wall behind the trench, a shovel across his lap. Thatcher and Luna climbed out of the front seat.

"I'll wait," Leaphorn said.

This was his new trouble. Lack of interest. It had been his trouble since his mind had reluctantly processed the information from Emma's doctor.

"There's no good way to tell this, Mr. Leaphorn," the voice had said. "We lost her. Just now. It was a blood clot. Too much infection. Too much strain. But if it's any consolation, it must have been almost instantaneous."

He could see the man's face—pink-white skin, bushy blond eyebrows, blue eyes reflecting the cold light of the surgical waiting room through the lenses of horn-rimmed glasses, the small, prim mouth speaking to him. He could still hear the words, loud over the hum of the hospital air conditioner. It was like a remembered nightmare. Vivid. But he could not remember getting into his car in the parking lot, or driving through Gallup to Shiprock, or any of the rest of that day. He could remember only reviving his thoughts of the days before the operation. Emma's tumor would be removed. His joy that she was not being destroyed, as he had dreaded for so long, by the terrible, incurable, inevitable Alzheimer's disease. It was just a tumor. Probably not malignant. Easily curable. Emma would soon be herself again, memory restored. Happy. Healthy. Beautiful.

"The chances?" the surgeon had said. "Very good. Better than ninety percent complete recovery. Unless something goes wrong, an excellent prognosis."

But something had gone wrong. The tumor and its placement were worse than expected. The operation had taken much longer than expected. Then infection, and the fatal clot.

Since then, nothing had interested him. Someday, he would come alive again. Or perhaps he would. So far he hadn't. He sat sideways, legs stretched, back against the door, watching. Thatcher and Luna talked to the white woman in the trench. Unusual name for a woman. Maxie. Probably short for something Leaphorn couldn't think of. The Navajo was putting on a denim jacket, looking interested in whatever was being said, the expression on his long-jawed face sardonic. Maxie was gesturing, her face animated. She climbed out of the trench, walked toward the pickup truck with the Navajo following, his shovel over his shoulder in a sort of military parody. In the deep shadow of the hat brim Leaphorn saw white teeth. The man was grinning.

Beyond him, the slanting light of the autumn afternoon outlined the contours of the Chaco Plateau with lines of darkness. The shadow of Fajada Butte stretched all the way across Chaco Wash now. Outside the shadow, the yellow of the cottonwood along the dry streambed glittered in the sun. They were the only trees in a tan-gray-silver universe of grass. (Where had they found their firewood, Leaphorn wondered, the vanished thousands of Old Ones who built these huge stone apartments? The anthropologists thought they'd carried the roof beams fifty miles on their shoulders from forests on Mount Taylor and the Chuskas—an incredible feat. But how did they boil their corn, roast venison, cure their pottery, and warm themselves in winter? Leaphorn remembered the hard labor each fall—his father and he taking their wagon into the foothills, cutting dead piñon and juniper, making the long haul back to their hogan. But the Anasazi had no horses, no wheels.)

Thatcher and Luna were back at the van now. Thatcher slammed the door on his coat, said something under his breath, reopened it and closed it again. When Luna started the engine the seat belt warning buzzed. "Seat belt," Thatcher said.

Luna fastened the seat belt. "Hate these things," he said.

The green pickup pulled ahead of them, raising dust.

"We're going down to look at what's-her-name's stuff," Thatcher said, raising his voice for Leaphorn. "This Ms. Davis doesn't think hyphenated could be a pot hunter. Said she collected pots, but it was for her work. Scientific. Legitimate. Said Ms. . . . Ms. Bernal hated pot hunters."

"Um," Leaphorn said. He could see the big reservation hat of the young man through the back window of the pickup ahead. Odd to see a Navajo digging in the ruins. Stirring up Anasazi ghosts. Probably someone on the Jesus Road, or into the Peyote Church. Certainly a traditional man wouldn't be risking ghost sickness—or even worse, the reputation of being a witch—by digging among the bones. If you believed in the skinwalker traditions, bones of the dead made the tiny missiles that the witches shot into their victims. Leaphorn was not a believer. Those who were were the bane of his police work.

"She thinks something happened to Ms. Bernal," Thatcher said, glancing in the rearview mirror at Leaphorn. "You ought to have that seat belt on."

"Yeah," Leaphorn said. He fumbled it around him, thinking that probably nothing had happened to the woman. He thought of the anonymous call that had provoked this trip. There would be a connection, somewhere. One thing somehow would link Dr. What's-Her-Name's departure from Chaco with the motive for the call. The departure had led to the call, or something had happened that provoked both.

"What do you think?" he would have asked Emma. "Woman takes off for Farmington and drops off the world. Two days later somebody nasty turns her in for stealing pots. It could be she'd done something to make him sore, and knew he'd find out about it and turn her in. So she took off. Or she went to Farmington, made him sore there, and took off. So what do you think?"

And Emma would have asked him three or four questions, and found out how little he knew about the woman, or about anything else to do with this, and then she would have smiled at him and used one of those dusty aphorisms from her Bitter Water Clan.

"Only yearling coyotes think there's just one way to catch a rabbit," she'd say. And then she'd say, "About next Tuesday the woman will call and tell her friends she ran away and got married, and it won't have anything to do with stealing pots." Maybe Emma would be right and maybe she'd be wrong, and that didn't really matter. It was a game they had played for years. Emma's astute mind working against his own intelligence, honing his thinking, testing his logic against her common sense. It helped him. She enjoyed it. It was fun.

Had been fun.

Leaphorn noticed it immediately—the cold, stagnant air of abandoned places. He was standing beside Thatcher when Thatcher unlocked the door to the apartment of Dr. Friedman-Bernal and pushed it open. The trapped air flowed outward into Leaphorn's sensitive nostrils. He sensed dust in it, and all that mixture of smells which humans leave behind them when they go away.

The Park Service calls such apartments TPH, temporary personnel housing. At Chaco, six of them were built into an L-shaped frame structure on a concrete slab—part of a complex that included maintenance and storage buildings, the motor pool, and the permanent personnel housing: a line of eight frame bungalows backed against the low cliff of Chaco Mesa.

"Well," Thatcher said. He walked into the apartment with Maxie Davis a step behind him. Leaphorn leaned against the door. Thatcher stopped. "Ms. Davis," he said, "I'm going to ask you to wait outside for a while. Under this search warrant here . . . well, it makes everything different. I may have to take an oath on what was in here when I opened the door." He smiled at her. "Things like that."

"I'll wait," Maxie Davis said. She walked past Leaphorn, smiling at him nervously, and sat on the porch railing in the slanting sunlight. Her face was somber. Again, Leaphorn noticed her striking beauty. She was a small young woman. Cap off now, her dark hair needed combing. Her oval face had been burned almost as dark as Leaphorn's. She stared toward the maintenance yard, where a man in coveralls was doing something to the front end of a flatbed truck. Her fingers tapped at the railing—small, battered fingers on a small, scarred hand. Her blue work shirt draped against her back. Under it, every line of her body was tense. Beyond her, the weedy yard, the maintenance shed, the tumbled boulders along the cliff, seemed almost luminous in the brilliant late-afternoon sunlight. It made the gloom inside Dr. Friedman-Bernal's apartment behind Leaphorn seem even more shadowy than it was.

Thatcher walked through the living room, pulled open the drapes and exposed sliding-glass doors. They framed Fajada Butte and the expanse of the Chaco Valley. Except for a stack of books on the coffee table in front of the bleak brown institutional sofa, the room looked unused. Thatcher picked up the top book, examined it, put it down, and walked into the bedroom. He stood just inside the doorway, shaking his head.

"It would help some," he said, "if you knew what the hell you're looking for."

The room held a desk, two chairs, and two double beds. One seemed to be for sleeping—the covers carelessly pulled back in place after its last use. The other was work space—covered now with three cardboard boxes and a litter of notebooks, computer printouts, and other papers. Beyond this bed other boxes lined the floor along the wall. They seemed to hold mostly broken bits of pottery. "No way on God's green earth of telling where she got any of this stuff," Thatcher said. "Not that I know of. It might be perfectly legal."

"Unless her field notes tell us something," Leaphorn said. "They might. In fact, if she collected that stuff as part of some project or other, they should tell exactly where she picked up every bit of that stuff. And it's going to be legal unless she's been selling the artifacts."

"And of course if she's doing it for a project, it's legal," Thatcher said. "Unless she doesn't have the right permit. And if she's selling the stuff, she sure as hell ain't going to write down anything incriminating."

"Nope," Leaphorn said.

A man appeared at the apartment door. "Finding anything?" he asked. He walked past Leaphorn without a glance and into the bedroom. "Glad to see you people getting interested in this," he said. "Ellie's been missing almost three weeks now."

Thatcher put a fragment of pot carefully back into its box. "Who are you?" he asked.

"My name's Elliot," he said. "I work with Ellie on the Keet Katl dig. Or did work with her. What's this Luna's been telling me? You think she's stealing artifacts?"

Leaphorn found himself interested—wondering how Thatcher would deal with this. It wasn't the sort of thing anticipated and covered in the law enforcement training Thatcher would have received. No chapter covering intrusion of civilian into scene of investigation.

"Mr. Elliot," Thatcher said, "I want you to wait outside on the porch until we get finished in here. Then I want to talk to you."

Elliot laughed. "For God's sake," he said, in a tone that canceled any misunderstanding the laugh might have caused. "A woman vanishes for almost a month and nobody can get you guys off your butts. But somebody calls in with an anonymous . . ."

"Talk to you in a minute," Thatcher said. "Soon as I'm done in here."

"Done what?" Elliot said. "Done stirring through her potsherds? If you get 'em out of order, get 'em mixed up, it will screw up everything for her."

"Out," Thatcher said, voice still mild.

Elliot stared at him.

Maybe middle thirties or a little older, Leaphorn thought. A couple of inches over six feet, slender, athletic. The sun had bleached his hair even lighter than its usual very light brown. His jeans were worn and so were his jean jacket and his boots. But they fit. They had been expensive. And the face fit the pattern—a little weatherbeaten but what Emma would have called "an upper-class face." A little narrow, large blue eyes, nothing crooked, nothing bent, nothing scarred. Not the face you'd see looking out of a truckload of migrant workers, or in a roofing crew, or the cab of a road grader.

"Of course this place is full of pots." Elliot's voice was angry. "Studying pots is Ellie's job. . . ."

Thatcher gripped Elliot at the elbow. "Talk to you later," he said mildly, and moved him past Leaphorn and out the door. He closed the door behind him.

"Trouble is," Thatcher said, "everything he says is true. Her business is pots. So she'll have a bunch of 'em here. So what the hell are we looking for?"

Leaphorn shrugged. "I think we just look," he said. "We find what we find. Then we think about it."

They found more boxes of potsherds in the closet, each shard bearing a label that seemed to identify it with the place it had been found. They found an album of photographs, many of them snapshots of people who seemed to be anthropologists working at digs. There were three notebooks—two filled and one almost half filled—in which little pencil drawings of abstract patterns and pots were interposed with carbon rubbings of what they agreed must be the surface patterns of potsherds. The notes that surrounded these were in the special shorthand scientists develop to save themselves time.

"You studied this stuff at Arizona State," Thatcher said. "Can't you make it out?"

"I studied anthropology," Leaphorn admitted. "But mostly I studied cultural anthropology. This is a specialty and I didn't get into it. We went on a few digs in a Southwestern Anthro class, but the Anasazi culture wasn't my thing. Neither were ceramics."

Among the papers on the bed were two Nelson's catalogs, both auctions of American Indian art, African art, and Oceanic art. Both facedown, both open to pages that featured illustrations of Mimbres, Hohokam, and Anasazi pots. Leaphorn studied them. The appraised prices ranged from $2,950 to $41,500 for a

Mimbres urn. Two of the Anasazi ceramics had been circled in red in one catalog, and one in the other. The prices were $4,200, $3,700, and $14,500.

"Heard of Nelson's all my life," Thatcher said. "Thought they were just a London outfit. Just auctioned art, masterpieces, the *Mona Lisa*, things like that."

"This is art," Leaphorn said.

"A painting is art," Thatcher said. "What kind of nut pays fourteen grand for a pot?" He tossed the catalog back on the bed.

Leaphorn picked it up.

The cover picture was a stylized re-creation of a pictograph—stick-figure Indians with lances riding horses with pipestem legs across a deerskin surface.

Across the top the legend read:

NELSON'S
FOUNDED 1744
Fine American Indian Art
New York
Auction May 25 and 26

It opened easily to the pottery pages. Ten photographs of pots, each numbered and described in a numbered caption. Number 242 was circled in red. Leaphorn read the caption:

242. Anasazi St. John's Polychrome bowl, circa
A.D. 1000–1250, of deep rounded form, painted on
the interior in rose with wavy pale "ghost lines."
Has a geometric pattern enclosing two interlocked
spirals. Two hatched, serrated rectangles below
the rim. Interior surface serrated. Diameter 7¼
inches (19 cm). $4,000/$4,200.

Resale offer by an anonymous collector.
Documentation.

Inside the scrawled red circle, the same pen
had put a question mark over "anonymous collector" and scribbled notations in the margin.
What looked like a telephone number. Words
that seemed to be names. "Call Q!" "See Houk."
Houk. The name made a faint echo in Leaphorn's
mind. He'd known someone named Houk. The
only notation that meant anything to him was:
"Nakai, Slick." Leaphorn knew about Slick
Nakai. Had met him a time or two. Nakai was a
preacher. A fundamentalist Christian evangelist.
He pulled a revival tent around the reservation in
a trailer behind an old Cadillac sedan, putting it
up here and there—exhorting those who came
to hear him to quit drinking, leave off fornica-
tion, confess their sins, abandon their pagan
ways, and come to Jesus. Leaphorn scanned the
other names, looking for anything familiar, read
the description of a Tonto Polychrome olla valued

at \$1,400/\$1,800. He put the catalog back on the bed. On the next page, a Mimbres black-on-white burial pot, with a "kill hole" in its bottom and its exterior featuring lizards chasing lizards, was advertised for \$38,600. Leaphorn grimaced and put down the catalog.

"I'm going to make a sort of rough inventory," Thatcher said, sorting through one of the boxes. "Just jot down some idea of what we have here, which we both know is absolutely nothing that is going to be of any use to us."

Leaphorn sat in the swivel chair and looked at the 365-day calendar on the desk. It was turned to October 11. "What day was it they said Dr. Hyphenated left here? Wasn't it the thirteenth?"

"Yeah," Thatcher said.

Leaphorn flipped over a page to October 13. "Do it!" was written under the date. He turned the next page. Across this was written: "Away." The next page held two notes: "Be ready for Lehman. See H. Houk."

H. Houk. Would it be Harrison Houk? Maybe. An unusual name, and the man fit the circumstances. Houk would be into everything and the Houk ranch—outside of Bluff and just over the San Juan River from the north side of the reservation—was in the heart of Anasazi ruins country.

The next page was October 16. It was blank. So

was the next page. That took him to Wednesday. Across this was written: "Lehman!!! about 4 P.M. dinner. sauerbraten, etc."

Leaphorn thumbed through the pages up to the present. So far Dr. Friedman-Bernal had missed two other appointments. She would miss another one next week. Unless she came home.

He put down the calendar, walked into the kitchen, and opened the refrigerator, remembering how Emma liked to make sauerbraten. "It's way too much work," he would say, which was better than telling her that he really didn't like it very well. And Emma would say: "No more work than Navajo tacos, and less cholesterol."

The smell of soured milk and stale food filled his nostrils. The worse smell came from a transparent ovenware container on the top shelf. It held a Ziploc bag containing what seemed to be a large piece of meat soaking in a reddish brown liquid. Sauerbraten. Leaphorn grimaced, shut the door, and walked back into the room where Thatcher was completing his inventory.

The sun was on the horizon now, blazing through the window and casting Thatcher's shadow black against the wallpaper. Leaphorn imagined Eleanor Friedman-Bernal hurrying through the sauerbraten process, getting all those things now shriveled and spoiled lined up on the refrigerator shelves so that fixing dinner for

Lehman could be quickly done. But she hadn't come back to fix that dinner. Why not? Had she gone to see Harrison Houk about a pot? Leaphorn found himself remembering the first, and only, time he'd encountered the man. Years ago. He'd been what? Officer Leaphorn working out of the Kayenta substation, obliquely involved in helping the FBI with the manhunt across San Juan.

The Houk killings, they had called them. Leaphorn, who forgot little, remembered the names. Della Houk, the mother. Elmore Houk, the brother. Dessie Houk, the sister. Brigham Houk, the killer. Harrison Houk, the father. Harrison Houk had been the survivor. The mourner. Leaphorn remembered him standing on the porch of a stone house, listening intently while the sheriff talked, remembered him climbing up from the river, staggering with fatigue, when it was no longer light enough to search along the bank for Brigham Houk. Or, almost certainly even then, Brigham Houk's drowned body.

Would it be this same H. Houk now whom Eleanor Friedman-Bernal had noted on her calendar? Was Harrison Houk some part of the reason for the uneaten banquet spoiling in the refrigerator? To his surprise Joe Leaphorn found his curiosity had returned. What had prevented Eleanor Friedman-Bernal from coming home for her party with a guest whose name deserved three exclamation points? What caused her to miss a dinner she'd worked so hard to prepare?

Leaphorn walked back into the closet and recovered the album. He flipped through it. Which one was Eleanor Friedman-Bernal? He found a page of what must have been wedding pictures—bride and groom with another young couple. He slipped one of them out of the corners that held it. The bride was radiant, the groom a good-looking Mexican, his expression slightly stunned. The bride's face long, prominent bones, intelligent, Jewish. A good woman, Leaphorn thought. Emma would have liked her. He had two weeks left on his terminal leave. He'd see if he could find her.

THREE

IT HAD BEEN A BAD DAY for Officer Jim Chee of the Navajo Tribal Police. In fact, it had been the very worst day of an abysmal week.

It had started going bad sometime Monday. Over the weekend it had dawned upon some dimwit out at the Navajo Tribal Motor Pool that a flatbed trailer was missing. Apparently it had been missing for a considerable time. Sunday night it was reported stolen.

"How long?" Captain Largo asked at Monday afternoon's briefing. "Tommy Zah don't know how long. Nobody knows how long. Nobody seems to remember seeing it since about a month ago. It came in for maintenance. Motor pool garage fixed a bad wheel bearing. Presumably it was then parked out in the lot. But it's not in the lot now. Therefore it has to be stolen. That's because it makes Zah look less stupid to declare it stolen. Better'n admitting he just don't know what the hell they did with it. So we're supposed to find it for 'em. After whoever took it had time to haul it about as far as Florida."

Looking back on it, looking for the reason all of what followed came down on him instead of some other officer on the evening shift, Chee could see it was because he had not been looking alert. The captain had spotted it. In fact, Chee had been guilty of gazing out of the assembly room window. The globe willows that shaded the parking lot of the Shiprock subagency of the Navajo Tribal Police were full of birds that afternoon. Chee had been watching them, deciding they were finches, thinking what he would say to Janet Pete when he saw her again. Suddenly he became aware that Largo had been talking to him.

"You see it out there in the parking lot?"

"Sir?"

"The goddam trailer," Largo said. "It out there?"

"No sir."

"You been paying enough attention to know what trailer we're talking about?"

"Motor pool trailer," Chee said, hoping Largo hadn't changed the subject.

"Wonderful," Largo said, glowering at Chee. "Now from what Superintendent Zah said on the telephone, we're going to get a memo on this today and the memo is going to say that they called our dispatcher way back sometime and reported pilfering out there at night and asked us to keep an eye on things. Long before they mislaid their trailer, you understand. That's to cover the superintendent's ass and make it our fault."

Largo exhaled a huge breath and looked at his audience—making sure his night shift understood what their commanding officer was dealing with here.

"Now, just about now," Largo continued, "they're starting to count all their stuff out there. Tools. Vehicles. Coke machines. God knows what. And sure as hell they're going to find other stuff missing. And not know when they lost it, and claim it got stolen five minutes ago. Or tomorrow if that's handier for 'em. Anyway, it will be at some time after—I repeat, after—we've been officially informed and asked to watch out for 'em. And then I'm going to be spending my weekends writing reports to send down to Window Rock." Largo paused. He looked at Chee.

"So, Chee . . ."

"Yes sir." Chee was paying attention now. Too late.

"I want you to keep an eye on that place. Hang around there on your shift. Get past there every chance you get. And make chances. Call the dispatcher to keep it on record that you're watching. When they finish their inventory and find out they've lost other stuff, I don't want 'em in a position to blame us. Understand?"

Chee understood. Not that it helped.

That was Monday afternoon. Monday evening it got worse. Even worse than it might have been, because he didn't learn about it until Tuesday.

As instructed, Chee had been hanging close to the motor pool. He would coast out Highway 550 maybe as far as the Hogback formation, which marked the eastern edge of the Big Reservation. Then he would drift back past the motor pool fence and into Shiprock. Stopping now and then to check the gate. Noticing that the summer's accumulation of tumbleweeds piled along the chain-link fence was undisturbed. Drifting down 550 again. Drifting back. Keeping Farmington-Shiprock traffic holding nervously in the vicinity of the speed limit. Boring himself into sleepiness. Calling in now and then to have the dispatcher record that he was diligently watching the motor pool and that all there remained serene.

"Unit Eleven checking at the motor pool," Chee called. "All quiet. No sign of entry."

"Since you're there on five-fifty," the dispatcher said, "see what's going on at the Seven-Eleven. Just had a disturbance call."

Chee had done a quick U-turn, boredom

replaced by the uneasiness that always preceded the probability of dealing with a drunk. Or two drunks. Or however many drunks it was taking to disturb the peace at the Shiprock 7-Eleven.

But the parking space in front of the convenience store had been quiet—empty except for an old Dodge sedan and a pickup truck. No drunks. Inside, no drunks either. The woman behind the cash register was reading one of those tabloids convenience stores sell. A green-ink headline proclaimed THE TRUTH ABOUT LIZ TAYLOR'S WEIGHT LOSS. Another declared SIAMESE TWINS BOTH PREGNANT. BLAME MINISTER. A teenaged boy was inspecting the canned soda pop in the cooler.

"What's the trouble?" Chee asked.

The teenager put down the Pepsi he'd selected, looking guilty. The cashier lowered her paper. She was a middle-aged Navajo woman. Towering House Clan, Chee remembered, named Gorman, or Relman, or something like that. Anglo-type name with six letters. Bunker. Walker. Thomas.

"What?" she asked.

"Somebody called in a disturbance here. What's the trouble?"

"Oh," the Towering House woman said. "We had a drunk in here. Where you been?"

"What'd he do? Any damages?"

"She," the woman said. "Old Lady George. She went away when she heard me calling the police."

The cashier's name was Gorman, Chee now remembered. But he was thinking of Old Lady George.

"Which way did she go?"

"Just went," Mrs. Gorman said. She gestured vaguely. "Didn't look. I was picking up the cans she knocked over."

So Chee had gone looking for Old Lady George. He knew her fairly well. She'd been a witness in an automobile theft case he'd worked on—a very helpful witness. Later, when he was looking for one of her grandsons on an assault warrant, she'd helped him again. Sent the boy down to the station to turn himself in. Besides, she was Streams Come Together Clan, which was linked to Chee's father's clan, which made her a relative. Chee had been raised knowing that you watch out for your relatives.

He had watched out for her, first up and down 550 and then up and down side streets. He found her sitting on a culvert, and talked her into the patrol car, and took her home and turned her over to a worried young woman who he guessed must be a granddaughter. Then he had gone back and established that the motor pool remained intact. At least it seemed to be intact as seen from the highway. But seen from the highway, it hadn't been possible to detect that someone had tinkered with the padlock securing the gate. He heard about that the next day when he reported for work.

Captain Largo's usually big voice was unusually quiet—an ominous sign.

"A backhoe," Largo said. "That's what they stole this time. About three tons. Bright yellow. Great big thing. I told Mr. Zah that I had one of my best men watching his place last night. Officer Jim Chee. I told Zah that it must be just another case of forgetting to put it down on the record when somebody borrowed it. You know what he said to me?"

"No sir," Chee said. "But nobody stole that on my shift. I was driving back and forth past there the whole time."

"Really," Largo said. "How nice." He picked up a sheet from the shift squeal report from his desk. He didn't look at it. "I'm pleased to hear that. Because you know what Zah said to me? He said"—Largo shifted his voice up the scale—" 'Oh, it was stolen last night all right. The guy that runs the service station across the street there told us about it.' " Largo's voice returned to normal. "This service station man stood there and watched 'em drive out with it."

"Oh," Chee said, thinking it must have been while he was at the 7-Eleven.

"This Zah is quite a comedian. He told me you'd think sneaking a big yellow backhoe out with one of my policemen watching would be like trying to sneak moonrise past a coyote."

Chee flushed. He had nothing to say to that. He had heard the simile before somewhere in another form. Hard as sneaking sunrise past a rooster, it had been. A moonrise without a coyote baying was equally impossible, and relating a coyote to Largo's police added a nicely oblique insult. You don't call a Navajo a coyote. The only thing worse is to accuse him of letting his kinfolks starve.

Largo handed Chee the squeal sheet. It confirmed what Zah had told Largo.

Subject Delbert Tsosie informed Officer Shorty that while serving a customer at the Texaco station at approximately 10 P.M. he noticed a man removing the chain from the gate of the motor pool maintenance yard across Highway 550. He observed a truck towing a flatbed trailer drive through the gate into the yard. Subject Tsosie said that approximately fifteen minutes later he noticed the truck driving out the gate towing a machine which he described as probably a backhoe or some sort of trenching machine loaded on the trailer. He said he did not report this to police because he presumed tribal employees had come to get the equipment to deal with some sort of emergency.

"That must have been while I was looking for Old Lady George," Chee said. He explained, hurrying through the last stages because of Largo's expression.

"Get to work," Largo said, "and leave this alone. Sergeant Benally will be chasing the backhoe. Don't mess with it."

That was Tuesday morning and should have been the very bottom of the week. The pits. It would have been, perhaps, had not Chee driven past the Texaco station on 550 and seen Delbert Tsosie stacking tires. Benally was handling it, but Chee sometimes bought gasoline from Tsosie. No harm in stopping to talk.

"No," Tsosie said. "Didn't see either one of them well enough to recognize 'em. But you could see one was Dineh—tall, skinny Navajo. Had on a cowboy hat. I know a lot of 'em that works at the motor pool. They come over here and use the Coke machine and buy candy. Wasn't none I knew and I was thinking it was a funny time to be coming to work. But I thought they must have forgotten something and was coming for it. And when I saw the backhoe I figured some pipe broke somewhere. Emergency, you know." Tsosie shrugged.

"You didn't recognize anybody?"

"Bad light."

"Guy in the truck. You see him at all?"

"Not in the truck," Tsosie said. "The skinny Navajo was driving the truck. This guy was following in a sedan. Plymouth two-door. About a '70, '71 maybe. Dark blue but they was doing some bodywork on it. Had an off-color right front fender. Looked white or gray. Maybe primer coat. And lots of patches here and there, like they was getting ready to paint it."

"Driver not a Navajo?"

"Navajo driving the truck. *Belagana* driving the Plymouth. And the white guy, I just barely got a look at him. They all sort of look alike anyway. All I notice is freckles and sunburn."

"Big or little?"

Tsosie thought. "About average. Maybe sort of short and stocky."

"What color hair?"

"Had a cap on. Baseball cap. With a bill."

None of which would have mattered since Benally was handling it, and Tsosie had already told Benally all of this, and probably more. But Saturday morning Chee saw the Plymouth two-door.

It was dark blue, about a '70 model. When it passed him going in the other direction—Shiprock-bound on 550—he saw the mismatched front fender and the patches of primer paint on its doors and the baseball cap on the head of the white man driving it. Without a thought, Chee did a U-turn across the bumpy divider.

He was driving Janet Pete's car. Not exactly Janet Pete's car. Janet had put down earnest money on a Buick Riviera at Quality Pre-owned Cars in Farmington and had asked Chee to test-drive it for her. She had to go to Phoenix Friday and when she got back Monday she wanted to close the deal.

"I guess I've already decided," Janet had told him. "It has everything I need and only fourteen thousand miles on it and the price seems reasonable and he's giving me a thousand dollars on my old Datsun and that seems fair."

To Chee the thousand for the Datsun seemed enough more than fair to arouse suspicion. Janet's Datsun was a junker. But it was clear that Janet was not going to be receptive to discouraging words. She described the Buick as "absolutely beautiful." As she described it, the lawyer in Janet Pete fell away. The girl emerged through the delight and enthusiasm, and Janet Pete became absolutely beautiful herself.

"It has the prettiest blue plush upholstery. Lovely color. Dark blue outside with a real delicate pinstripe down the side, and the chrome is just right." She looked slightly guilty at this. "I don't usually like chrome," she said. "But this . . ." She performed a gesture with shoulder and face that depreciated this lapse from taste. ". . . But this . . . well, I just love it."

She paused, examining Chee and transforming herself from girl to lawyer. "I thought maybe you would check it out for me. You drive all the time and you know all about mechanical things. If you don't mind doing it, and there's something seriously wrong with the engine, or something like that, then I could . . ."

She had left the awful statement unfinished. And Chee had accepted the keys and said sure, he'd be glad to do it. Which wasn't exactly the case. If there was something seriously wrong with the engine, telling her about it wasn't going to make him popular with Janet Pete. And Chee wanted to be popular. He wondered about her. He wondered about a woman lawyer. To be more precise, he wondered if Janet Pete, or any woman, could fill the gap Mary Landon seemed to be leaving in his life.

That was Friday evening. Saturday morning he drove the Buick down to Bernie Tso's garage and put it on the rack. Bernie was not impressed.

"Fourteen thousand miles, my ass," Bernie said. "Look at the tread on those tires. And here." Bernie rattled the universal joint. "Arizona don't have a law about running back the odometer, but New Mexico does," he said. "And she got this junker over in New Mexico. I'd say they fudged the first number a little. Turned her back from forty-four thousand, or maybe seventy-four."

He finished his inspection of the running gear and lowered the hoist. "Steering's slack, too," he said. "Want me to pull the head and take a look there?"

"Maybe later," Chee said. "I'll take it out and see what I can find and then I'll let her decide if she wants to spend any money on it."

And so he had driven Janet Pete's blue Buick out Highway 550 toward Farmington, glumly noting its deficiencies. Slow response to the gas pedal. Probably easy to fix with an adjustment. Tendency to choke on acceleration. Also fixable. Tendency to steer to the right on braking. Suspension far too soft for Chee, who was conditioned to the cast-iron springing of police cars and pickup trucks. Maybe she liked soft suspension, but this one was also uneven—suggesting a bad shock absorber. And, as Bernie had mentioned, slack steering.

He was measuring this slack, swaying down the Farmington-bound lanes of 550, when he saw the Backhoe Bandit. And it was the slack steering, eventually, that did him in.

He noticed the off-color fender first. He noticed that the car approaching him, Shiprock-bound, was a blue Plymouth sedan of about 1970 vintage. As it passed, he registered the patches of gray-white primer paint on its door. He got only a glimpse of the profile of the driver—youngish, long blond hair emerging from under a dark billed cap.

Chee didn't give it a thought. He did a U-turn across the bumpy divider and followed the Plymouth.

He was wearing his off-duty work clothes—greasy jeans and a Coors T-shirt with a torn armpit. His pistol was locked securely in the table beside the cot in his trailer at Shiprock. No radio in the Buick, of course. And it was no chase car. He would simply tag along, determine where the Backhoe Bandit was going, take whatever opportunity presented itself. The Plymouth was in no particular hurry. It did a left turn off 550 on the access road to the village of Kirtland. It crossed the San Juan bridge, did another turn onto a dirt road, and made the long climb up the mesa toward the Navajo Mine and the Four Corners Power Plant. Chee had fallen a quarter-mile back, partly to avoid eating the Plymouth's dust and partly to avoid arousing suspicion. But by the time he reached the escarpment the Backhoe Bandit seemed to have sensed he was being followed. He did another turn onto a poorly graded dirt road across the sagebrush, driving much faster now and producing a rooster tail of dust. Chee followed, pushing the Buick, sending it bouncing and lurching over the humps, fighting the steering where the road was rutted. Through the dust he became belatedly aware the Plymouth had made another turn—a hard right. Chee braked, skidded, corrected the skid, collected the slack in the steering, and made the turn. He was a little late.

Oops! Right wheel onto the rocky track. Left wheel in the sagebrush. Chee bounced painfully against the Buick's blue plush roof, bounced again, saw through the dust the rocks he should have been avoiding, frantically spun the slack steering wheel, felt the impact, felt something go in the front end, and then simply slid along—his hat jammed low onto his forehead by its kiss with the ceiling.

Janet Pete's beautiful blue Buick slid sideways, plowing a sedan-sized gash through the sage. It stopped in a cloud of dirt. Chee climbed out.

It looked bad, but not as bad as it might have been. The left front wheel was horizontal, the tie-rod that held it broken. Not as bad as a broken axle. The rest of the damage was, to Chee's thinking, superficial. Just scrapes, dents, and scratches. Chee found the chrome strip that Janet Pete had so admired about fifteen yards back in the brush, peeled off by a limb. He laid it carefully on the backseat. The plume of dust produced by the Plymouth was receding over the rim of the mesa. Chee watched it, thinking about his immediate problem—getting a tow truck out here to haul in the Buick. Thinking about the five or six miles he would have to walk to get to a telephone, thinking about the seven or eight hundred dollars it was going to cost to patch up the damaged Buick. Thinking about such things was far more pleasant than considering his secondary problem, which was how to break the news to Janet Pete.

"Absolutely beautiful," Janet Pete had said. "I fell in love with it," she'd said. "Just what I'd always wanted." But he would think about that later. He was staring into the diminishing haze of dust, but his vision was turned inward—imprinting the Backhoe Bandit in his memory. The profile, the suggestion of pockmarks on the jaw, the hair, the cap. This had become a matter of pride. He would find the man again, sooner or later.

By midafternoon, with the Buick back at Bernie Tso's garage, it seemed it would be sooner. Tso knew the Plymouth. Had, in fact, once towed it in. And he knew a little about the Backhoe Bandit.

"Everything that goes around comes around," Chee said, happily. "Everything balances out."

"I wouldn't say that," Tso said. "What's it going to cost you to balance out this Buick?"

"I mean catching the son of a bitch," Chee said. "At least I'm going to be able to do that. Lay that on the captain's desk."

"Maybe your girlfriend can take it back to the

dealer," Tso said. "Tell 'em she doesn't like the way that front wheel looks."

"She's not my girlfriend," Chee said. "She's a lawyer with DNA. Tribal legal services. I ran into her last summer." Chee described how he had picked up a man who came to be Janet Pete's client, and had tried to have him kept in the Farmington jail until he had a chance to talk to him, and how sore Pete had been about it.

"Tough as nails," Chee said. "Not my type. Not unless I kill somebody and need a lawyer."

"I don't see how you're going to catch him with what little I know about him," Tso said. "Not even his name. All I remember is he works out in the Blanco gas field the other side of Farmington. Or said he did."

"And that you pulled him in when he had transmission troubles. And he paid you with two hundred-dollar bills. And he told you when you got it fixed to leave it at Slick Nakai's revival tent."

"Well, yeah," Tso said.

"And he said you could leave the change with Slick 'cause he saw Slick pretty often."

And now it was Saturday night. Slick Nakai's True Gospel had long since left the place near the Hogback where Tso had gone to tow in the Plymouth. But it was easy enough to locate by asking around. Nakai had loaded his tent, and his portable electric organ, and his sound system into his four-wheel trailer and headed southeast. He had left behind fliers tacked to telephone poles and Scotch-taped to store windows announcing that all hungering for the Word of the Lord could find him between Nageezi and the Dzilith-Na-O-Dith-Hie School.

FOUR

FULL DARKNESS CAME LATE on this dry autumn Saturday. The sun was far below the western horizon but a layer of high, thin cirrus clouds still received the slanting light and reflected it, red now, down upon the ocean of sagebrush north of Nageezi Trading Post. It tinted the patched canvas of Slick Nakai's revival tent from faded tan to a doubtful rose and the complexion of Lieutenant Joe Leaphorn from dark brown to dark red.

From a lifetime of habit, Leaphorn had parked his pickup a little away from the cluster of vehicles at the tent and with its nose pointing outward, ready for whatever circumstances and duty might require of it. But Leaphorn was not on duty. He would never be on duty again. He was in the last two weeks of a thirty-day "terminal leave." When it ended, his application to retire from the Navajo Tribal Police would be automatically accepted. In fact he was already retired. He felt retired. He felt as if it were all far, far behind him. Faded in the distance. Another life in another world, nothing to do with the man now standing under this red October sunset, waiting for the sounds coming from the True Gospel revival tent to signal a break in the preaching.

He had come to Slick Nakai's revival to begin his hunt. Where had that hyphenated woman gone? Why had she abandoned a meal so carefully prepared, an evening so obviously anticipated? It didn't matter, and yet it did. In a way he couldn't really understand, it would say good-by to Emma. She would have prepared such a meal in anticipation of a treasured guest. Often had done so. Leaphorn couldn't explain it, but his mind made a sort of nebulous connection between Emma's character and that of a woman who probably was quite different. And so he would use the final days of his final leave to find that woman. That had brought him here. That, and boredom, and his old problem of curiosity, and the need for a reason to get away from their house in Window Rock and all its memories.

Whatever had moved him, he was here, on the very eastern fringe of the Navajo Reservation— more than a hundred miles from home. When circumstances allowed, he would talk to a man whose very existence annoyed him. He would ask questions the man might not answer and which might mean nothing if he did. The alternative was sitting in their living room, the television on for background noise, trying to read. But Emma's absence always intruded. When he raised his eyes, he saw the R. C. Gorman print she'd hung over the fireplace. They'd argued about it. She liked it, he didn't. The words would sound in his ears again. And Emma's laughter. It was the same everywhere he looked. He should sell that house, or burn it. It was in the tradition of the Dineh. Abandon the house contaminated by the dead, lest the ghost sickness infect you, and you died. Wise were the elders of his people, and the Holy People who taught them the Navajo Way. But instead, he would play this pointless game. He would find a woman. If alive, she wouldn't want to be found. If dead, it wouldn't matter.

Abruptly, it became slightly more interesting. He had been leaning on the door of his pickup, studying the tent, listening to the sounds coming from it, examining the grounds (another matter of habit). He recognized a pickup, parked like his own behind the cluster of vehicles. It was the truck of another tribal policeman. Jim Chee's truck. Chee's private truck, which meant Chee was also here unofficially. Becoming a born-again Christian? That hardly seemed likely. As

Leaphorn remembered it, Chee was the antithesis of Slick Nakai. Chee was a *hatathali*. A singer. Or would be one as soon as people started hiring him to conduct their curing ceremonials. Leaphorn looked at the pickup, curious. Was someone sitting in it? Hard to tell in the failing light. What would Chee be doing here?

The sound of music came from the tent. A surprising amount of music, as if a band were playing. Over that an amplified male voice leading a hymn. Time to go in.

The band proved to be two men. Slick Nakai, standing behind what seemed to be a black plastic keyboard, and a thin guitarist in a blue checked shirt and a gray felt hat. Nakai was singing, his mouth a quarter-inch from a stand-mounted microphone, his hands maintaining a heavy rhythm on the keyboard. The audience sang with him, with much swaying and clapping of hands.

"Jesus loves us," Nakai sang. "That we know. Jesus loves us. Everywhere."

Nakai's eyes were on him, examining him, sorting him out. The guitarist was looking at him, too. The hat looked familiar. So did the man. Leaphorn had a good memory for faces, and for just about everything else.

"We didn't earn it," Nakai sang. "But He don't care. His love is with us. Everywhere."

Nakai emphasized this with a flourish at the

keyboard, shifting his attention now from Leaphorn to an elderly woman wearing wire-rimmed
glasses who was sway-dancing, eyes closed, too
caught up with emotion to be aware she had
danced into the tangle of electrical cables linking
Nakai's sound system to a generator outside the
tent. A tall man with a thin mustache standing
by the speaker's podium noticed Nakai's concern.
He moved quickly, steering the woman clear of
the cables. Third member of the team, Leaphorn
guessed.

When the music stopped, Nakai introduced
him as "Reverend Tafoya."

"He's Apache. I tell you that right out," Nakai
said. "Jicarilla. But that's all right. God made the
Apaches, and the *belagana*, and the blacks, and
the Hopis, and us Dineh and everybody else just
the same. And he inspired this Apache here to
learn about Jesus. And he's going to tell you about
that."

Nakai surrendered the microphone to Tafoya.
Then he poured water from a thermos into a Sty-
rofoam cup and carried it back toward where
Leaphorn was standing. He was a short man,
sturdily built, neat and tidy, with small, round
hands, small feet in neat cowboy boots, a round,
intelligent face. He walked with the easy grace of
a man who walks a lot.

"I haven't seen you here before," Nakai said.

"If you came to hear about Jesus you're welcome. If you didn't come for that you're welcome anyway." He laughed, showing teeth that conflicted with the symphony of neatness. Two were missing, one was broken, one was black and twisted. Poor people's teeth, Leaphorn thought. Navajo teeth.

"Because that's about all you hear around me anyway . . . Jesus talk," Nakai said.

"I came to see if you can help me with something," Leaphorn said. They exchanged the soft, barely touching handshake of the Navajo—the compromise of the Dineh between modern convention and the need to be careful with strangers who might, after all, be witches. "But it can wait until you're through with your revival. I'd like to talk to you then."

At the podium, Reverend Tafoya was talking about the Mountain Spirits of the Apaches. "Something like your *yei*, like your Holy People. But some different, too. That's who my daddy worshiped, and my mother, and my grandparents. And I did too, until I got this cancer. I don't have to tell you people here about cancer. . . ."

"The Reverend will take care of it for a while," Nakai said. "What do you need to know? What can I tell you?"

"We have a woman missing," Leaphorn said. He showed Nakai his identification and told him about Dr. Eleanor Friedman-Bernal. "You know her?"

"Sure," Nakai said. "For maybe three years, or four." He laughed again. "But not very well. Never made a Christian out of her. It was just business." The laugh went away. "You mean seriously missing? Like foul play?"

"She went to Farmington for the weekend a couple of weeks ago and nobody's heard from her since," Leaphorn said. "What was the business you had with her?"

"She studied pots. That was her business. So once in a while she would buy one from me." Nakai's small, round face was registering concern. "You think something went wrong with her?"

"You never know about that with missing people," Leaphorn said. "Usually they come back after a while and sometimes they don't. So we try to look into it. You a pot dealer?"

Leaphorn noticed how the question sounded, but before he could change it to "dealer in pots," Nakai said, "Just a preacher. But I found out you can sell pots. Pretty big money sometimes. Had a man I baptized over near Chinle give me one. Didn't have any money and he told me I could sell it in Gallup for thirty dollars. Told me where." Nakai laughed again, enjoying the memory. "Sure enough. Went to a place there on Railroad Avenue and the man gave me forty-six dollars for it." He made a bowl of his hands, grinning at Leaphorn. "The Lord provides," he said. "Not too well sometimes, but he provides."

"So now you go out and dig 'em up?"

"That's against the law," Nakai said, grinning. "You're a policeman. I bet you knew that. With me, it's once in a long while people bring 'em in. Several times at revivals I mentioned that fella who gave me the pot, and how it bought gasoline for a week, and the word got around among the born-again people that pots would give me some gasoline money. So now and then when they got no money and want to offer something, they bring me one."

"And the Friedman-Bernal woman buys them?"

"Mostly no. Just a time or two. She told me she wanted to see anything I got when I was preaching over around Chinle, or Many Farms—any of that country over around Chinle Wash. And out around here in the Checkerboard, and if I get up into Utah—Bluff, Montezuma Creek, Mexican Hat. Up in there."

"So you save them for her?"

"She pays me a little fee to take a look at them, but mostly she doesn't buy any. Just looks. Studies them for a couple of hours. Magnifying glass and all. Makes notes. The deal is, I have to know exactly where they came from."

"How do you manage that?"

"I tell the people, 'You going to bring in a pot to offer to the Lord, then you be sure you tell me where you found it.'" Nakai grinned his small, neat grin at Leaphorn. "That way, too, I know it's a legal pot. Not dug up off of government land."

Leaphorn didn't comment on that.

"When's the last time you saw her?" The answer should be late September, or something like that. Leaphorn knew the date he'd seen on Friedman's calendar, but it wasn't something Nakai would be likely to remember.

Nakai extracted a well-worn pocket notebook from his shirt and fingered his way through its pages. "Be last September twenty-third."

"More than a month ago," Leaphorn said. "What did she want?"

Nakai's round face filled with thought. Behind him, the Reverend Tafoya's voice rose into the high tenor of excitement. It described an old preacher at a revival tent in Dulce calling Tafoya to the front, laying on his hands, "right there on the place where that skin cancer was eating into my face. And I could feel the healing power flowing. . . ."

"Well," Nakai said, speaking very slowly. "She brought back a pot she'd gotten from me back in the spring. A piece of a pot, really. Wasn't all there. And she wanted to know everything I knew about it. Some of it stuff I had already told her. And she'd written it down in her notebook. But she asked it all again. Who I'd got it from. Everything he'd said about where he'd found it. That sort of stuff."

"Where was it? I mean where you met. And what did this notebook look like?"

"At Ganado," Nakai said. "I got a place there. I got home from a revival over by Cameron and I had a note from her asking me to call, saying it was important. I called her there at Chaco Canyon. She wasn't home so I left a message when I'd be back at Ganado again. And when I got back, there she was, waiting for me."

He paused. "And the notebook. Let's see now. Little leather-covered thing. Small enough to go in your shirt pocket. In fact that's where she carried it."

"And she just wanted to talk to you about the pot?"

"Mostly where it came from."

"Where was that?"

"Fella's ranch between Bluff and Mexican Hat."

"Private land," Leaphorn said, his voice neutral.

"Legal," Nakai agreed.

"Very short visit then," Leaphorn said. "Just repeating what you had already told her."

"Not really. She had a lot of questions. Did I

know where she could find the person who had brought it? Could he have gotten it from the south side of the San Juan instead of the north side? And she had me look at the design on it. Wanted to know if I'd seen any like it."

Leaphorn had discovered that he was liking Nakai a little, which surprised him. "And you told her he couldn't have found it south of the San Juan because that would be on the Navajo Reservation, and digging up a pot there would be illegal?" He was smiling when he said it and Nakai was smiling when he answered.

"Didn't have to tell Friedman something like that," Nakai said. "That sort of thing, she knew."

"What was special about this pot?"

"It was the kind she was working on, I guess. Anasazi pot, I understand. They look pretty much alike to me, but I remember this one had a pattern. You know, sort of abstract shapes painted onto its surface. That seemed to be what she was interested in. And it had a sort of mixed color. That's what she always had me watching out for. That pattern. It was sort of an impression of Kokopelli, tiny, repeated and repeated and repeated."

Nakai looked at Leaphorn quizzically. Leaphorn nodded. Yes, he knew about Kokopelli, the Humpbacked Flute Player, the Watersprinkler, the fertility symbol. Whatever you called him, he was a frequent figure in strange pictographs the

Anasazi had painted on cliffs across the Colorado Plateau.

"Anytime anyone brought one in like that— even a little piece of the pot with that pattern on it—then I was to save it for her and she'd pay a minimum of fifty dollars."

"Who found that pot?"

Nakai hesitated, studied Leaphorn.

"I'm not out hunting pot hunters," Leaphorn said. "I'm trying to find this woman."

"It was a Paiute Clan man they call Amos Whistler," Nakai said. "Lives out there near south of Bluff. North of Mexican Water."

Suddenly Reverend Tafoya was shouting "Hallelujah," his voice loud and hoarse, and the crowd was joining him, and the thin man with the hat was doing something with the guitar.

"Anything else? I can talk to you later," Nakai said. "I need to help out now."

"Was that the last time you saw her? The last contact?"

"Yeah," Nakai said. He started toward the speaker's platform, then turned back. "One other contact," he said. "More or less. A man who works with her came by when I was preaching over at the Hogback there by Shiprock. Fella named . . ." Nakai couldn't come up with the name. "Anyway he was a *belagana*. An Anglo. He said he wanted to pick up a pot I had for her. I didn't have any. He said he understood I had one, or maybe it was some, from over on the San Juan, around Bluff. I said no." Nakai turned again.

"Was it a tall man? Blond. Youngish. Named Elliot?"

"That's him," Nakai said.

Leaphorn watched the rest of it. He unfolded a chair at the back of the tent and sat, studied Nakai's techniques, and sorted out what he had learned, which wasn't much.

Nakai's congregation here on the fringe of the Checkerboard Reservation included perhaps sixty people—all Navajos apparently, but Leaphorn wouldn't swear that a few of them weren't from the Jicarilla Reservation, which bordered on Navajo territory here. They were about sixty percent women, and most middle-aged or older. That surprised Leaphorn a little. Without really thinking about it, because this aspect of his culture interested Leaphorn relatively little, he had presumed that those attracted to fundamentalist Christianity would be the young who'd been surrounded by the white man's religion off the reservation. That wasn't true here.

At the microphone, Nakai was gesturing toward the north. "Right up the highway here—you could see it from right here if it wasn't dark—right up here you have Huerfano Mesa. We been taught, us Navajos, that that's where First Woman lived, and First Man, and some of the other Holy People, they lived there. An' so when I was a boy, I would go with my uncle and we'd carry a bundle of *aghaal* up there, and we'd stick those prayer sticks up in a shrine we made up there and we'd chant this prayer. And then sometimes we'd go over to Gobernador Knob. . . ." Nakai gestured toward the east. "Over there across Blanco Canyon where First Woman and First Man found the Asdza'a' Nadleehe', and we would leave some of those *aghaal* over there. And my uncle would explain to me how this was a holy place. But I want you to remember something about Huerfano Mesa. Just close your eyes now and remember how that holy place looked the last time you saw it. Truck road runs up there. It's got radio towers built all over the top of it. Oil companies built 'em. Whole forest of those antennae all along the top of our holy place."

Nakai was shouting now, emphasizing each word with a downward sweep of his fist. "I can't pray to the mountain no more," he shouted. "Not after the white man built all over the top of it. Remember what the stories tell us. Changing Woman left us. She's gone away. . . ."

Leaphorn watched the thin man with the guitar, trying to find a place for him in his memory. He studied the audience, looking for familiar faces, finding a few. Even though he'd rarely worked this eastern Checkerboard side of the Big Reservation, this didn't surprise him. The reservation occupied more space than all of New England but it had a population of no more than 150,000. In a lifetime of policing it, Leaphorn had met, in one way or another, a lot of its inhabitants. And these fifty or sixty assembled under Nakai's old canvas to try the Jesus Road seemed approximately typical. Fewer children than would have been brought to a ceremonial of the traditional Navajo religion, none of the teenagers who would have been hanging around the fringes of a Night Chant playing the mating game, none of the drunks, and certainly no one who looked even moderately affluent. Leaphorn found himself wondering how Nakai paid his expenses. He'd collect whatever donations these people would make, but that wouldn't be much. Perhaps the church he represented paid him out of some missionary fund. Leaphorn considered the pots. What he'd seen in the Nelson's catalog made it clear that some of them brought far, far more than fifty-five dollars. But most of them would have little value and Leaphorn couldn't imagine Nakai getting many of them. Even if they were totally converted, still these were born Navajo. The pots came from burials, and Navajos were conditioned almost from infancy to avoid the dead and to have a special dread of death.

It was exactly what Nakai was talking about. Or, more accurately, shouting. He gripped the microphone stand with both of his small, neat hands, and thundered into it.

"The way I was taught, the way you were taught, when my mother died my uncles came there to the place where we lived out there near Rough Rock and they took the body away and put it somewhere where the coyotes and the ravens couldn't get to it." Nakai paused, gripped the microphone stand, looked down. "You remember that?" he asked, in a voice that was suddenly smaller. "Everybody here remembers somebody dying." Nakai looked up, recovering both composure and voice. "And then there's the four days when you don't do nothing but remember. And nobody speaks the name of the dead. . . . Because there's nothing left of them but the *chindi*, that ghost that is everything that was bad about them and nothing that was good. And I don't say my mother's name anymore—not ever again— because that *chindi* may hear me calling it and come back and make me sick. And what about what was good about my mother? What about what was good about your dead people? What about that? Our Holy People didn't tell us much about that. Not that I know about, they didn't. Some of the Dineh, they have a story about a young man who followed Death, and looked down into the underworld, and saw the dead people sitting around down there. But my clan, we didn't have that story. And I think it got borrowed from the Hopi People. It is one of their beliefs."

Early in this discourse, Leaphorn had been interested in Nakai's strategy. Methods of persuasion intrigued him. But there seemed to be nothing particularly unique in it, and he'd let his attention wander. He had reviewed what little he'd learned from Nakai, and what he might do next, if anything, and then simply watched the audience reaction. Now Leaphorn found himself attentive again. His own Red Forehead Clan had no such story either—at least he hadn't been told it in his own boyhood introduction into the Navajo Way. He had heard it often in his days as an anthropology student at Arizona State. And he'd heard it since from Navajos around Window Rock. But Nakai was probably right. Probably it was another of the many stories the Dineh borrowed from the cultures that surrounded them—borrowed and then refined into abstract philosophical points. The Navajo Way was devoted to the harmony of life. It left death simply terrifying black oblivion.

"We learn this story about how Monster Slayer corners Death in his pit house. But he lets Death live. Because without death there wouldn't be enough room for the babies, for young people.

But I can tell you something truer than that."
Nakai's voice had risen again to a shout.

"Jesus didn't let Death live. Hallelujah! Praise
the Lord!" Nakai danced across the platform,
shouting, drawing from the audience answering
shouts. "When we walk through the Valley of
Death, he is with us, that's what Jesus teaches. We
don't just drift away into the dark night, a ghost
of sickness. We go beyond death. We go into a
happy world. We go where there ain't no hunger.
There ain't no sorrow. Ain't no drunks. No fighting. No seeing relatives run over out here on the
highway. We go into a world where last are first,
and the poor are the rich, and the sick are well,
and the blind, they see again. . . ."

Leaphorn didn't hear the last of it. He was hurrying out through the tent flap into the darkness.
He stood for a while, allowing his eyes to adjust,
breathing the cool, clean high-altitude air. Smell-
ing dust, and sagebrush, shaken, remembering
the day they brought Emma's body home from
the hospital.

It had still been unreal to him, what had happened at Gallup, what the doctor had told him. It
had left him stunned. Emma's brothers had come
to talk to him about it. He'd simply told them
that he knew Emma would want a traditional
burial, and they'd left.

They'd taken the body to her mother's place

over near Blue Gap Chapter House, on the edge of Black Mesa. Under the brush arbor her old aunt had washed her, and combed out her hair, and dressed her in her best blue velvet skirt, and her old squash-blossom necklace, put on her rings, and wrapped her in a blanket. He had sat in the hogan, watching. Her brothers had picked her up then, and put the body in the back of their truck, and driven down the track toward the cliffs. In about an hour they came back without her and took their cleansing sweat bath. He didn't know—would never know—where they'd left her. In a crevice somewhere, probably. High. Protected by deadwood from the predators. Hidden away. He had stayed for two days of the silent days of mourning. Tradition demanded four days, to give the dead time to complete their journey into the oblivion of death. Two days was all he could stand. He'd left them.

And her. But no more of this.

Chee's pickup was still there. Leaphorn walked to it.

"*Ya te'eh,*" Chee said, acknowledging him.

"*Ya te,*" Leaphorn said. He leaned on the truck door. "What brings you out to the Reverend Slick Nakai's revival?"

Chee explained about the backhoe loader, and the abortive chase, and what Tso had told him about where the Backhoe Bandit might be found.

"But I don't think he is going to show up tonight," Chee said. "Getting too late."

"You going to go in and ask Nakai who this fellow is?" Leaphorn asked.

"I'm going to do that," Chee said. "When he's through preaching and when I get a look at the people coming out of the tent."

"You think Nakai would tell you he didn't know this guy, and then tip him off you're looking for him?"

Long silence. "He might," Chee said. "But I think I'll risk it."

Leaphorn didn't comment. It was the decision he would have made. Handle it on Navajo time. No reason to rush in there.

There was no hurry for him either, but he went back into the tent. He'd hear the rest of Nakai's sermon, and see how much money he took in at his collection. And how many, if any, pots. Leaphorn was thinking that maybe he'd learned a little more than he'd first realized. Something had jogged his memory. The thin Navajo with the guitar was the same man he'd seen helping Maxie Davis at the excavation at Chaco Canyon. That answered one small question. A Christian Navajo wouldn't be worrying about stirring up the *chindi* of long-dead Anasazi. But it also made an interesting connection—a man who dug up scientific pots at Chaco worked for a man who sold theoretically legal pots. And a man who sold theoretically legal pots linked to a man who stole a backhoe. Backhoes were machines notoriously useful in uprooting Anasazi ruins and despoiling their graves.

It was just about then, as he walked out of the darkness into the tent, that he became aware of something in his attitude about all this.

He felt an urgency now. The disappearance of Dr. Eleanor Friedman-Bernal had been merely something curious—an oddity. Now he sensed something dangerous. He had never been sure he could find the woman. Now he wondered if she'd be alive if he did.

FIVE

"REMEMBER, BOY," Uncle Frank Sam Nakai would sometimes tell Chee, "when you're tired of walking up a long hill you think about how easy it's going to be walking down." Which was Nakai's Navajo way of saying things tend to even up. For Chee this proved, as his uncle's aphorisms often did, to be true. Chee's bad luck was followed by good luck.

Early Monday a San Juan County sheriff's deputy, who happened to have read the paperwork about the stolen flatbed trailer and backhoe, also happened to get more or less lost while trying to deliver a warrant. He turned off on an access road to a Southern Union pump site and found the trailer abandoned. The backhoe apparently had been unloaded, driven about twenty yards on its own power, and then rolled up a makeshift ramp—presumably into the back of a truck. The truck had almost new tires on its dual rear wheels. The tread pattern was used by Dayton Tire and Rubber, with a single dealer in Farmington and none in Shiprock. The dealer had no trouble remembering. The only truck tires he sold for a month had been to Farmington U-Haul. The company had three trucks out at the moment with dual rear wheels. Two had been recently reshod with Daytons. One was rented to a Farmington furniture company. The other, equipped with a power winch, was rented to Joe B. Nails, P.O. Box 770, Aztec, using a MasterCard.

Farmington police had a record on Nails. One driving while intoxicated. It was enough to provide an employer's name. Wellserve, Inc., a contractor maintaining the Gasco collection system. But Wellserve was a former employer. Nails had quit in August.

Chee learned all of this good news second-hand. He'd spent the morning hanging around Red Rock, worrying about what he'd tell Janet Pete when she got back from Phoenix, and waiting for a witness he was supposed to deliver to the FBI office in Farmington. With that done two hours behind schedule, he had stopped at the Shiprock headquarters and got the first half of the news about the trailer. He'd spent the afternoon hunting around Teec Nos Pos for a fellow who'd broken his brother-in-law's leg. No luck on that. When he pulled back into Shiprock to knock off for the day, he ran into Benally going off shift.

"I guess we got your Backhoe Bandit," Benally said. And he filled Chee in on the rest of it. "U-Haul calls us when he checks the truck in."

That struck Chee as stupid. "You think he'll have the backhoe in it when he returns it?" Chee said. "Otherwise, no proof of anything. What you charge him with?"

Benally had thought of that and so had Captain Largo.

"We bring him in. We tell him we have witnesses who saw him taking the thing out, and we can connect it to the truck he rented, and if he'll cooperate and tell us where it is so we can recover it, and snitch on his buddy, then we go light on him." Benally shrugged, not thinking it would work either. "Better than nothing," he added. "Anyway, the call's out on the U-Haul truck. Maybe we catch him with the backhoe in it."

"I doubt it," Chee said.

Benally agreed. He grinned. "The best plan would have been for you to have grabbed him when he was driving out of the yard with it."

Chee called Pete's office from the station phone. He'd break it by degrees. Tell her first that a lot of things were wrong with the Buick, sort of slip into the part about tearing it up. But Miss Pete wasn't in, wasn't back from Phoenix, had called in and said she'd be held over for a day.

Wonderful. Chee felt immense relief. He put the Buick out of his mind. He thought about the Backhoe Bandit, who was going to get away with it. He thought about what the preacher had told him Saturday night.

The preacher said he didn't know the name of the man who owned the patched-up car. He thought he'd heard him called Jody, or maybe Joey. He thought the man worked in the Blanco field—maybe for Southern Union Gas, but maybe not. The man sometimes brought him a pot which the preacher said he sometimes bought. The last time he saw him, the man had asked if the preacher would buy a whole bunch of pots if the man could get them. "And I told him maybe I could and maybe I couldn't. It would depend on whether I had any money."

"So maybe he'll come back again and maybe he won't."

"I think he'll be back," the preacher had said. "I told him if I couldn't handle it, I knew somebody who could." And he told Chee about the woman anthropologist, and that led him to Lieutenant Leaphorn. The preacher was a talkative man.

Chee sat now in his pickup truck beside the

willows shading the police parking lot. He felt relief on one hand, pressure on the other. The dreaded meeting with Janet Pete was off, at least until tomorrow. But when it came, he wanted to conclude his story by telling Pete how he had nailed the man to blame for all this. It didn't seem likely that was going to happen. Largo's solution was sensible if you were patient, even though it probably wouldn't produce an indictment. Aside from what it had done to Chee, the crime was relatively minor. Theft of equipment worth perhaps $10,000 in its badly used condition. Hardly an event to provoke all-out deployment of police to run down evidence. So the Backhoe Bandit would get away with it. Unless the rent-a-truck could be found with the backhoe on it. Where would it be?

Chee shifted sideways in the seat, leaned a knee against the dashboard, thought. Nails was a pot hunter. Probably he wanted the backhoe for digging up burials to find a lot of them. With the teeth removed from the shovel to minimize breakage, they were a favorite tool of the professionals. And from what the preacher said, Nails must be going professional. He must have found a likely ruins. What Nails had told the preacher suggested he'd found a wholesale source. Therefore it was a safe presumption that he'd stolen the backhoe to dig them.

So far it was easy. The hard question was where?

The willow branches dangling around Chee's pickup had turned yellow with the season. Chee studied them a moment to rest the brain. Surely he must know something helpful. How about the trailer? Stolen. Then brought back to haul out the backhoe. Then abandoned in favor of the truck? The night the trailer was stolen the backhoe was still being repaired. Had the head off the engine, in fact. So they took the trailer, and brought it back when the backhoe was ready to roll. Pretty stupid, on the face of it. But Chee had checked and learned the trailer was scheduled to haul equipment to a job at Burnt Water the next day. The Backhoe Bandit knew a hell of a lot about what went on in that maintenance yard. Interesting, but it didn't help now.

The next answers did. The question was why steal the trailer at all? Why not simply rent the U-Haul truck earlier, and haul the backhoe out on that? And why not rent the backhoe, instead of stealing it? As Chee thought it through, the answers connected. Rental trucks were easy to trace, so the Backhoe Bandit avoided the risk of having the truck seen at the burglary. A rented backhoe would also be easy to trace. But there would be no reason to trace it if it was checked back in after it was used. So why . . . ? Chee's orderly mind sorted through it. The truck was needed instead of the trailer because the trailer couldn't be pulled where the backhoe was needed. Could it be the dig site was somewhere from which the backhoe couldn't be extricated? Of course. It would be at the bottom of someplace, and that would explain why Nails had rented a truck with a power winch. Running a backhoe down the steep slope of a canyon could well be possible where pulling it out wouldn't be.

Chee climbed out of the cab, trotted into the office, and called the Farmington office of Wellserve, Inc. Yes, they could provide the police with a copy of their well-service route map. Yes, the service superintendent could mark the route Nails had served.

When Chee left Wellserve with the map folded on the seat beside him he had three hours left before sundown. Then there would be a half-moon. A good night for a pot hunter to work, and a good night to hunt pot hunters. He stopped at the sheriff's office and found out who was patrolling where tonight. If Nails was off reservation land, he'd need a deputy along to make an arrest. Then he drove up the San Juan River valley through the little oil town of Bloomfield, and out of the valley into the infinity of sagebrush that covers the Blanco Plateau. He was remembering he'd read somewhere of somebody estimating more than a hundred thousand Anasazi sites on the Colorado Plateau—only a few of them excavated, only a few thousand even mapped. But it wouldn't be impossible. He would guess Nails had found sites along the service roads he traveled and would be looting them. Chee knew some of those sites himself. And he knew what attracted the Anasazi. A cliff faced to catch the winter sun and shaded in the summer, enough floodplain to grow something, and a source of water. That, particularly the water, narrowed it a lot.

He scouted Canyon Largo first, and Blanco Canyon, and Jasis Canyon. He found two sites that had been dug into fairly recently. But nothing new and no sign of the tire tread pattern he was looking for. He moved north then and checked Gobernador Canyon and La Jara and the Vaqueros Wash eastward in the Carson National Forest. He found nothing. He skipped westward, driving far faster than the speed limit down New Mexico Highway 44. The light was dying now—a cloudless autumn evening with the western sky a dull copper glow. He checked out a couple of canyons near Ojo Encino, restricting himself always to the access roads gouged out to reach the gas wells and pump stations Nails had been serving.

By midnight he finished checking the roads leading from the Star Lake Pump Station, driving slowly, using his flashlight to check for tracks at every possible turnoff. He circled back past the sleeping trading post the maps called White Horse Lake. He crossed the Continental Divide, and dropped into the network of arroyos that drain Chaco Mesa. Again he found nothing. He circled back across Chaco Wash and picked up the gravel road that leads northwestward toward Nageezi Trading Post.

Beyond Betonnie Tsosie Wash he stopped the pickup in the middle of the road. He climbed out wearily, stretched, and turned on the flash to check the turnoff of an access trail. He stood in the light of the half-moon, yawning, his flash reflecting from the chalky dust. It showed, clear and fresh, the dual tracks of an almost new Dayton tire tread.

Chee's watch showed 2:04 A.M. At 2:56 he found the place where, maybe a thousand years ago, a little band of Anasazi families had lived, and built their cluster of small stone shelters and living spaces, and died. Chee had been walking for more than a mile. He had left his pickup by a pump site and followed the twin tracks on foot. The pump marked the dead end of this branch of the service road—if two ruts wandering through the sage and juniper could be called that. From here, the dual tires had made their own road. Away from the hard-packed ruts, they were easy to follow now—crushed tumbleweeds, broken brush, the sharp smell of bruised sage.

They led up a long slope, and Chee guessed they wouldn't lead far. He walked carefully and quietly, moon over his shoulder, flash off. The slow huffing of the pump motor diminished behind him. He stopped, listening for the sound the backhoe motor would be making. He heard a coyote, and then its partner. One behind him, one on the ridge to his left. It was work time for predators, with all the little nocturnal rodents out braving death to find a meal.

He didn't see the truck until he was within fifty feet of it. Nails had nosed it into a cluster of juniper just over the crest of the hill. The doors of its van box stood open, a square black shape with the ramp used to unload the backhoe still in place. Chee stared, listening, feeling a mixture of excitement, exultation, and uneasiness. He put his hand on the pistol in his jacket pocket. Chee did not like pistols in general, and the one he had carried since being sworn into the force was no exception. But now the heavy hard metal was reassuring. He walked to the truck, placing each step carefully, stopping to listen. The cab was empty, the doors unlocked. The wire cable from the winch spool extended down the steep slope, slack. If the backhoe was down there, as it must be, the engine wasn't running. The silence was almost total. From far behind him, he could hear the faint sound of the walking beam pump. No coyote sounds now. The air was moving up the slope past his face, a faint coolness.

Chee held the cable in his left hand and started down the slope, following the path broken by the backhoe, trying to keep his weight on his feet, trying to avoid the noise sliding would make.

The slope was too steep. He slid a few feet, regained control. Slid again as the earth gave way under his feet. Then he lay on his back, motionless, breathing dust, cursing under his breath at the noise he had made. He listened, hand gripping the cable. Down here under the ridge, he could no longer hear the distant pump motor. The coyote yipped somewhere off to his left and provoked an answering yip from its partner. He saw the backhoe, partially visible through the brush, its motor silent. The half-moon lit the roof of its cab, the shovel, and part of the jointed arm that controlled it. Nails apparently had been frightened away. It didn't matter. He had the backhoe. He had the truck that had hauled it here, and the record would show Nails had rented the truck.

Chee gripped the cable and shifted his free hand to push himself erect. He felt cloth under his fingers. And a button. And the hard bone and cold skin of a wrist. He scrambled away from it.

The form lay facedown, head upslope, in the deep darkness cast by a juniper—its left hand stretching out toward the cable. A man, Chee saw. He squatted, controlling the shock. And when it was controlled, he leaned forward and felt the wrist.

Dead. Dead long enough to be stiff. He bent low over the corpse and turned on his flash. It wasn't Nails. It was a Navajo. A young man, hair cut short, wearing a blue checked shirt with two stains on its back. Chee touched one of them with a tentative finger. Stiff. Dried blood. The man had apparently been shot twice. In the middle of the back and just above the hip.

Chee snapped off the light. He thought of the Navajo's ghost, hovering nearby. He turned his mind away from that. The *chindi* was out there, representing all that was evil in the dead man's being. But one did not think of *chindis* out in the darkness. Where was Nails? Most likely, hours away from here. But why did he leave the truck? This Navajo must be the one seen with Nails when they'd stolen the backhoe. Maybe the Navajo had driven the truck, Nails had come in his own car. Odd, but possible.

Chee moved cautiously the few remaining yards to the bottom of the hill. It was full dark here, the moonlight blocked by the high ground. Just enough reflected light to guide his feet. A falling out of thieves, Chee thought. A fight. Nails pulls a gun. The Navajo runs. Nails shoots him. He didn't believe Nails would still be here, or anywhere near here. But he walked carefully.

Even so he almost tripped over the bag before he saw it. It was black plastic, the sort sold in little boxes of a dozen to line wastebaskets. Chee untwisted the wire securing its top and felt inside. Fragments of pottery, just as he'd expected. Between him and the backhoe, more such bags were clustered. Chee walked past them to look at the machine.

It had been turned off with the shovel locked high over the trench it had been digging into a low, brush-covered mound. Scattered along the excavation was a clutter of flat stones. Once they must have formed the wall of an Anasazi settlement. He didn't notice the bones until he turned on his flash.

They were everywhere. A shoulder blade, a thigh bone, part of a skull, ribs, four or five connected vertebrae, part of a foot, a lower jaw.

Jim Chee was modern man built upon traditional Navajo. This was simply too much death. Too many ghosts disturbed. He backed away from the excavation, flashlight still on, careful no longer. He wanted only to be away from here. Into the sunlight. Into the cleansing heat of a sweat bath. To be surrounded by the healing, curing sounds of a Ghostway ceremonial. He started up the slope, pulling himself up by the cable.

The panic receded. First he would check the backhoe cab. He trotted to it, guided by the flash. He checked the metal serial-number plate and the Navajo Nation Road Department number painted on its side. Then he flashed the light into the cab.

A man was sitting there, slumped sideways against the opposite door, his open eyes reflecting white in Chee's flash. The left side of his face was black with what must be blood. But Chee could see his mustache and enough of his face to know that he had found Joe Nails.

SIX

LEAPHORN CAME HOME to Window Rock long after midnight. He hadn't bothered to turn on the lights. He drank from his cupped palms in the bathroom and folded his clothing over the bedside chair (where Emma had so often sat to read or knit, to do the thousand small things that Emma did). He had turned the bed ninety degrees so that his eyes would open in the morning to the shock of a different view. That broke his lifelong habit, the automatic waking thought of "Where's Emma?" and what then followed. He had moved from his side of the bed to Emma's—which had eliminated that once-happy habit of reaching out to touch her when he drifted into sleep.

Now he lay flat on his back, feeling tired muscles relax, thinking about the food in Eleanor

Friedman-Bernal's refrigerator, drifting from that to her arrangement with Nakai to inspect contributed pots and from that to the notebook Nakai had described. He hadn't noticed a pocket-sized leather notebook in her apartment—but then it might be almost anywhere in the room. Thatcher had made no real search. On the long drive homeward across the Checkerboard from Huerfano Mesa, he had thought of why Elliot hadn't mentioned being sent by Friedman to see Nakai and collect a pot. It must have seemed odd to Elliot, this abortive mission. Why not mention it? Before Leaphorn could come to any conclusion, he drifted off to sleep, and it was morning.

He showered, inspected his face, decided he could go another few days without a shave, made himself a breakfast of sausage and fried eggs—violating his diet with the same guilty feelings he always had when Emma was away visiting her family. He read the mail that Saturday had brought him, and the Gallup *Independent*. He snapped on the television, snapped it off again, stood at the window looking out on the autumn morning. Windless. Cloudless. Silent except for a truck rolling down Navajo Route 3. The little town of Window Rock was taking Sunday off. Leaphorn noticed the glass was dusty—a condition Emma had never tolerated. He got a handkerchief from his drawer and polished the pane.

He polished other windows. Abruptly he walked to the telephone and called Chaco Canyon.

Until recently telephone calls between the world outside and Chaco had traveled via a Navajo Communications Company telephone line. From Crownpoint northeast, the wire wandered across the rolling grassland, attached mostly to fence posts and relying on its own poles only when no fence was available going in the right direction. This system made telephone service subject to the same hazards as the ranch fence on which it piggybacked. Drifts of tumbleweeds, winter blizzards, dry rot, errant cattle, broke down both fences and communications. When it was operating, voices sometimes tended to fade in and out with the wind velocity. But recently this system had been modernized. Calls were now routed two hundred miles east to Santa Fe, then beamed to a satellite and rebroadcast to a receiving dish at Chaco. The space age system, like the National Aeronautics and Space Administration which made it possible, was frequently out of operation. When it operated at all, voices tended to fade in and out with the wind velocity. Today was no exception.

A woman's voice answered, strong at first, then drifting away into space. No, Bob Luna wasn't in. No use ringing his number because she'd seen him driving away and she hadn't seen him return.

How about Maxie Davis?

Just a minute. She might not be up yet. It was, after all, early Sunday morning.

Maxie Davis was up. "Who?" she asked. "I'm sorry. I can hardly hear you."

Leaphorn could hear Maxie Davis perfectly—as if she were standing beside him. "Leaphorn," he repeated. "The Navajo cop who was out there a couple of days ago."

"Oh. Have you found her?"

"No luck," Leaphorn said. "Do you remember a little leather-covered notebook she used? Probably carried in her shirt pocket?"

"Notebook? Yeah. I remember it. She always used it when she was working."

"Know where she keeps it? When it's not with her?"

"No idea. Probably in a drawer somewhere."

"You've known her long?"

"Off and on, yes. Since we were graduate students."

"How about Dr. Elliot?"

Maxie Davis laughed. "We're sort of a team, I guess you'd say." And then, perhaps thinking Leaphorn would misunderstand, added: "Professionally. We're the two who are going to write the bible on the Anasazi." She laughed again, the sound fading in and out. "After Randall Elliot and me, no more need for Anasazi research."

"Not Friedman-Bernal? She's not part of it?"

"Different field," Davis said. "She's ceramics. We're people. She's pots."

They had decided, he and Emma, to install the telephone in the kitchen. To hang it on the wall beside the refrigerator. Standing there, listening to Maxie Davis, Leaphorn inspected the room. It was neat. No dishes, dirty or otherwise, were in sight. Windows clean, sink clean, floor clean. Leaphorn leaned forward to the full reach of the telephone receiver cord and plucked a napkin from the back of the chair. He'd used it while he'd eaten his eggs. He held the receiver against his ear with his shoulder while he folded it.

"I'm going to come back out there," he said. "I'd like to talk to you. And to Elliot if he's there."

"I doubt it," Maxie Davis said. "He's usually out in the field on Sunday."

But Elliot was there, leaning against the porch support watching Leaphorn as he parked his pickup in the apartment's courtyard.

"Ya tay," Elliot said, getting the pronunciation of the Navajo greeting almost right. "Didn't know policemen worked on Sunday."

"They don't tell you that when they recruit you," Leaphorn said, "but it happens now and then."

Maxie Davis appeared at the door. She was wearing a loose blue T-shirt decorated with a figure copied from a petroglyph. Short dark hair fell around her face. She looked feminine, intelligent, and beautiful.

"I'll bet I know where she keeps that notebook," Davis said. "Do you still have the key?"

Leaphorn shook his head. "I'll get one from headquarters." Or, he thought, failing that, it would be simple enough to get into the apartment. He'd noticed that when Thatcher had unlocked the door.

"Luna's away," Elliot said. "We can get in through the patio door."

Elliot managed it with the long blade of his pocketknife, simply sliding the blade in and lifting the latch.

"Something you learn in graduate school," he said.

Or in juvenile detention centers, Leaphorn thought. He wondered if Elliot had ever been in one of those. It didn't seem likely. Jail is not socially acceptable for prep school boys.

Everything seemed exactly as it had been when he'd been here with Thatcher—the same stale air, the same dustiness, the boxes of pots, the disarray. Thatcher had searched it, in his tentative way, looking for evidence that Dr. Eleanor Friedman-Bernal was a violator of the Federal Antiquities Act. Now Leaphorn intended to search it in his own way, looking for the woman herself.

"Ellie kept her purse in the dresser," Maxie Davis said. She opened a bottom drawer. "In here. And I remember seeing her drop that notebook in it when she came in from work."

Davis extracted a purse and handed it to Leaphorn. It was beige leather. It looked new and it looked expensive. Leaphorn unsnapped it, checked through lipstick, small bottles, package of sugarless gum, Tums, small scissors, odds and ends. No small leather notebook. Emma had three purses—a very small one, a very good one, and a worn one used in the workaday world of shopping.

"She had another purse?" Leaphorn said, making it half a question.

Davis nodded. "This was her good one." She checked into the drawer. "Not here."

Leaphorn's mild disappointment at not finding the notebook was offset by mild surprise. The wrong purse was missing. Friedman-Bernal had not taken her social purse with her for the weekend. She had taken her working purse.

"I want to take a sort of rough inventory," Leaphorn said. "I'm going to rely on your memory. See if we can determine what she took with her."

There were the disclaimers he expected, from both Maxie Davis and Elliot, that they really didn't know much about Ellie's wardrobe or Ellie's possessions. But within an hour, they had a rough list on the back of an envelope. Ellie had taken no suitcase. She had taken a small canvas gym bag. She'd probably taken no makeup or cosmetics. No skirt was missing. No dress. She had taken only jeans and a long-sleeved cotton shirt.

Maxie Davis sat on the bed, examining her jottings, looking thoughtful. "No way of knowing about socks or underwear or things like that. But I don't think she took any pajamas." She motioned toward the chest of drawers. "There's an old blue pair in there I've seen her wear, and a sort of worn-out checked set, and a fancy new pair. Silk." Davis looked at him, checking the level of Leaphorn's understanding of such things. "For company," she explained. "I doubt if she would have a fourth set, or bring it out here anyway."

"Okay," Leaphorn said. "Did she have a sleeping bag?"

"Yeah," Davis said. "Of course." She sorted through the things on the closet shelf. "That's gone too," she said.

"So she was camping out," Leaphorn said. "Sleeping out. Probably nothing social. Probably working. Who did she work with?"

"Nobody, really," Elliot said. "It was a one-woman project. She worked by herself."

"Let's settle down somewhere and talk about that," Leaphorn said.

They settled in the living room. Leaphorn perched on the edge of a sofa that looked and felt as if it would fold outward into a bed, Davis and Elliot on the Park Service Purchasing Office low-bid overstuffed couch. Much of what Leaphorn heard he already knew from his own studies a lifetime ago at Arizona State. He had considered telling the two about his master's degree and decided against it. The time that might have saved had no value to Leaphorn now. And sometimes something might be gained by seeming to know less than you did. And so Leaphorn listened patiently to basic stuff, mostly from Davis, about how the Anasazi culture had risen on the Colorado Plateau, almost certainly a progression from the small, scattered families of hunters and seed collectors who lived in pit houses, and somehow learned to make baskets, and then the rudiments of agriculture, and then how to irrigate their crops by controlling runoff from rain, and—probably in the process of caulking baskets with fire-dried mud to make them waterproof—how to make pottery.

"Important cultural breakthrough," Elliot inserted. "Improved storage possibilities. Opened a door to art." He laughed. "Also gave anthropology something a lot more durable than baskets to hunt, and measure, and study, and all that. But you already know a lot about this, don't you?"

"Why do you say that?" Leaphorn never allowed a subject to shift him from the role of interrogator unless Leaphorn wanted to be shifted.

"Because you don't ask any questions," Elliot said. "Maxie isn't always perfectly clear. Either you're not interested in this background, or you already know it."

"I know something about it," Leaphorn said. "You've said Friedman's interest was in pottery. Apparently she was interested mostly in one kind of pot. Pots which have a kind of corrugated finish. Probably some other revealing details. Right?"

"Ellie thought she had identified one specific potter," Elliot said. "A distinctive individual touch."

Leaphorn said nothing. That sounded mildly interesting. But—even given the intense interest of anthropologists in the Anasazi culture and its mysterious fate—it didn't seem very important. His expression told Elliot what he was thinking.

"One potter. Dead probably seven hundred and fifty years." Elliot put his boots on the battered coffee table. "So what's the big deal? The big deal is, Ellie knows where he lived. Out there at BC57, across the wash from Pueblo Bonito, because she found a lot of his pots there broken in the process of being made. Must have been where he worked. . . ."

"She," Maxie Davis said. "Where she worked."

"Okay, she." Elliot shook his head, regaining his chain of thought, showing no sign of irritation. It was part of a game they played, Leaphorn thought. Elliot's boots were dusty, scarred, flat-heeled, practical. A soft brown leather, perfectly fitted, extremely expensive.

Davis was leaning forward, wanting Leaphorn to understand this. "Nobody before had ever found a way to link the pot with the person who made it—not before Ellie began noticing this peculiar technique repeated in a lot of those BC57 pots. She had already noticed it in a couple of others from other places—and now she had found the source. Where they came from. And she was lucky in another way. Not only was this potter prolific, she was good. Her pots traded around. Ellie tracked one back to the Salmon Ruins over on the San Juan, and she thinks one came out of a burial near the White House Ruin in Canyon de Chelly, and . . ."

If Elliot had any objection to Maxie Davis's commandeering his story, his face hadn't showed it. But now he said: "Get to the important point."

Maxie looked at him. "Well, she's not sure about that," she said.

"Maybe not, but this BC57 site was one of the last ones built—just before everybody disappeared. They dated a roof beam to 1292, and some of the charcoal in what might have been a kiln fire to 1298. So she was working just about the time they turned out the lights here and walked away. And Ellie is beginning to think she might be able to pin down where she went."

"That's the really big deal out here." Davis waved her arms. "Where'd the Anasazi go? The big huge mystery that all the magazine writers write about."

"Among a couple of other big questions," Elliot said. "Like why they built roads when they didn't have wheels, or pack animals, and why they left, and why they lived in this place in the first place with so damn little wood, or water, or good land, and . . ." Elliot shrugged. "The more we learn, the more we wonder."

"This man who was coming out to see her the week after she disappeared, do you know who he was?"

"Lehman," Davis said. "He came." She smiled ruefully. "Plenty sore about it. He came on a Wednesday and it had rained Tuesday night and you know how that road gets."

"And he's . . ." Leaphorn began to ask.

"He's the hotshot in Ellie's field," Elliot said. "I think he was chairman of her dissertation committee when she got her doctorate at Madison. Now he's a professor at University of New Mexico. Two or three books on Mimbres, and Hohokam, and Anasazi pottery evolution. Top guru in the ceramics field."

"Ellie's equivalent of our Devanti," Davis said. "She pretty well had to persuade Lehman she knew what she was talking about. Like in migrations, Elliot and I have to deal with our top honcho."

"Doctor Delbert Devanti," Elliot said. "Arkansas's answer to Einstein." The tone was sardonic.

"He's proved some things," Maxie Davis said, her voice flat. "Even if he didn't go to Phillips Exeter Academy, or Princeton."

There was silence. Elliot's long, handsome face had become stiff and blank. Maxie glanced at him. In the glance Leaphorn read . . . what? Was it anger? Malice? She turned to Leaphorn. "Please note the blue blood's lofty contempt for the plebeians. Devanti is definitely a plebe. He sounds like corn pone."

"And is often wrong," Elliot said.

Davis laughed. "There is that," she said.

"But you give people the right to be wrong if they came out of the cotton patch," Elliot said. His voice sounded normal, or almost normal, but Leaphorn could see the tension in the line of his jaw.

"More of an excuse for it," Maxie said, mildly. "Maybe he overlooked something while he was working nights to feed his family. No tutors to do his digging in the library."

To that, Randall Elliot said nothing. Leaphorn watched. Where would this tension lead? Nowhere, apparently. Maxie had nothing more to say.

"You two work as a team," Leaphorn said. "That right?"

"More or less," Davis said. "We have common interests in the Anasazi."

"Like how?" Leaphorn asked.

"It's complicated. Actually it involves food economics, nutrition tolerances, population sizes, things like that, and you spend a lot more time working on programming statistical projections in the computer than you do digging in the field. Really dull stuff, unless you're weird enough to be into it." She smiled at Leaphorn. A smile of such dazzling charm that once it would have destroyed him.

"And Randall here," she added, "is doing something much more dramatic." She poked him with her elbow—a gesture that almost made what she was saying mere teasing. "He is revolutionizing physical anthropology. He is finding a way to solve the mystery, once and for all, of what happened to these people."

"Population studies," Elliot said in a low voice. "Involves migrations and genetics."

"Rewrites all the books if it works," Maxie Davis said, smiling at Leaphorn. "Elliots do not spend their time on small things. In the navy they are admirals. In universities they are presidents. In politics they are senators. When you start at the top you have to aim high. Or everybody is disappointed."

Leaphorn was uncomfortable. "It would be a problem," he said.

"But not one I had," Maxie Davis said. "I'm white trash."

"Maxie never tires of reminding me of the silver spoon in my crib," Elliot said, managing a grin. "It doesn't have much to do with finding Ellie, though."

"But you have a point," Leaphorn said. "Dr. Friedman wouldn't have missed that appointment with Lehman without a good reason."

"Hell, no," Maxie said. "That's what I told that idiot at the sheriff's office."

"Do you know why he was coming? Specifically."

"She was going to bring him up-to-date," Elliot said.

"She was going to hit him with a bombshell," Maxie said. "That's what I think. I think she finally had it put together."

There was something in Elliot's expression. Maybe skepticism. Or disapproval. But Davis was enthusiastic.

"What did she tell you?"

"Nothing much, really. But I could just sense it. That things were working out. But she wouldn't say much."

"It's not traditional," Elliot said. "Not among us scientists."

Leaphorn found himself as interested in what was going on with Elliot as in the thrust of the conversation. Elliot's tone now was faintly mocking. Davis had caught it, too. She looked at Elliot and then back at Leaphorn, speaking directly to him.

"That's true," she said. "Before one boasts, one must have done something to boast about."

She said it in the mildest of voices, without looking at Elliot, but Elliot's face flushed.

"You think she had found something important," Leaphorn said. "She didn't tell you anything, but something caused you to think that. Something specific. Can you think what it was?"

Davis leaned back on the couch. She caught her lower lip between her teeth. She laid her hand, in a gesture that looked casual, on Elliot's thigh. She thought.

"Ellie was excited," she said. "Happy, too. For a week, maybe a little longer, before she left." She got up from the couch and walked past Leaphorn into the bedroom. Infinite grace, Leaphorn thought.

"She'd been over in Utah. I remember that. To

Bluff, and Mexican Hat and—" Her voice from the bedroom was indistinct.

"Montezuma Creek?" Leaphorn asked.

"Yes, all that area along the southern edge of Utah. And when she came back"—Davis emerged from the bedroom carrying a Folgers Coffee carton—"she had all these potsherds." She put the box on the coffee table. "Same ones, I think. At least, I remember it was this box."

The box held what seemed to Leaphorn to be as many as fifty fragments of pots, some large, some no more than an inch across.

Leaphorn sorted through them, looking for nothing in particular but noticing that all were reddish brown, and all bore a corrugated pattern.

"Done by her potter, I guess," Leaphorn said. "Did she say where she got them?"

"From a Thief of Time," Elliot said. "From a pot hunter."

"She didn't say that," Davis said.

"She went to Bluff to look for pot hunters. To see what they were finding. She told you that."

"Did she say which one?" Leaphorn asked. Here might be an explanation of how she had vanished. If she had been dealing directly with a pot hunter, he might have had second thoughts. Might have thought he had sold her evidence that would put him in prison. Might have killed her when she came back for more.

"She didn't mention any names," Davis said.

"Hardly necessary," Elliot said. "Looking for pot hunters around Bluff, you'd go see Old Man Houk. Or one of his friends. Or hired hands."

Bluff, Leaphorn thought. Maybe he would go there and talk to Houk. It must be the same Houk. The surviving father of the drowned murderer. The memories flooded back. Such tragedy burns deep into the brain.

"Something else you might need to know," Davis said. "Ellie had a pistol."

Leaphorn waited.

"She kept it in the same drawer with that purse."

"It wasn't there," Leaphorn said.

"No. It wasn't," Davis said. "I guess she took it with her."

Yes, Leaphorn thought. He would go to Bluff and talk to Houk. As Leaphorn remembered him, he was a most unusual man.

SEVEN

JIM CHEE SAT on the edge of his bunk, rubbed his eyes with his knuckles, cleared his throat, and considered the uneasiness that had troubled his sleep. Too much death. The disturbed earth littered with too many bones. He put that thought aside. Was there enough water left in the tank of his little aluminum trailer to afford a shower? The answer was perhaps. But it wasn't a new problem. Chee long ago had developed a method for minimizing its effects. He filled his coffeepot ready for perking. He filled a drinking glass as a tooth-brushing reserve and a mustard jar for the sweat bath he was determined to take.

Chee climbed down the riverbank carrying the jar, a paper cup, and a tarpaulin. At his sweat bath in the willows beside the San Juan, he collected enough driftwood to heat his rocks, filled the cup with clean, dry sand, started his fire, and sat, legs crossed, waiting and thinking. No profit in thinking of Janet Pete—that encounter represented a humiliation that could be neither avoided nor minimized. Any way he figured it, the cost would be $900, plus Janet Pete's disdain. He thought instead of last night, of the two bodies being photographed, being loaded into the police van by the San Juan County deputies. He thought of the pots, carefully wrapped in newspapers inside the garbage bags.

When the rocks were hot enough and the fire had burned itself down to coals, he covered the sweat bath frame with the tarp, slid under it. He squatted, singing the sweat bath songs that the Holy People had taught the first clans, the songs to force contamination and sickness from the body. He savored the dry heat, conscious of muscles relaxing, perspiration seeping from his skin, trickling behind his ears, down his back, wet against his flanks. He poured a palmful of water from the jar into his hand and sprinkled it onto the rocks, engulfing himself in an explosion of steam. He inhaled this hot fog deeply, felt his body slick with moisture. He was dizzy now, free. Concern for bones and Buicks vanished in the hot darkness. Chee was conscious instead of his lungs at work, of open pores, supple muscles, of his own vigorous health. Here was his *hozro*—his harmony with what surrounded him.

When he threw back the tarp and emerged, rosy with body heat and streaming sweat, he felt light of head, light of foot, generally wonderful. He rubbed himself down with the sand he'd collected, climbed back to the trailer, and took his shower. Chee added to the desert dweller's habitual frugality with water the special caution that those who live in trailers relearn each time they cover themselves with suds and find there's nothing left in the reservoir. He soaped a small area, rinsed it, then soaped another, hurried by the smell of his coffee perking. His Navajo genes spared him the need to shave again for probably a week, but he shaved anyway. It was a way to delay the inevitable.

That was delayed a bit more by the lack of a telephone in Chee's trailer. He used the pay phone beside the convenience store on the highway. Janet Pete wasn't at her office. Maybe, the receptionist said, she had gone down to the Justice building, to the police station. She had been worried about her new car. Chee dialed the station. Three call-back messages for him, two from Janet Pete of DNA, the tribal legal service, one from Lieutenant Leaphorn. Leaphorn had just called and talked to Captain Largo. The captain then had left the message for Chee to call Leaphorn at his home number in Window Rock after 6:00 P.M. Had Pete left any messages? Yes, with the last call she had said to tell him she wanted to pick up her car.

Chee called Pete's home number. He tapped his fingers nervously as the telephone rang. There was a click.

"Sorry I can't come to the phone now," Pete's voice said. "If you will leave a message after the tone sounds, I will call you."

Chee listened to the tone, and the silence following it. He could think of nothing sensible to say, and hung up. Then he drove over to Tso's garage. Surely the damage hadn't been as bad as he remembered.

The damage was exactly as he'd remembered. The car squatted on Tso's towing dolly, discolored with dust, the front wheel grotesquely misaligned, paint scraped from the fender, the little clips that once held Janet Pete's favorite chrome strip holding nothing. A small dent in the door. A large dent marring the robin's-egg blue of the rear fender. Looking crippled and dirty.

"Not so terrible," Tso said. "Nine fifty to eleven hundred dollars and it's good as it was. But she really ought to fix all those problems it had when you first drove it in." Tso was wiping the grease from his hands in a gesture that reminded Chee of greedy anticipation. "Grabby brakes, slack steering, all that."

"I'm going to need some credit," Chee said.

Tso thought about that, his face full of remembered debts, of friendships violated. Chee's thoughts of Tso, always warm, began turning cool. While they did, Janet Pete's motor pool sedan pulled up beside the building. The front door opened. Janet Pete emerged. She looked at the Buick, at two other cars awaiting Tso's ministrations, and gave Chee a dazzling smile.

"Where's my Buick?" she asked. "How did it run? Did you . . ."

The question trailed off. Janet Pete looked again at the Buick.

"My God," she said. "Was anybody killed?"

"Well," Chee said. He cleared his throat. "You see, I was driving down . . ."

"Bad shocks," Tso said. "Slack steering. But Chee here took it out anyway. Sort of a safety check." Tso shrugged, made a wry face. "Could have been killed," he said.

Which, if you thought about it right, was perhaps true, Chee thought. His displeasure with Tso was swept away by a wave of gratitude.

He made a depreciating gesture. "I should have been more careful," he said. "Tso warned me."

Janet was staring at the Buick, reconciling what she saw with what she had left. "They told me everything was fine," she said.

"Odometer set back," Tso said. "Brake lining unevenly worn. U-joint loose. Steering loose. Needed lots of work."

Janet Pete bit her lip. Thought. "Can I use your telephone?"

Chee overheard only part of it. Getting past the salesman to the sales manager to the general manager. It seemed to Chee that the general manager mostly listened.

"Officer Chee doesn't seem to be too badly hurt, but I haven't heard from his lawyer . . . mechanic's list of defects shows . . . that's a third-degree misdemeanor in New Mexico, odometer tampering is. Yes, well, a jury can decide that for us. I think the fine is five thousand dollars. You can pick it up at Tso's garage in Shiprock. He tells me he won't release it until you pay his costs. Towing, inspection, I guess. My lawyer told me to make sure that none of your mechanics worked on it until he decides . . ."

On the way to get a cup of coffee in Janet Pete's motor pool sedan, Chee said, "He'll have his mechanics fix everything."

"Probably," Janet said. "Wouldn't be much of a lawsuit anyway. Not worth it."

"Just letting him sweat a little?"

"You know, they wouldn't try that on you. You're a man. They pull that crap on women. They figure they can sell a woman on the baby blue paint and the chrome stripe. Sell us a lemon."

"Um," Chee said, which provoked a period of silence.

"What really happened?" Janet asked.

"Steering failed," Chee said, feeling uneasy.

"Come on," Janet said.

"Tried to make a turn," Chee said. "Missed it."

"How fast? Come on. What was going on?"

So Jim Chee explained it, all about the missing trailer, and the missing backhoe, and Captain Largo, and that led to what he had found last night.

Janet had heard about it on the radio. Over coffee she was full of questions, not all of them about the crime.

"I heard you were a *hatathali*," she said. "That you sing the Blessing Way."

"I'm still learning," Chee said. "The only one I performed was in the family. A relative. But I know it now. If anybody wants one done."

"How do you get time off? Isn't that a problem? Eight days, isn't it? Or do you sing the shorter version?"

"No problem yet. No customers."

"Another thing I hear about you—you have a *belagana* girlfriend. A teacher over at Crown-point."

"She's gone away," Chee said, and felt that odd sensation of hearing, from some external point, his voice saying the words. "Gone away to be a graduate student in Wisconsin."

"Oh," Janet said.

"We write," Chee said. "I sent her a pregnant cat once."

Janet looked surprised. "Testing her patience?"

Chee tried to think how to explain it. A stupid thing to send to Mary Landon, stupid to mention it now.

"At the time I thought it had some symbolism," he said.

Janet let the silence live, Navajo fashion. If he had more he wanted to say about Mary Landon and the cat, he would say it. He liked her for that. But he had nothing more to say.

"It was that cat you told me about? Last summer when you'd arrested that old man I was representing. The cat the coyote was after?"

Chee was stirring his coffee, head down but conscious that Janet Pete was studying him. He nodded, remembering. Janet Pete had suggested he provide his stray cat with a coyote-proof home and they had gone to a Farmington pet store and bought one of those plastic and wire cages used to ship pets on airliners. He had used it, eventually, to ship the abandoned white man's cat back to the white man's world.

"Symbolism," Janet Pete said. Now she was stirring her coffee, looking down at the swirl the spoon made.

To the top of her head, Chee said: "*Belagana* cat can't adapt to the Navajo ways. Starves. Eaten by coyote. My stray cat experiment fails. I accept the failure. Cat goes back to the world of the *belaganas*, where there's more to eat and the coyote doesn't get you." It was more than Chee had intended to say. He was torn. He wanted to talk about Mary Landon, about the going away of Mary Landon. But he wasn't comfortable talking about it to Janet Pete.

"She didn't want to stay on the reservation. You didn't want to leave," Janet Pete said. "You are saying you understand her problem."

"Our problem," Chee said. "My problem."

Janet Pete sipped her coffee. "Mine was a law professor. Assistant professor, to be technical." She put the cup down and considered. "You know," she said, "maybe it was the same symbolic cat problem. Let me see if I can make it fit."

Chee waited. Like Mary Landon, Janet Pete had large, expressive eyes. Dark brown instead of blue. Now they were surrounded by frown lines as Janet Pete thought.

"Doesn't fit so well," she said. "He wanted a helpmate." She laughed. "Adam's rib. Something to hold back the loneliness of the young man pursuing his brilliant career at law. The Indian maiden." The words sounded bitter, but she smiled at Chee. "You remember. Few years ago, Indian maidens were in with the Yuppies. Like squash-blossom necklaces and declaring yourself to be part Cherokee or Sioux if you wanted to write romantic poetry."

"Not so much now," Chee said. "I gather you agreed to disagree."

"Not really," she said. "The offer remains open. Or so he tells me."

"Fits in a way," Chee said. "I wanted her to be my Navajo."

"She was a schoolteacher? At Crownpoint?"

"For three years," Chee said.

"But didn't want to make a career out of it. I can see her point."

"That wasn't exactly the problem. It was raising kids out here. More than that, too. I could leave. Had an offer from the FBI. Better money. Sort of a choice involved, as she saw it. Did I want her enough to quit being a Navajo?"

Outside the dusty front window of the Navajo Nation Café the dazzling late-day sunlight turned dark with cloud shadow. A Ford 250 pickup rolled past slowly, its front seat crowded with four Navajos, its rear bumper crowded by the van of an impatient tourist. Chee caught the eye of the waitress and got their coffees refilled. What would he say if Janet Pete pressed the question. If she said: "Well, do you?" what would he say?

Instead, she stirred her coffee.

"How has the professor's brilliant career developed?" Chee asked.

"Brilliantly. He's now chief legal counsel of Davidson-Bart, which I understand is what is called a multinational conglomerate. But mostly involved with the commercial credit end of export-import business. Makes money. Lives in Arlington."

Through the dusty window came the faint sound of thunder, a rumble that faded away.

"Wish it would rain," Janet Pete said.

Chee had been thinking exactly the same thing. Sharing a Navajo thought with another Navajo. "Too late to rain," he said. "It's October thirty-first."

Janet Pete dropped him at the garage. He stopped at the station to call Lieutenant Leaphorn on his way back to the trailer.

"Largo told me you found the bodies of those pot hunters," Leaphorn said. "He was a little vague about what you were doing out there."

He left the question implied and Chee thought a moment before answering. He knew Leaphorn's wife had died. He'd heard the man was having trouble coping with that. He'd heard—everybody in the Navajo Tribal Police had heard—that Leaphorn had quit the force. Retired. So what was he doing in this affair? How official was this? Chee exhaled, taking another second for thought. He thought, quit or not, this is still Joe Leaphorn. Our legendary Leaphorn.

"I was looking for that fellow who stole that backhoe here at Shiprock," Chee said. "I found out he was a pot hunter now and then, and I was trying to catch him out digging. With the stolen property."

"And you knew where to look?" Leaphorn, Chee remembered, never believed in coincidence.

"Some guessing," Chee said. "But I knew what gas company he worked for, and where his job would have taken him, and where there might be some sites in the places he would have been."

The word that spread among the four hundred employees of the Navajo Tribal Police was that Joe Leaphorn had lost it. Joe Leaphorn had a nervous breakdown. Joe Leaphorn was out of it. To Jim Chee, Leaphorn's voice sounded no different. Neither did the tone of his questions. A kind of skepticism. As if he knew he wasn't being told all he needed to know. What would Leaphorn ask him now? How he knew the man would be digging last night?

"You have anything else to go on?"

"Oh," Chee said. "Sure. We knew he rented a truck with new tires on double back wheels."

"Okay," Leaphorn said. "Good. So there were tracks to look for." Now his voice sounded more relaxed. "Makes a lot of difference. Otherwise you spend the rest of your life out there running down the roads."

"And I figured he might be out digging last night because of something he said to Slick Nakai. The preacher bought pots from him, now and then. And he sort of told the preacher he'd have some for him quick," Chee said.

Silence.

"Did you know I'm on leave? Terminal leave?"

"I heard it," Chee said.

"Ten more days and I'm a civilian. Right now, matter of fact, I guess I'm unofficial."

"Yes sir," Chee said.

"If you can make it tomorrow, would you drive out there to the site with me? Look it over with me in daylight. Tell me how it was before the sheriff's people and the ambulance and the FBI screwed everything up."

"If it's okay with the captain," Chee said, "I'd be happy to go."

EIGHT

LEAPHORN HAD BEEN AWARE of the wind most of the night, listening to it blow steadily from the southeast as he waited for sleep, awakening again and again to notice it shifting, and gusting, making *chindi* sounds around the empty house. It was still blowing when Thatcher arrived to pick him up, buffeting Thatcher's motor pool sedan.

"Cold front coming through," Thatcher said. "It'll die down."

And as they drove northward from Window Rock it moderated. At Many Farms they stopped for breakfast, Thatcher reminiscing about Harrison Houk, cattleman, pillar of the Church of Jesus Christ of Latter-day Saints, potent Republican, subject of assorted gossip, county commissioner, holder of Bureau of Land Management grazing permits sprawling across the southern Utah can-

yon country, legendary shrewd operator. Leaphorn mostly listened, remembering Houk from
long ago, remembering a man stricken. When
they paid their check, the western sky over Black
Mesa was bleak with suspended dust but the
wind was down. Fifty miles later as they crossed
the Utah border north of Mexican Water, it was
no more than a breeze, still from the southeast but
almost too faint to stir the sparse gray sage and
the silver cheat grass of the Nokaito Bench. The
sedan rolled across the San Juan River bridge below Sand Island in a dead calm. Only the smell of
dust recalled the wind.

"Land of Little Rain," Thatcher said. "Who
called it that?"

It wasn't the sort of friendship that needed answers. Leaphorn looked upstream, watching a
small flotilla of rubber kayaks, rafts, and wooden
dories pushing into the stream from the Sand Island launching site. A float expedition down into
the deep canyons. He and Emma had talked of
doing that. She would have loved it, getting him
away from any possibility of telephone calls. Getting him off the end of the earth. And he would
have loved it, too. Always intended to do it but
there was never enough time. And now, of course,
the time was all used up.

"One of your jobs?" Leaphorn asked, nodding
toward the flotilla below.

"We license them as tour boatmen. Sell 'em trip permits, make sure they meet the safety rules. So forth." He nodded toward the stream. "That must be the last one of the season. They close the river down just about now."

"Big headache?"

"Not this bunch," Thatcher said. "This is Wild Rivers Expeditions out of Bluff. Pros. More into selling education. Take you down with a geologist to study the formations and the fossils, or with an anthropologist to look at the Anasazi ruins up the canyons, or maybe with a biologist to get you into the lizards and lichens and the bats. That sort of stuff. Older people go. More money. Not a bunch of overaged adolescents hoping to get scared shitless going down the rapids."

Leaphorn nodded.

"Take great pride in cleaning up after themselves. The drill now is urinate right beside the river, so it dilutes it fast. Everything else they carry out. Portable toilets. Build their camp fires in fireboxes so you don't get all that carbon in the sand. Even carry out the ashes."

They turned upriver toward Bluff. Off the reservation now. Out of Leaphorn's jurisdiction and into Thatcher's. Much of the land above the bluffs lining the river would be federal land—public domain grazing leases. The land along the river had been homesteaded by the Mormon families who'd settled this narrow valley on orders from Brigham Young to form an outpost against the hostile Gentile world. This stony landscape south of the river had been Leaphorn's country once, when he was young and worked out of Kayenta, but it was too waterless and barren to support the people who would require police attention.

History said 250 Mormons had settled the place in the 1860s, and the last census figures Leaphorn had seen showed its current population was 240—three service stations strung along the highway, three roadside cafés, two groceries, two motels, the office and boathouse of Wild Rivers Expeditions, a school, a ward meetinghouse, and a scattering of houses, some of them empty. The years hadn't changed much at Bluff.

Houk's ranch house was the exception. Leaphorn remembered it as a big, solid block of a building, formed of cut pink sandstone, square as a die and totally neat. It had been connected to the gravel road from Bluff by a graded dirt driveway, which led through an iron gate, curved over a sagebrush-covered rise, and ended under the cottonwoods that shaded the house. Leaphorn noticed the difference at the gate, painted then, rusted now. He unlatched it, refastened it after Thatcher drove through. Then he pulled the chain, which slammed the clapper against the big iron church bell suspended on the pole that took the electric line to the house. That told Houk he had visitors.

The driveway now was rutted, with a growth of tumbleweeds, wild asters, and cheat grass along the tracks. The rabbit fence, which Leaphorn remembered surrounding a neat and lush front yard garden, was sagging now and the garden a tangle of dry country weeds. The pillars that supported the front porch needed paint. So did the pickup truck parked beside the porch. Only the solid square shape of the house, built to defy time, hadn't been changed by the years. But now, surrounded by decay, it stood like a stranger. Even the huge barn on the slope behind it, despite its stone walls, seemed to sag.

Thatcher let the sedan roll to a stop in the shade of the cottonwood. The screen door opened and Houk appeared. He was leaning on a cane. He squinted from the shadows into blinding sunlight, trying to identify who had rung the yard bell. At first look, Leaphorn thought that Houk, like the pink sandstone of his house, had been proof against time. Despite the cane, his figure in the shadow of the porch had the blocky sturdiness Leaphorn remembered. There was still the round bulldog face, the walrus mustache, the small eyes peering through wire-rimmed glasses. But now Leaphorn saw the paunch, the slight slump, the deepened lines, the grayness, the raggedness of the mustache which hid his mouth. And as Houk shifted his weight against the cane, Leaphorn saw the grimace of pain cross his face.

"Well, now, Mr. Thatcher," Houk said, recognizing him. "What brings the Bureau of Land Management all the way out here so soon? Wasn't it only last spring you was out here to see me?" And then he saw Leaphorn. "And who . . ." he began, and stopped. His expression shifted from neutral, to surprise, to delight.

"By God," he said. "I don't remember your name, but you're the Navajo policeman who found my boy's hat." Houk stopped. "Yes I do. It was Leaphorn."

It was Leaphorn's turn for surprise. Almost twenty years since he'd been involved in the hunt for Houk's boy. He had talked to Houk only two or three times, and only briefly. Giving him the wet blue felt hat, soggy with muddy San Juan River water. Standing beside him under the alcove in the cliff that tense moment when the state police captain decided they had Brigham Houk cornered. And finally, on this very porch when it was all over and no hope remained, listening to the man examine his conscience, finding in his own flaws the blame for his boy's murderous rage. Three meetings, and a long, long time ago.

Houk ushered them into what he called the

parlor, a neat room that smelled of furniture polish. "Don't use this room much," Houk said loudly, and he pulled back the curtains, raised the blinds, and pushed up the sash windows to admit the autumn. But the room was still dim—its walls a gallery of framed photographs of people, of bookshelves lined mostly with pots. "Don't get much company," Houk concluded. He sat himself in the overstuffed armchair that matched the sofa, creating another faint puff of dust. "In just a minute the girl will be in here with something cold to drink." He waited then, his fingers tapping at the chair arm. It was their turn to speak.

"We're looking for a woman," Thatcher began. "Anthropologist named Eleanor Friedman-Bernal."

Houk nodded. "I know her." He looked surprised. "What she do?"

"She's been missing," Thatcher said. "For a couple of weeks." He thought about what he wanted to say next. "Apparently she came out here just a little while before she disappeared. To Bluff. Did you see her?"

"Let's see now. I'd say it was three, four weeks when she was out here last," Houk said. "Something like that. Maybe I could figure it out exactly."

"What did she want?"

It seemed to Leaphorn that Houk's face turned

slightly pinker than its usual hue. He stared at Thatcher, his lip moving under the mustache, his fingers still drumming.

"You fellas didn't take long to get out here," he said. "I'll say that for you." He pushed himself up in the chair, then sat back down again. "But how the hell you connect it with me?"

"You mean her being missing?" Thatcher said, puzzled. "She had your name down in her notes."

"I meant the killings," Houk said.

"Killings?" Leaphorn asked.

"Over in New Mexico," Houk said. "The pot hunters. It was on the radio this morning."

"You think we're connecting those with you?" Leaphorn asked. "Why do you think that?"

"Because it seems to me that every time the feds start thinking about pot stealing, they come nosing around here," Houk said. "Those folks get shot stealing pots, stands to reason it's going to get the BLM cops, and the FBI, and all off their butts and working. Since they don't know what the hell they're doing, they bother me." Houk surveyed them, his small blue eyes magnified by the lenses of his glasses.

"You fellas telling me this visit hasn't nothing to do with that?"

"That's what we're telling you," Leaphorn said. "We're trying to find an anthropologist. A woman named Eleanor Friedman-Bernal. She disappeared the thirteenth of October. Some references in her notes about coming out here to Bluff to see Mr. Harrison Houk. We thought if we knew what she came out here to see you about, it might tell us something about where to look next."

Houk thought about it, assessing them. "She came to see me about a pot," he said.

Leaphorn sat, waiting for his silence to encourage Houk to add to that. But Thatcher was not a Navajo.

"A pot?"

"To do with her research," Houk said. "She'd seen a picture of it in a Nelson auction catalog. You know about that outfit? And it was the kind she's interested in. So she called 'em, and talked to somebody or other, and they told her they'd got it from me." Houk paused, waiting for Thatcher's question.

"What did she want to know?"

"Exactly where I found it. I didn't find it. I bought it off a Navajo. I give her his name."

A middle-aged Navajo woman came into the room, carrying a tray with three water glasses, a pitcher of what appeared to be ice water, and three cans of Hires root beer.

"Drinking water or root beer," Houk said. "I guess you knew I'm Latter-day Saints."

Everybody took water.

"Irene," Houk said. "You want to meet these

fellas. This is Mr. Thatcher here. The one from the BLM who comes out here now and then worrying us about our grazing rights. And this fella here is the one I've told you about. The one that found Brigham's hat. The one that kept those goddam state policemen from shooting up into that alcove. This is Irene Musket."

Irene put down the tray and held her hand out to Thatcher. "How do you do," she said. She spoke in Navajo to Leaphorn, using the traditional words, naming her mother's clan, the Towering House People, and her father's, the Paiute Dineh. She didn't hold out her hand. He wouldn't expect it. This touching of strangers was a white man's custom that some traditional Navajos found difficult to adopt.

"You remember what day it was that anthropology woman was out here?" Houk asked her. "Almost a month ago, I think."

Irene considered. "On a Friday," she said. "Four weeks ago last Friday." She picked up the tray and left.

"Great friend of my wife, Irene was. After Alice passed on, Irene stayed on and looked after things," Houk said.

They sipped the cold water. Behind Houk's gray head, the wall was lined with photographs. Houk and his wife and their children clustered on the front porch. Brigham, the youngest, standing in front. The brother and sister he was destined to kill standing behind him, smiling over his shoulders. Brigham's mouth looked slightly twisted, as if he had been ordered to smile. Houk's face was happy, boyish. His wife looked tired, strain showing in the lines around her mouth. A wedding picture, the bride with the veil raised above her face, Houk with the mustache much smaller, older couples flanking them. A picture of Brigham on a horse, his smile strained and lopsided. A picture of the sister in a cheerleader's uniform. Of the brother in a Montezuma Creek High School football jacket. Of Brigham holding up a dead bobcat by its back legs, his eyes intense. Of Houk in an army uniform. Of the Houks and another couple. But mostly the pictures were of the three children. Dozens of them, at all ages. In most of them, Brigham stood alone, rarely smiling. In three of them, he stood over a deer. In one, over a bear. Leaphorn remembered Houk talking endlessly on the porch the day Brigham had drowned.

"Always outdoors," Houk had said. "From the very littlest. Shy as a Navajo. Wasn't happy around people. We shouldn't have made him go to school there. We should have gotten him some help."

Now Houk put down his glass. Thatcher asked, "When she left here, was she going to see the Navajo? The one who found the pot?"

"I reckon," Houk said. "That was her intention. She wanted to know where he got it. All I knew is what he told me. That he didn't break any law getting it." Houk was talking directly to Thatcher. "Didn't get it off public domain land, or off the reservation. Got to be off private land or I won't have nothing to do with it."

"What was his name?" Thatcher asked.

"Fella named Jimmy Etcitty," Houk said.

"Live around here?"

"South, I think," Houk said. "Across the border in Arizona. Between Tes Nez Iah and Dinnehotso, I think he said." Houk stopped. It seemed to Leaphorn that it was to decide whether he had told them enough. And this time Thatcher didn't interrupt the silence. Houk thought. They waited. Leaphorn studied the room. Everything was dusty except the piano. It glowed with wax. Like most of the bookshelves, a shelf above the piano was lined with pots.

"I think I told her she should stop at the Dinnehotso Chapter House and ask how to get to the Mildred Roanhorse outfit," Houk added. "Etcitty's her son-in-law."

"I noticed in the Nelson catalog that they give the customer some sort of documentation on their artifacts," Leaphorn said. He left the question implied, and Houk let it hang a moment while he thought about how to answer it.

"They do," Houk said. "If I happen to find something myself—or sometimes when I have personal knowledge where it came from—then I fill out this sort of statement, time and place and all that, and I sign it and send it along. Case like this, I just give the documentation form to the finder—whoever I'm buying it from. I have them fill it in and sign it."

"You show that paper to the lady?" Leaphorn asked.

"Didn't have it," Houk said. "Usually I just have the finder send the letter directly to whoever is buying from me. This case, I gave Etcitty the Nelson form and told him to take care of it."

They sat and considered this.

"Cuts out the middleman on that," Houk said.

And, Leaphorn thought, insulates Harrison Houk from any charge of fraud.

"Might as well get it from the horse's mouth," Houk added, somberly. But he winked at Leaphorn.

There was still plenty of the day left to drive south to the Dinnehotso Chapter House and get directions to the Mildred Roanhorse outfit and find Jimmy Etcitty. On the porch Houk touched Leaphorn's sleeve.

"Always wanted to say something to you about what you did," he said. "That evening I wasn't in any condition to think about it. But it was a kindly thing. And brave too."

"It was just my job," Leaphorn said. "That highway patrolman was a traffic man. Green about that kind of work. And scared too, I guess. Somebody needed to keep it cool."

"Turned out it didn't matter," Houk said. "Brigham wasn't hiding up there anyway. I guess he was already drowned by then. But I thank you."

Thatcher was standing at the foot of the steps, waiting and hearing all this. Embarrassing. But he didn't bring it up until they were out of Bluff driving toward Mexican Water into the blinding noontime sun.

"Didn't know you were involved in that Houk case," he said. He shook his head. "Hell of a thing. The boy was crazy, wasn't he?"

"That's what they said. Schizophrenia. Heard voices. Unhappy around anyone but his dad. A loner. But Houk told me he was great at music. That piano in there, that was the boy's. Houk said he was good at it and played the guitar and the clarinet."

"But dangerous," Thatcher said. "Ought to been put in a hospital. Locked up until he was safe."

"I remember that's what Houk said they should've done. He said his wife wanted to, but he wouldn't do it. Said he thought it would kill the boy. Locking him up. Said he wasn't happy except when he was outdoors."

"What'd you do to make such an impression on Houk?"

"Found the boy's hat," Leaphorn said. "Washed up on the reservation side of the river. It was already pretty clear he'd tried to swim across."

Thatcher drove for a while. Turned on the radio. "Catch the noon news," he said. "See what they got to say about those pot hunters getting shot."

"Good," Leaphorn said.

"There was more to it than that," Thatcher said. "More than finding his goddamned hat."

Might as well get it over with. The memories had been flooding back anyway—another of those many things a policeman accumulates in the mind and cannot erase. "You remember the case," Leaphorn said. "Houk and one of his hired hands came home that night, and found the bodies, and the youngest boy, Brigham, missing, with some of his stuff. And the shotgun he'd done it with was missing too. Big excitement. Houk was even more important then than he is now—legislator and all that. Bunches of men out everywhere looking. This Utah highway patrol officer—a captain or lieutenant or something—

he and a bunch he was handling thought they had the boy cornered in a sort of alcove-cave up in a box canyon. Saw something or heard something, and I guess the kid had used the place before as a sort of hangout. Anyway, they'd called for him to come out, and no answer, so this dumb captain is going to have everybody shoot into there, and I said first I'd get a little closer and see what I could see, and turned out nobody was in there."

Thatcher looked at him.

"No big deal," Leaphorn said. "Nobody was there."

"So you didn't get shot with a shotgun."

"I happened to have a pretty clear idea of how far a shotgun will shoot. Not very far."

"Yeah," Thatcher said.

The tone irritated Leaphorn. "Hell, man," he said. "The boy was only fourteen."

Thatcher had no comment on that. The woman reading the noon news had gotten to the pot hunter shooting. The San Juan County Sheriff's Office said they had no suspects in the case as yet but they did have promising leads. Casts had been made of the tire tracks of a vehicle believed used by the killer. Both victims had now been identified. They were Joe B. Nails, thirty-one, a former employee of Wellserve in Farmington, and Jimmy

Etcitty, thirty-seven, whose address was given as Dinnehotso Chapter House on the Navajo Reservation.

"Well now," Thatcher said. "I guess we can skip stopping at Dinnehotso."

NINE

THIS IS JUST ABOUT where they'd left the U-Haul truck parked," Chee said. He turned off the ignition, set the parking brake. "Pulled up to the edge of the slope with the winch cable run out. Apparently they eased the backhoe down on the cable."

The front of Chee's pickup was pointed down the steep slope. Fifty feet below, the grassy, brushy hump where a little Anasazi pueblo had stood a thousand years ago was a chaos of trenches, jumbled stones, and what looked like broken sticks. Bones reflecting white in the sunlight.

"Where was the backhoe?"

Chee pointed. "See the little juniper? At the end of that shallow trench there."

"The sheriff hauled everything off, I guess," Leaphorn said. "After they got their photographs."

"That was the plan when I left."

Leaphorn didn't comment. He sat silently, considering the destruction below. This ridge was much higher than it had seemed to Chee in the darkness. Shiprock stuck up like a blue thumb on the western horizon seventy miles away. Behind it, the dim outline of the Carrizo Mountains formed the last margin of the planet. The sagebrush flats between were dappled with the shadow of clouds, drifting eastward under the noon sun.

"The bodies," Leaphorn said, "The *belagana* in the backhoe? Right? Named Nails. And the Navajo partway up this slope under us? Jimmy Etcitty. Which one was shot first?"

Chee opened his mouth, closed it. His impulse had been to say the coroner would have to decide. Or about the same time. But he realized what Leaphorn wanted.

"I'd guess the Navajo was running for his life," he said. "I'd say he'd seen the white man shot in the machine. He was running for the truck."

"Do much checking before you called it in to the sheriff?"

"Hardly any," Chee said.

"But some," Leaphorn said.

"Very little."

"The killer parked up here?"

"Down by the oil well pump."

"Tire tracks mean anything?"

"Car or pickup. Some wear." Chee shrugged. "Dusty dry and in the dark. Couldn't tell much."

"How about his tracks? Or hers?"

"He parked on the sandstone. No tracks right at the vehicle. After that, mostly scuff marks."

"Man?"

"Probably. I don't know." Chee was remembering how shaken he had been. Too much death. He hadn't been using his head. Now he felt guilty. Had he concentrated, he surely could have found at least something to indicate shoe size.

"Not much use going over it again," Leaphorn said. "Too many deputy sheriffs and paramedics and photographers been trampling around."

And so they scrambled down the hill—Leaphorn losing his footing and sliding twenty feet in a shower of dislodged earth and gravel. Standing there, amid the dislodged stones, amid the scattered bones, Chee felt the familiar uneasiness. Too many *chindi* had taken to the air here, finding freedom from the bodies that had housed them. Leaphorn was standing at a narrow trench the backhoe had dug beside a crumbled wall, looking thoughtful. But then Leaphorn didn't believe in *chindi*, or in anything else.

"You studied anthropology, didn't you? At New Mexico?"

"Right," Chee said. So had Leaphorn, if the word around the Navajo Tribal Police was true. At Arizona State. A BA and an MS.

"Get into the Anasazi much? The archaeological end of it?"

"A little," Chee said.

"The point is, whoever did this work knew something about what he was doing," Leaphorn said. "Anasazi usually buried their dead in the trash midden with the garbage, or right against the walls, sometimes inside the rooms. This guy worked the midden. . . ." Leaphorn gestured to the torn earth beyond them. "And he worked along the walls. So I'd guess he knew they buried pottery with their corpses, and he knew where to find the graves."

Chee nodded.

"And maybe he knew this was a late site, and that—rule of thumb—the later the site, the better the pot. Glazed, multicolored, decorated, so forth." He bent, picked up a shard of broken pottery the size of his hand and inspected it.

"Most of the stuff I've seen here is like this," he said, handing the shard to Chee. "Recognize it?"

The interior surface was a rough gray. Under its coating of dust the exterior glowed a glossy rose, with ghostly lines of white wavering through it. Chee touched the glazed surface to his tongue—the automatic reaction of a former anthropology student to a potsherd—and inspected the clean spot. A nice color, but his memory produced nothing more than a confused jumble of titles: Classical. Pueblo III. Incised. Corrugated, etc. He handed the shard to Leaphorn, shook his head.

"It's a type called St. John's Polychrome," Leaphorn said. "Late stuff. There's a theory it originated in one of the Chaco outlier villages. I think they're pretty sure it was used for trading."

Chee was impressed and his face showed it.

Leaphorn chuckled. "I can't remember stuff like that either," he said. "I've been doing some reading."

"Oh?"

"We seem to have a sort of overlap here," he said. "You were looking for a couple of men who stole our backhoe. I'm looking for an anthropologist. A woman who works at Chaco and took off one day three weeks ago to go to Farmington and never came back."

"Hadn't heard about that," Chee said.

"She prepared this big, elaborate dinner. Had a guest coming to visit. A man very important to her. She put it in the fridge and she didn't come back." Leaphorn had been looking out across the grassland toward the distant thunderheads. It must have occurred to him that this would sound strange to Chee. He glanced at him. "It's a San

Juan County missing person's case," he said. "But I'm on leave, and it sounded interesting."

"You mentioned you were quitting," Chee said. "I mean resigning."

"I'm on terminal leave," Leaphorn said. "A few more days and I'm a civilian."

Chee could think of nothing to say. He didn't particularly like Leaphorn, but he respected him.

"But I'm not a civilian yet," he added, "and what we have here is peculiar. This overlap, I mean. We have Dr. Friedman-Bernal being a ferocious collector of this kind of pottery." Leaphorn tapped the potsherd with his forefinger. "We have Jimmy Etcitty killed here digging up this sort of pot. This same Jimmy Etcitty worked over at Chaco where Friedman-Bernal worked. This same Jimmy Etcitty found a pot somewhere near Bluff which he sold to a collector who sold it to an auction house. This pot got Friedman-Bernal excited enough a month ago to send her driving to Bluff looking for Etcitty. And on top of that we have Friedman-Bernal buying from Slick Nakai, the evangelist, and Nails selling to Slick, and Etcitty playing guitar for Nakai."

Chee waited, but Leaphorn seemed to have nothing to add.

"I didn't know any of that," Chee said. "Just knew Nails and a friend stole the backhoe when

I was supposed to be watching the maintenance yard."

"Nice little tangle of strings, and right here is the knot," Leaphorn said.

And none of it any of Leaphorn's business, Chee thought. Not if he had resigned. So why was he out here, sitting on that stone wall with his legs in the sun, with almost two hundred miles of driving already behind him today? He must enjoy it or he wouldn't be here. So why has he resigned?

"Why did you resign?" Chee asked. "None of my business, I guess, but . . ."

Leaphorn seemed to be thinking about it. Almost as if for the first time. He glanced at Chee, shrugged. "I guess I'm tired," he said.

"But you're using leave time out here, chasing after whatever it is we have here."

"I've been wondering about that myself," Leaphorn said. "Maybe it's the fire horse syndrome. Lifelong habit at work. I think it's because I'd like to find this Friedman-Bernal woman. I'd like to find her and sit her down and say: 'Dr. Bernal, why did you prepare that big dinner and then go away and let it rot in your refrigerator?' "

To Chee, the answer to why Dr. Bernal let her dinner spoil was all too easy. Especially now. Dr. Bernal was dead.

"You think she's still alive?"

Leaphorn considered. "After what we have here, it doesn't seem likely, does it?"

"No," Chee said.

"Unless she did it," Leaphorn said. "She had a pistol. She took it with her when she left Chaco."

"What caliber?" Chee asked. "I heard this one was small."

"All I know is small," Leaphorn said. "Small handgun. She carried it in her purse."

"Sounds like twenty-two caliber," Chee said. "Or maybe a twenty-five or a small thirty-two."

Leaphorn rose, stiffly, to his feet. Stretched his back, flexed his shoulders. "Let's see what we can find," he said.

They found relatively little. The investigators from the county had taken the bodies and whatever else had interested them, which probably hadn't been much. The victims seemed to be clearly identified, and that would be checked with people who knew them for confirmation. The FBI would be asked to do a run on their fingerprints, just in case. The backhoe had been hauled away and would be gone over carefully for prints in the event the killer had been careless with his hands when he shot Nails. The rental truck would receive the same treatment. So would the two plastic sacks in which Chee had seen the pots carefully packed. And just in case, a cord had been run around the dig site, with the little tags dangling to warn citizens away from a homicide site. If some afterthought brought an investigator back to check on something, nothing would be disturbed.

What interested Chee was outside the cord—a new cardboard carton bearing the red legend SU-PERTUFF and the sublegend WASTEBASKET LINERS, and several other messages: "Why Pay More For Something You'll Throw Away? Six free in this carton. Thirty for the price of twenty-four!"

The cardboard was smudged with white. Chee squatted beside it and recognized fingerprint powder. Someone had checked it and found the cardboard too rough to show prints. Chee picked it up, extracted the carefully folded plastic sacks. Counted them. Twenty-seven. Twenty-seven plus two filled with pots made twenty-nine. He slipped the sacks back into the box and replaced it. One sack unaccounted for. Filled with what? Had the killer taken one set of pots and left the other two? Had Nails's girlfriend, if he had a girlfriend, borrowed one? It was one of those imponderables.

He watched Leaphorn prowling along the trenches, inspecting digging procedures, or perhaps the human bones. Chee had been avoiding the bones without realizing it. Now almost at his foot he noticed the weathered flat surface of a scapula, broken off below the shoulder joint. Just beyond was a very small skull, complete except for the lower jaw. A child, Chee guessed, unless the Anasazi had been even smaller than he remembered. Beyond the skull, partly buried by the excavation dirt, were ribs, and part of a spinal column, the small bones of a foot, three lower jaws placed in a row.

Chee stared. Why had that happened? He strolled over and looked down at them. One was broken, a small jaw with part of its left side missing. The other two were complete. Adult, Chee guessed. An expert would be able to tell the sex of their owners, the approximate ages at death, something about their diet. But why had someone lined them up like this? One of the pot hunters, Chee guessed. It didn't seem the sort of thing one of the deputies would have done. Then Chee noticed another jawbone, and three more, and finally a total of seventeen within a few yards of the juniper where he was standing. He could see only three craniums. Someone—again surely the pot hunters—had sorted out the jaws. Why? Chee walked over to where Leaphorn was standing, studying something in the trench.

"Find anything?" Leaphorn asked, without looking up.

"Nothing much," Chee said. "One of those plastic bags seems to be missing."

Leaphorn looked up at him.

"The box said contents thirty. There were still twenty-seven folded in it. I saw two with pots in them."

"Interesting," Leaphorn said. "We'll ask about that at the sheriff's office. Maybe they took one."

"Maybe," Chee said.

"You notice anything about the skeletons?" Leaphorn was squatting now in the shallow trench, examining bones.

"Somebody seemed to be interested in the jawbones," Chee said.

"Yes," Leaphorn said. "Now why would that be?" He stood up, holding in both hands a small skull. It was gray with the clay of the grave, and the jaw was missing. "Why in the world would that be?"

Chee had not the slightest idea, and said so.

Leaphorn bent into the grave again, poking at something with a stick. "I think this is what they call a Chaco outlier site," he said. "Same people who lived in the great houses over in the canyon, or probably the same. I think there is some evidence, or at least a theory, that these outliers traded back and forth with the great-house people, maybe came into Chaco for their religious ceremonials. Nobody really knows. This was probably one of the sites being reserved for digging sometime in the future." He sounded, Chee thought, like an anthropology lecturer.

"You have anything pressing to do in Shiprock tonight?" Chee denied it with a negative motion of his head.

"How about stopping off at the Chaco Center on the way home then," Leaphorn said. "Let's see what we can find out about this."

TEN

FROM THE DESPOILED OUTLIER SITE to the eastern
boundary of the Chaco Culture National Historic
Park would be less than twenty-five miles if a
road existed across the dry hills and Chaco Mesa.
None did. By the oil company roads that carried
Leaphorn and Chee back to Highway 44, thence
northwest to Nageezi, and then southwest over
the bumpy dirt access route, it was at least sixty
miles. They arrived at the visitors' center just after
sundown, found it closed for the day, and drove
up to the foot of the bluff where employee housing was located.

The Luna family was starting supper—the superintendent, his wife, a son of perhaps eleven,
and a daughter a year or two younger. Supper
centered on an entrée involving macaroni,
cheese, tomatoes, and things that Leaphorn could

not readily identify. That he and Chee would eat was a foregone conclusion. Good manners demanded the disclaimer of hunger from the wayfarer, but the geography of the Colorado Plateau made it an obvious lie. Out here there was literally no place to stop to eat. And so they dined, Leaphorn noticing that Chee's appetite was huge and that his own had returned. Perhaps it was the smell of the home cooking—something he hadn't enjoyed since Emma's sickness reached the point where it was no longer prudent for her to be in the kitchen.

Bob Luna's wife, a handsome woman with a friendly, intelligent face, was full of questions about Eleanor Friedman-Bernal. After polite feelers established that questions were not out of order, she asked them. The Luna son, Allen, a blond, profusely freckled boy who looked like a small copy of his blond and freckled mother, put down his fork and listened. His sister listened without interrupting her supper.

"We haven't learned much," Leaphorn said. "Maybe the county has done better. It is their jurisdiction. But I doubt it. No sheriff ever has enough officers. In San Juan County it's worse than normal. You're worried to death with everything from vandalism of summer cabins up on Navajo Lake to people tapping distillate out of the gas pipelines, or stealing oil field equipment, things like that. Too much territory. Too few people. So missing persons don't get worked on." He stopped, surprised at hearing himself deliver this defense of the San Juan County Sheriff's Office. Usually he was complaining about it. "Anyway," he added, lamely, "we haven't learned anything very useful."

"Where could she have gone?" Mrs. Luna said. Obviously it was something she had often thought about. "So early in the morning. She told us she was going to Farmington, and got the mail we had going out, and our shopping lists, and then just vanished." She glanced from Chee to Leaphorn and back. "I'm afraid it isn't going to have a happy ending. I'm afraid Ellie got in over her head with a man we don't know about." She attempted a smile. "I guess that sounds odd—to say that about a woman her age—but at this place, it's so small—so few of us live here, I mean—that everybody tells everybody everything. It's the only thing we have to be interested in. One another."

Luna laughed. "It's pretty hard to have secrets here," he said. "You have experienced our telephone. You don't get any secret calls. And you don't get any secret mail—unless it happens to show up at Blanco the day you happen to pick it up." He laughed again. "And it would be pretty hard to have any secret visitors."

But not impossible, Leaphorn thought. No

more impossible than driving out to make your calls away from here, or setting up a post office box in Farmington.

"You just get to know everything by accident even if people don't mention it," Mrs. Luna said. "For example, going places. I hadn't thought to tell anybody when I was going to Phoenix over the Fourth to visit my mother. But everybody knew because I got a postcard that mentioned it, and Maxie or somebody picked up the mail that day." If Mrs. Luna resented Maxie or somebody reading her postcard, it didn't show. Her expression was totally pleasant—someone explaining a peculiar, but perfectly natural, situation. "And when Ellie made that trip to New York, and when Elliot went to Washington. Even if they don't mention it, you just get to know." Mrs. Luna paused to sip her coffee. "But usually they tell you," she added. "Something new to talk about." At that she looked slightly abashed. She laughed. "That's about all we have to do, you know. Speculate about one another. TV reception is so bad out here we have to be our own soap operas."

"When was the trip to New York?" Leaphorn asked.

"Last month," Mrs. Luna said. "Ellie's travel agent in Farmington called and said the flight schedule had been changed. Somebody takes the message, so everybody knows about it."

"Does anyone know why she went?" Leaphorn asked.

Mrs. Luna made a wry face. "You win," she said. "I guess there are some secrets."

"How about why Elliot went to Washington?" Leaphorn added. "When was that?"

"No secret there," Luna said. "It was last month. A couple of days before Ellie left. He got a call from Washington, from his project director I think it was. Left a message. There was a meeting of people working on archaic migration patterns. He was supposed to attend."

"Do you know if Ellie's going to New York had anything to do with her pots? Is that logical?"

"Just about everything she did had something to do with her pots," Luna said. "She was sort of obsessive about it."

Mrs. Luna's expression turned defensive. "Well now," she said, "Ellie was about ready to make a really important report. As least she thought so. And so do I. She pretty well had the proof that would connect a lot of those St. John Polychromes from the Chetro Ketl site with Wijiji and Kin Nahasbas. And more important than all that, she was finding that this woman must have moved away from Chaco and was making pots somewhere else."

"This woman?" Luna said, eyebrows raised. "She tell you her potter was a woman?"

"Who else would do all that work?" Mrs. Luna got up, got the coffeepot, and offered all hands, including the children, a refill.

"She was excited, then?" Leaphorn asked. "About something she'd found recently? Did she talk to you about it?"

"She was excited," Mrs. Luna said. She looked at Luna with an expression Leaphorn read as reproach. "I really do believe that she'd found something important. To everybody else those people are just a name. Anasazi. Not even their real name, of course. Just a Navajo word that means . . ." She glanced at Chee. "Old Ones. Ancestors of our enemies. Something like that?"

"Close enough," Chee said.

"But Ellie has identified a single human being in what has always just been statistics. An artist. Did you know that she'd arranged her pots chronologically . . . showing how her technique developed?"

The question was aimed at Luna. He shook his head.

"And it's very logical. You can see it. Even if you don't know much about pots, or glazing, or inscribing, or any of those decorative techniques."

Luna seemed to have decided about then that his self-interest dictated a change in posture on this issue.

"She's done some really original work, Ellie

has," he said. "Pretty well pinned down where this potter worked, up Chaco Wash at a little ruins we call Kin Nahasbas. She did that by establishing that a lot of pots made with this potter's technique had been broken there before they were fully baked in the kiln fire. Then she tied a bunch of pots dug up at Chetro Ketl and Wijiji to the identical personal techniques. Trade pots, you know. One kind swapped to people at Chetro Ketl and another sort to Wijiji. Both with this man's—this potter's peculiar decorating strokes. Hasn't been published yet, but I think she has it pinned."

It gave Leaphorn a sense of déjà vu, as if he remembered a graduate student over some supper in a dormitory at Tempe saying exactly these same words. The human animal's urge to know. To leave no mysteries. Here, to look through the dirt of a thousand years into the buried privacy of an Anasazi woman. "To understand the human species," his thesis chairman liked to say. "To understand how we came to behave the way we do." But finally it had seemed to Leaphorn he could understand this better among the living. It was the spring he'd met Emma. When the semester ended in May he'd left Arizona State and his graduate fellowship and his intentions of becoming Dr. Leaphorn, and joined the recruit class of the Navajo Tribal Police. And he and Emma . . .

Leaphorn noticed Chee watching him. He cleared his throat. Sipped coffee.

"Did you have any clear idea of what she was excited about?" Leaphorn asked. "I mean just before she disappeared. We know she drove over to Bluff and talked to a man over there named Houk. Man who sometimes deals in pots. She asked him about a pot she'd seen advertised in an auction catalog. Wanted to know where it came from. Houk told us she was very intense about it. He told her how to get the documentation letter. Did she say why she was going to New York?"

"Not to me, she didn't," Mrs. Luna said.

"Or why she was excited?"

"I know some more of those polychrome pots had turned up. Several, I think. Same potter. Some identical and some with a more mature style. Later work. And it turned out they came from somewhere else—away from the Chaco. She thought she could prove her potter had migrated."

"Did you know Ellie had a pistol?"

Luna and his wife spoke simultaneously. "I didn't," she said. Luna said: "It doesn't surprise me. I'd guess Maxie has one, too. For snakes," he added, and laughed. "Actually it's for safety."

"Do you know if she ever hired Jimmy Etcitty to find pots for her?"

"Boy, that was a shock," Luna said. "He hadn't

worked here long. Less than a year. But he was a good hand. And a good man."

"And he didn't mind digging around graves."

"He was a Christian," Luna said. "A fundamentalist born-again Christian. No more *chindi*. But no, I doubt if he worked for Ellie. Hadn't heard of it."

"Had you ever heard he might be a Navajo Wolf?" Leaphorn asked. "Into any kind of witchcraft. Being a skinwalker?"

Luna looked surprised. And so, Leaphorn noticed, did Jim Chee. Not at the question, Leaphorn guessed. That fooling around with the bones they'd found at the ruins would suggest witchcraft to anyone who knew the Navajo tradition of skinwalkers robbing graves for bones to grind into corpse powder. But Chee would be surprised at Leaphorn's thinking. Leaphorn was aware that his contempt for the Navajo witchcraft business was widely known throughout the department. Chee, certainly, was aware of it. They had worked together in the past.

"Well," Luna said. "Not exactly. But the other men who worked here didn't have much to do with him. Maybe that was because he was willing to dig around the burials. Had given up the traditional ways. But they gossiped about him. Not to me but among themselves. And I sort of sensed they were wary of him."

"Davis told me Lehman came. The man she had the appointment with."

"Her project supervisor? Yeah."

"Did he say what the meeting was about?"

"She'd told him she had one more piece of evidence to get and then she'd be ready to publish. And she wanted to show it all to him and talk it over. He stuck around the next day and then drove back to Albuquerque."

"I'll get his address from you," Leaphorn said. "Did he have any idea what that one piece of evidence was?"

"He thought she'd probably found some more pots. Ones that fit. He said she was supposed to have them when they met."

Leaphorn thought about that. He noticed Chee had marked it, too. It seemed to mean that when Ellie left Chaco it was to pick up those final pots.

"Would Maxie Davis or Elliot be likely to know any more about all this?"

Mrs. Luna answered that one. "Maxie, maybe. She and Ellie were friends." She considered that statement, found it too strong. "Sort of friends. At least they'd known each other for years. I don't think they'd ever worked together—as Maxie and Elliot sometimes do. Teamed."

"Teamed," Leaphorn said.

Mrs. Luna looked embarrassed. "Sue," she said.

"Allen. Don't you two have any homework? To-morrow is a school day."

"Not me," Allen said. "I did mine on the bus."

"Me either," Sue said. "This is interesting."

"They're friends," Mrs. Luna said, looking at Sue, but meaning Maxie and Elliot.

"When Mr. Thatcher and I talked to them it seemed pretty obvious that Elliot wanted it that way," Leaphorn said. "I wasn't so sure about Miss Davis."

"Elliot wants to get married," Mrs. Luna said. "Maxie doesn't."

She glanced at her children again, and at Luna.

"Kids," Luna said. "Sue, you better see about your horse. And Allen, find something to do."

They pushed back their chairs. "Nice to have met you," Allen said, nodding to Leaphorn and to Chee.

"Great children," Leaphorn said, as they disappeared down the hallway. "They ride the bus? To where?"

"Crownpoint," Mrs. Luna said.

"Wow!" Chee said. "I used to ride a school bus about twenty-five milcs and that seemed forever."

"About sixty miles or so, each way," Luna said. "Makes an awful long day for 'em. But that's the nearest school."

"We could teach them out here," Mrs. Luna said. "I have a teacher's certificate. But they need to see other children. Nothing but grownups at Chaco."

"Two young women and one young man," Leaphorn said. "Was there any friction between the women over that? Any sort of jealousy?"

Luna chuckled.

Mrs. Luna smiled. "Eleanor wouldn't be much competition in that race," she said. "Unless the man wants an intellectual, and then it's about even. Besides, I think in Randall Elliot you have one of those one-woman men. He left a job in Washington and worked his way into a project out here. Just following her. I think he's sort of obsessive about it."

"Delete the 'sort of,'" Luna said. "Make it downright obsessive. And sad, too." He shook his head. "Elliot's a sort of macho guy most ways. Played football at Princeton. Flew a navy helicopter in Vietnam. Won a Navy Cross and some other decorations. And he's made himself a good name in physical anthropology for a man his age. Got stuff published about genetics in archaic populations. That sort of stuff. And Maxie refuses to take anything he does seriously. It's the game she plays."

From down the hall came the high, sweet sound of a harmonica—and then the urgent nasal whine of Bob Dylan. Almost instantly the volume was muted.

"Not a game," Mrs. Luna said, thoughtfully. "It's the way Maxie is."

"Reverse snob, you mean?" Luna asked.

"More to it than that. Kind of a sense of justice. Or injustice, maybe."

Luna looked at Leaphorn and Chee. "To explain what we're talking about, and maybe why we're doing this gossiping, there's no way Maxie would be jealous of Dr. Friedman. Or anybody else, I think. Maxie is the ultimate self-made woman from what I've heard about her. Off of some worn-out farm in Nebraska. Her father was a widower, so she had to help raise the little kids. Went to a dinky rural high school. Scholarship to University of Nebraska, working her way through as a housekeeper in a sorority. Graduate scholarship to Madison, working her way through again. Trying to send money home to help Papa and the kids. Never any help for her. So she meets this man from old money, Exeter Academy, where the tuition would have fed her family for two years. Where you have tutors helping you if you need it. And then Princeton, and graduate school at Harvard, all that." Luna sipped his coffee. "Opposite ends of the economic scale. Anyway, nothing Elliot can do impresses Maxie. It was all given to him."

"Even the navy career?"

"Especially the navy," Mrs. Luna said. "I asked her about that. She said, 'Of course, Randall has an uncle who an admiral, and an aunt who's married to an undersecretary of the navy, and somebody else who's on the Senate Armed Services Committee. So he starts out with a commission.' And I said something like, 'You can hardly blame him for that,' and she said she didn't blame him. She said it was just that Randall has never had a chance to do anything himself." Mrs. Luna shook her head. "And then she said, 'He might be a pretty good man. Who knows? How can you tell?' Isn't that odd?"

"It sounds odd to me," Leaphorn said. "In Vietnam, he was evacuating the wounded?"

"I think so," Luna said.

"That was it," Mrs. Luna said. "I asked Maxie about that. She said, 'You know, he probably could have done something on his own if he had the chance. But officers give each other decorations. Especially if it pleases Uncle Admiral.' 'Uncle Admiral,' that's what she said. And then she told me her younger brother was in Vietnam, too. She said he was an enlisted man. She said a helicopter flew his body out. But no uncles gave him any decorations."

Mrs. Luna looked sad. "Bitter," she said. "Bitter, I remember the night we'd been talking about this. I'd said something about Randall flying a helicopter and she said, 'What chance do you think you or I would have had to be handed a helicopter to fly?' "

Leaphorn thought of nothing to say about that. Mrs. Luna rose, asked about coffee refills, and began clearing away the dishes. Luna asked if they'd like to spend the night in one of the temporary personnel apartments.

"We better be getting back home," Leaphorn said.

The night was dead still, lit by a half-moon. From the visitor camping area up the canyon there was the sound of laughter. Allen was walking up the dirt road toward his house. As he watched him, it occurred to Leaphorn how everyone knew Eleanor Friedman-Bernal had left so early on her one-way trip.

"Allen," Leaphorn called. "What time do you catch the bus in the morning?"

"It's supposed to get here about five minutes before six," Allen said. "Usually about then."

"Down by the road?"

Allen pointed. "At the intersection down there."

"Did you see Ellie drive away?"

"I saw her loading up her car," Allen said.

"You talk to her?"

"Not much," Allen said. "Susy said hello. And

she said something about you kids have a good day at school and we said for her to have a good weekend. Something like that. Then we went down and caught the bus."

"Did you know she was going away for the weekend?"

"Well," Allen said, "she was putting her stuff in her car."

"Sleeping bag, too?" Maxie said she owned one, but he hadn't found it in her apartment.

"Yeah," Allen said. "Whole bunch of stuff. Even a saddle."

"Saddle?"

"Mr. Arnold's," Allen said. "He used to work here. He's a biologist. Collects rocks with lichens on them, and he used to live in one of the temporary apartments. Dr. Friedman had his saddle. She was putting it in her car."

"She'd borrowed it from him?"

"I guess so," Allen said. "She used to have a horse. Last year it was."

"Do you know where this Mr. Arnold lives now?"

"Up in Utah," Allen said. "Bluff."

"How'd she sound? Okay? Same as usual? Nervous?"

"Happy," Allen said. "I'd say she sounded happy."

ELEVEN

FOR MOST OF HIS LIFE—since his early teens at least—knowing that he was smarter than most people had been a major source of satisfaction for Harrison Houk. Now, standing with his back pressed against the wall of the horse stall in the barn, he knew that for once he had not been smart enough. It was an unusual feeling, and chilling. He thought of that aphorism of southern Utah's hard country—if you want to be meaner than everybody else without dying young, you have to be smarter than everybody else. More than once Harrison Houk had heard that rule applied to him. He enjoyed the reputation it implied. He deserved it. He had gotten rich in a country where almost everybody had gotten poor. It had made him enemies, the way he had done it. He controlled grazing leases in ways that might not have stood grand jury scrutiny. He bought livestock, and sold livestock, under sometimes peculiar circumstances. He obtained Anasazi pots from people who had no idea what they were worth and sometimes sold them to people who only thought they knew what they were getting. He had arranged deals so lopsided that, when daylight hit them, they brought the high councilor of his Latter-day Saints stake down from Blanding to remind him of what was said about such behavior in the Book of Mormon. Even his stake president had written once exhorting him to make things right. But Houk had been smart enough not to die young. He was old now, and he intended to become very, very old. That was absolutely necessary. Things remained for him to do.

Now more than ever. Responsibilities. Matters of clearing his conscience. He hadn't stopped at much, but he'd never had a human life on his hands before. Not this directly. Never before.

He stood against the wall, trying to think of a plan. He should have recognized the car more quickly, and understood what it must mean. Should have instantly made the link between the killing of Etcitty and the rest of it. He would have when he was younger. Then his mind worked like lightning. Now the killings had made him nervous. They could have been motivated by almost anything, of course. Greed among thieves. Malice over a woman. God knows what. Almost anything. But the instinct that had served him so well for so long suggested something more sinister. An erasing of tracks. A gathering in of strings. That certainly would involve him, and he should have seen. Nor should he have thought so slowly when he saw the car turning through his gate. Maybe he would have had enough time then to hobble back to the house, to the pistol in his dresser drawer or the rifle in the closet. He could only wait now, and hope, and try to think of some solution. There could be no running for it, not with the arthritis in his hip. He had to think.

Quickly. Quickly. He'd left a note for Irene. He thought Irene would be coming back for her squash and she'd wonder where he'd gone. Pinned it on the screen door, telling her he'd be out in the barn working. It was right there in plain view. The worst kind of bad luck.

He looked around him for a hiding place. Houk was not a man subject to panic. He could climb into the loft but there was no cover there. Behind him bales of alfalfa were stacked head-high. He could restack some of them, leave himself a cave. Would there be time? Not without luck. He began a new stack against the wall, leaving a space just wide enough to hold him, groaning as he felt the weight of the heavy bales grinding his hip socket. As he worked, he realized the futility. That would only delay things a few minutes. There was really no place to hide.

He noticed the pitchfork then, leaning beside the door where he'd left it. He limped over, got it, limped back to the horse stall. Maybe there would be some chance to use it. Anyway, it was better than hiding and just waiting.

He gripped the fork handle, listening. His hearing wasn't what it once had been but he could detect nothing except, now and then, the breeze blowing through the slats. The smell of the barn was in his nostrils. Dust. Dry alfalfa. The faint acid of dried horse urine. The smell of a dry autumn.

"Mr. Houk," the voice called. "You in the barn?"

Add it all together, average it out, it had been a good enough life. The first fifty years, close to wonderful, except for Brigham being sick. Even that you could live with, given the good wife he'd been blessed with. Except for the downswings of the schizophrenia, Brigham had been happy enough, most of the time. The rages came and went, but when he was out in the wild country, hunting, living alone, he seemed full of joy. Thinking back, Houk was impressed again with the memory. He'd been pretty good himself outdoors as a kid. But not like The Boy. By the time he was ten, Brigham could go up a cliff that Houk wouldn't have tried with ropes. And he knew what to eat. And how to hide. That brought back a rush of memories, and of the old, old sorrow. The Boy, the summer he was seven, missing long after suppertime. All of them hunting him. Finding him in the old coyote den under the saltbush. He'd been as terrified at being found as if he had been a rabbit dug out by a dog.

That had been the day they no longer lied to themselves about it. But nothing the doctors tried had worked. The piano had helped for a while. He had a talent for it. And he could lose himself for hours just sitting there making his music. But the rages came back. And putting him away had been unspeakable and unthinkable.

"Houk?" the voice said. Now it was just beyond the barn wall. "I need to talk to you."

And now he could hear footsteps, the door with the draggy hinge being pulled open.

One thing he had to do. He couldn't leave it undone. He should have handled it yesterday, as soon as he found out about it. Yesterday—personally. It had to be taken care of. It wasn't something you went away and left—not a human life.

He took out his billfold, found a business card from a well-drilling outfit in it, and began writing on its back, holding the card awkwardly against the billfold.

"Houk," the voice said. It was inside the barn

now. "I see you there, through the slats. Come out."

No time now. He couldn't let the note be found, except by the police. He pushed it down inside his shorts. Just as he did, he heard the stall door opening.

TWELVE

It was raining in New York. L. G. Marcy, the director of public affairs to whom Joe Leaphorn was referred, proved to be a slender, stylish woman with gray hair, and eyes as blue as blade steel. On drier days, the expanse of glass behind her desk looked out upon the rooftops of midtown Manhattan. She examined Leaphorn's card, turned it over to see if the back offered more information, and then glanced up at him.

"You want to see the documentation on an artifact," she said. "Is that correct?" She glanced down at the open catalog Leaphorn had handed her.

"That's all. Just this Anasazi pot," Leaphorn said. "We need to know the site it came from."

"I can assure you it was legal," Ms. Marcy said.

"We do not deal in pots collected in violation of the Antiquities Preservation Act."

"I'm sure that's true," said Leaphorn, who was equally sure no sane pot hunter would ever certify that he had taken a pot illegally. "We presume the pot came from private land. We simply need to know which private land. Whose ranch."

"Unfortunately, that pot sold. All pots went in that auction. So we don't have the documentation. The documentation went to the buyer. Along with the pot," L. G. Marcy said. She smiled, closed the catalog, handed it to Leaphorn. "Sorry," she said.

"Who was the buyer?"

"We have a problem there," she said. "It is Nelson's policy to cooperate with the police. It is also Nelson's policy to respect the confidence of our customers. We never tell anyone the identity of buyers unless we have their advance clearance to do so." She leaned across the desk to return Leaphorn's card. "That rarely happens," she said. "Usually, none of the parties concerned wants publicity. They value privacy. On rare occasions, the object involved is so important that publicity is inevitable. But rarely. And in this case, the object is not the sort that attracts the news media."

Leaphorn put the card in the pocket of his uniform shirt. The shirt was damp from the rain Leaphorn had walked through from his hotel toward this office building before ducking for shelter into a drugstore. To his surprise, the store sold umbrellas. Leaphorn had bought one, the first he'd ever owned, and continued his journey under it—tremendously self-conscious—thinking he would own the only umbrella in Window Rock, and perhaps the only umbrella on the reservation, if not in all of Arizona. He was conscious of it now, lying wetly across his lap, while he waited silently for L. G. Marcy to add to her statement. Leaphorn had learned early in his career that this Navajo politeness often clashed with white abhorrence for conversational silences. Sometimes the resulting uneasiness caused *belagana* witnesses to blurt out more than they intended to say. While he waited, he noticed the prints on the wall. All, if Leaphorn could judge, done by female artists. The same for the small abstract sculpture on the Marcy desk. The silence stretched. It wasn't going to work with this *belagana*.

It didn't.

The pause caused L. G. Marcy's smile to become slightly bent. Nothing more. She outwaited him. About his own age, Leaphorn thought, but she looked like a woman in her mid-thirties.

Leaphorn stirred. Moved the umbrella off his lap. "I believe the FBI notified your company that we are investigating two homicides," he said.

"This particular pot seems to figure into it. Your client won't be embarrassed. Not in any way. We simply . . ."

"I'm not sure the FBI exactly notified us of anything," Ms. Marcy said. "An FBI agent called from . . ." She examined a notebook. ". . . Albuquerque, New Mexico, and told us that a representative of the Navajo Tribal Police would call today about an artifact we had handled. He said our cooperation would be appreciated. The call was referred to me, and when I questioned him about what the federal government interest might be, this agent, this Mr. Sharkey, he, well . . ." Ms. Marcy hunted politely for a word politer than "weaseled." "He made it appear that his call was not official at all. It was intended as a sort of a personal introduction."

Leaphorn simply nodded. Sharkey hadn't wanted to make the call, had foreseen embarrassment, had been talked into it. Having been caught at it, Sharkey would be angry and hard to deal with. But then in a few more days, nothing like that would matter. Leaphorn would be a civilian. He nodded again.

"There's a system for dealing with problems like this, of course," Ms. Marcy said. "One petitions the appropriate court for an injunction. You then serve this order on us, and we provide you with the information. The requirement that we make available evidence needed in a judicial proceeding supersedes our own need to maintain a confidential relationship with our customers." Her expression was bland.

After a moment, Leaphorn said, "Of course that's a possibility. We'd like to avoid it if we could." He shrugged. "The paperwork. We'd like to avoid all the delay." And, he thought, the problem of persuading the court that an item circled in a Nelson's catalog has anything at all to do with anything.

"That's understandable," Ms. Marcy said. "I think you can also understand our position. Our clients rely on us to keep transactions confidential. For many good reasons." She made an inclusive gesture with small white hands. "Burglars," she said, "for one example. Former wives. Business reasons. So you must understand . . ."

Ms. Marcy began pushing back her chair. When she rises, Leaphorn thought, she will tell me that without a court order she cannot give me any information. He did something he almost never did. He interrupted.

"Our problem is time," he said. "A woman's life may be at stake."

Ms. Marcy lowered herself back into the chair. That little motion brought to Leaphorn's nostrils an awareness of perfume, and powder, and fine feminine things. It reminded him, with overpowering force, of Emma. He closed his eyes, and opened them.

"A woman who was very interested in this particular pot—the woman who drew the circle around it in your catalog—she's been missing for weeks," Leaphorn said. He took out his wallet, extracted his photograph of Dr. Eleanor Friedman-Bernal, the bride. He handed it to Ms. Marcy. "Did she come in to see you? This autumn? Or call?"

"Yes," Ms. Marcy said. "She was in." She studied the photograph, frowning. Leaphorn waited until she looked up.

"Dr. Eleanor Friedman-Bernal," he said. "An anthropologist. Published a lot of papers in the field of ceramics—and of primitive ceramic art. We gather that Dr. Friedman-Bernal believes she has discovered an Anasazi potter whose work she can specifically identify. Did she tell you all that?"

As he related this, Leaphorn was aware of how mundane and unimportant it must sound to a layman. In fact, it sounded trivial to him. He watched Ms. Marcy's face.

"Some of it," Ms. Marcy said. "It would be fascinating if she can prove it."

"From what we can find out, Dr. Friedman-Bernal identified a decorative technique in the finishing of a kind of pottery called St. John Polychrome—a kind made in the last stages of the Anasazi civilization. She found that technique was peculiar to one single specific Anasazi potter."

"Yes. That's what she said."

Leaphorn leaned forward. If his persuasion didn't work, he'd wasted two days on airplanes and a night in a New York hotel.

"I gather that this woman, this Anasazi potter, had some special talent which the doctor spotted. Dr. Friedman-Bernal was able to trace her work backward and forward in time through scores of pots, arranging them chronologically as this talent developed. The potter worked at Chaco Canyon, and her work turned up at several of the villages there. But recently—probably earlier this year—Friedman-Bernal began finding pots that seemed to come from somewhere else. And they were later pots—with the woman's style matured. Your spring auction catalog carried a photograph of one of these pots. We found the catalog in Dr. Friedman-Bernal's room, with the photograph circled."

Ms. Marcy was leaning forward now. "But those pots, they were so stylized," she said. "So much alike. How . . . ?" She didn't complete the question.

"I'm not sure," Leaphorn said. "I think she does it the way graphologists identify handwriting. Something like that."

"It makes sense," Ms. Marcy said.

"From what we know, from what Friedman-Bernal told other anthropologists, she seems to have believed that she could find the place to which this potter moved when the Chaco civilization collapsed," Leaphorn said.

"About right," Ms. Marcy said. "She said she thought this pot was the key. She said she had come across several shards, and one complete pot, which she was sure came from a late phase in this potter's work—an extension and refinement and maturing of her techniques. The pot she'd seen in our catalog seemed to be exactly identical to this work. So she wanted to study it. She wanted to know where she could go to see it, and she wanted to see our documentation."

"Did you tell her?"

"I told her our policy."

"So you didn't tell her who had bought it? Or how to contact the buyer?"

Ms. Marcy sighed, allowed her expression to show a flash of impatience.

"I told her the same thing I am telling you. One of the reasons people have been dealing with Nelson's for more than two hundred years is because of our reputation. They know they can depend, absolutely and without a qualm of doubt, on Nelson's keeping transactions in confidence."

Leaphorn leaned forward.

"Dr. Friedman-Bernal flew back to Albuquerque after she talked to you. Then she drove back to Chaco Canyon, where she lives and works. The following Friday she got up very early, put her sleeping bag into her car, and drove away. She'd told her friends she'd be gone for a day or two. We suspect that somehow she found out where this pot had come from and went to see if she could find something to prove it. Probably to see if there were other such pots, or potsherds, at the place."

He leaned back, folded his hands across his chest, wondering if this would work. If it didn't, he was near a dead end. There was Chee, of course. He'd asked Chee to find the Reverend Slick Nakai—to learn from Nakai everything the man knew about where those damned pots were coming from. Chee seemed interested. Chee would do his best. But how smart was Chee? He should have waited, done it himself, not risked having it all screwed up.

"She vanished," Leaphorn said. "No trace of the woman, or car, or anything. Not a word to anyone. As if Eleanor Friedman-Bernal had never existed."

Ms. Marcy picked up the photograph and studied it. "Maybe she just went away," she said, looking up at Leaphorn. "You know. Too much work. Too much stress. Suddenly you just want to say to hell with it. Maybe that was it." She said it as a woman who knows the feeling.

"Possibly," Leaphorn said. "However, the evening before she left she spent a lot of time fixing a dinner. Marinated the meat entrée, all that. The professor she had worked with was coming in from Albuquerque. She fixed this fancy dinner and put it in the refrigerator. And at dawn the next morning she put her sleeping bag and things like that in her car and drove away."

Ms. Marcy considered. She took the picture of Eleanor Friedman as a bride from the desk and looked at it again.

"Let me see what I can do," she said. She picked up the telephone. "Will you wait outside just a moment?"

The reception room had no view of the rain. Just walls displaying abstract prints, and a receptionist in whom Leaphorn's damp Navajo Tribal Police uniform had aroused curiosity. He sat against the wall, glancing through an *Architectural Digest*, aware of the woman staring at him, wishing he had worn civilian clothes. But maybe it wasn't the uniform. Maybe it was the damp Navajo inside it.

Ms. Marcy came out in a little less than ten minutes. She handed Leaphorn a card. It bore a name, Richard DuMont, and an address on East Seventy-eighth Street.

"He said he would see you tomorrow morning," she said. "At eleven."

Leaphorn stood. "I appreciate this," he said.

"Sure," she said. "I hope you'll let me know. If you find her I mean."

Leaphorn spent the rest of the afternoon prowling through the Museum of Modern Art. He sat, finally, where he could see the patio of sculpture, the rain-stained wall behind it, and the rainy sky above. Like all dry-country people, Leaphorn enjoyed rain—that rare, longed for, refreshing blessing that made the desert bloom and life possible. He sat with his head full of thoughts and watched the water run down the bricks, drip from the leaves, form its cold pools on the flagstones, and give a slick shine to Picasso's goat.

The goat was Leaphorn's favorite. When they were young and he was attending the FBI Academy, he had brought Emma to see New York. They had discovered Picasso's goat together. He had already been staring at it when Emma had laughed, and plucked at his sleeve, and said: "Look. The mascot of the Navajo Nation."

He had an odd sensation as he remembered this, as if he could see them both as they had been then. Very young, standing by this glass wall looking out into the autumn rain. Emma, who was even more beautiful when she laughed, was laughing.

"Perfect for us Dineh," she'd said. "It's starved, gaunt, bony, ugly. But look! It's tough. It endures." And she had hugged his arm in the delight of her discovery, her face full of the joy, and the beauty, that Leaphorn had found nowhere else. And of course, it was true. That gaunt goat would have been the perfect symbol. Something to put on a pedestal and display. Miserable and starved, true enough. But it was also pregnant and defiant— exactly right to challenge the world at the entrance of the ugly octagonal Tribal Council meeting hall at Window Rock. Leaphorn remembered their having coffee at the museum café and then walking out and patting the goat. The sensation came back to him now—wet, cold metal slick under his palm—utterly real. He got up and hurried out of the museum into the rain, leaving the umbrella hanging forgotten on the chair.

Leaphorn took a cab to the Seventy-eighth Street address, got there a quarter of an hour early, and spent the time prowling the neighborhood—a territory of uniformed doormen and expensive dogs walked by persons who seemed to have been hired for the job. He rang the door chimes at eleven exactly. He waited on the steps, looking at the sky down the street. It would rain again, and soon—probably before noon. An old man, stooped and gray in a wrinkled gray suit, opened the door and stood silently, looking at him patiently.

"My name is Leaphorn," he said. "I have an appointment with Richard DuMont."

"In the study," the man said, motioning Leaphorn in.

The study was a long, high-ceilinged room down a long, high-ceilinged hall. A man in a dark blue dressing gown was sitting at the end of a long library table. Light from a floor lamp beside his chair reflected off the white of a breakfast cloth, and china, and silver.

"Ah, Mr. Leaphorn," the man said, smiling. "You are most punctual. I hope you will excuse me for not getting up to greet you." He tapped the arms of the wheelchair in which he was sitting. "And I hope you will join me for some breakfast."

"No thank you," Leaphorn said. "I've eaten."

"Some coffee, then?"

"I have never refused coffee. Never will."

"Nor I," DuMont said. "Another of my vices. But seat yourself." He gestured toward a blue plush chair. "The woman at Nelson's told me you are hunting a missing woman. An anthropologist. And that murder is involved." DuMont's small gray eyes peered at Leaphorn, avid with interest. Unusual eyes set in a pinched, narrow face under eyebrows almost identical in color to his pale skin. "Murder," he repeated, "and a missing woman." His voice was clear, precise, easy to understand. But like his face it was a small voice. Any background noise would bury it.

"Two pot hunters were killed," Leaphorn said. Something about DuMont was unpleasant. Too much interest? But interest in such a man seemed natural enough. After all, he was a collector. "Including the man who found my pot," DuMont said, with what seemed to Leaphorn to be a sort of pleasure. "Or so that woman at Nelson's told me."

"We think so," Leaphorn said. "Ms. Marcy told me you would be willing to let me see the documentation he sent in. We want to know where he found the pot."

"The document," DuMont said. "Yes. But tell me how the man was killed. How the woman is missing." He raised his arms wide apart, his small mouth grinning. "Tell me all of that."

Behind DuMont, on both sides of a great formal fireplace, shelves formed the wall. The shelves were lined with artifacts. Pots, carved stone images, baskets, fetishes, masks, primitive weapons. Just behind the man, a pedestal held a massive stone head—Olmec, Leaphorn guessed. Smuggled out of Mexico in defiance of that country's antiquities act.

"Mr. Etcitty and a companion were digging up an Anasazi ruin, apparently collecting pots. Someone shot them," Leaphorn said. "An anthropologist named Friedman-Bernal was specializing in this sort of ceramics. In fact, she was interested in this pot you bought. She disappeared. Left Chaco Canyon—she worked there—for a weekend and hasn't come back."

Leaphorn stopped. He and DuMont looked at each other. The stooped, gray man who had admitted Leaphorn appeared at his elbow, placed a small table beside his chair, spread a cloth upon it, put a silver tray on the cloth. The tray held a cup of paper-thin china sitting on a translucent saucer, a silver pot from which steam issued, two smaller silver containers, and a silver spoon. The gray man poured coffee into Leaphorn's cup and disappeared.

"One doesn't buy merely the object," DuMont said. "One wants what goes with it. The history. This head, for example, came out of the jungles in northern Guatemala. It had decorated the doorway to a chamber in a temple. The room where captives were held until they were sacrificed. I'm told the Olmec priests strangled them with a cord."

DuMont covered the lower part of his small face with his napkin and produced a small cough, his avid eyes on Leaphorn.

"And this Anasazi pot of yours. Why is it worth five thousand dollars?" He laughed, a small, tinkling sound. "It's not much of a pot, really. But the Anasazi! Such mysterious people. You hold this pot, and think of the day it was made. A civilization that had grown a thousand years was dying." He stared into Leaphorn's eyes. "As ours is surely dying. Its great houses were standing empty. No more great ceremonials in the kivas. This is about when my pot was made—so my appraisers tell me. Right at the end. The twilight. In the dying days."

DuMont did something at the arm of his wheelchair and said: "Edgar."

"Yes sir." Edgar's voice seemed to come from under the table.

"Bring me that pot we bought last month. And the documents."

"Yes sir."

"So stories are important to me," DuMont said to Leaphorn. "What you could tell me has its value here. I show my new pot to my friends. I tell them not just of the Anasazi civilization, but of murder and a missing woman." He grinned a small, prim grin, showing small, perfect teeth.

Leaphorn sipped his coffee. Hot, fresh, excellent. The china was translucent. To the right of DuMont a row of high windows lined the wall.

The light coming through them was dim, tinted green by the vines that covered them. Rain streamed down the glass.

"Did I make my point?" DuMont said.

"I think so," Leaphorn said.

"Tit for tat. You want information from me. In exchange it seems to me only fair that you give me my story. The story to go with my pot."

"I did," Leaphorn said.

DuMont raised two white hands, fluttered them. "Details, details, details," he said. "All the bloody details. The details to pass along."

Leaphorn told him the details. How the bodies were found. How the men had been killed. Who they were. He described the scene. He described the bones. DuMont listened, rapt.

". . . and there we are," Leaphorn concluded. "No leads, really. Our missing woman might be a lead to the killer. More likely she's another victim. But it's all vague. We know just that she was interested in the same pots. Just that she's missing."

Edgar had returned early in this account and stood beside DuMont, holding a pot and a manila folder. The pot was small, about the size of a man's head. A little larger than DuMont's skull.

"Hand the pot to Mr. Leaphorn," DuMont said. "And the documents, please."

Edgar did so. And stood there, stooped and

gray, his presence making Leaphorn edgy. Why didn't the man sit down? Leaphorn placed the pot carefully on the table, noticing the smooth feel of the glazing, aware that it had nothing to tell him. He opened the folder.

It contained what appeared to be two bills of sale, one from Harrison Houk to Nelson's and one from Nelson's to DuMont, and a form with its blanks filled in by an awkward hand. It was signed by Jimmy Etcitty.

Leaphorn checked the date. The previous June. He checked the space marked "Place of recovery." The entry read:

About eight or ten miles down San Juan from Sand Island. From mouth of canyon on north side of river go up the canyon about five and a half miles to the place where there are three ruins on the left side of the canyon at a low level. Right there by the lower ruin are a bunch of pictures of Anasazi *yei* figures and one looks like a big baseball umpire holding up a pink chest protector. On the north side of the canyon one of the ruins is built against the cliff on the shelf above the canyon bottom. Above it on the higher shelf there is a cave under the cliff with a ruin built in it, and above that in a smaller cave there is another ruin. All these ruins are on private land under lease to my friend Harrison Houk of Bluff, Utah. This

pot came from a trench beside the south wall of
the ruin against the cliff. It was faceup, with three
other pots, all broken, and a skeleton, or part of a
skeleton. When found, the pot had nothing but
dirt in it.

Leaphorn was surprised at the intensity of his
disappointment. It was exactly what he should
have expected. He checked the other blanks and
found nothing interesting. DuMont was watching him, grinning.

"A problem?"

"A little case of lying," Leaphorn said.

"Just what Dr. Friedman said." DuMont chuckled. "False, false, false."

"You talked to Dr. Friedman?"

"Just like this," DuMont said, delighted with
Leaphorn's amazement. "Your missing lady was
right here. In that same chair. Edgar, was she
drinking from the same cup?"

"I have no idea, sir," Edgar said.

"Same questions, anyway." DuMont gestured.
"Fascinating."

"How did she find you?"

"As you did, I presume. Through Nelson's. She
called, and identified herself, and made an appointment."

Leaphorn didn't comment. He was remembering her note. "Call Q!" Ellie seemed to have had a

pipeline into the auction house that got her past Ms. Marcy.

"She said the certification was false? The location?"

"She said that canyon isn't where Mr. . . . Mr. . . ."

"Etcitty," Edgar said.

"Where Mr. Etcitty said it was." DuMont laughed. "Running the wrong way, she said. Too far down the river. Things like that."

"She was right," Leaphorn said. If that false location had an effect on DuMont's five-thousand-dollar pot, it had no effect on his humor. He was grinning his small white grin.

"She was quite upset," he said. "Disappointed. Are you?"

"Yes," Leaphorn said. "But I shouldn't be. It's exactly what I should have expected."

"Edgar has made you a copy of that," DuMont said. "To take with you."

"Thank you," Leaphorn said. He pushed himself out of the chair. He wanted to get out of this room. Away. Out into the clean rain.

"And Edgar will give you my card," DuMont said from behind him. "Call me with all the details. When you find her body."

THIRTEEN

FINDING THE REVEREND SLICK NAKAI had not been easy. At the Nageezi site Chee found only the trampled place where the revival tent had stood, and the trash left behind. He asked around, learned that Nakai was known at the Brethren Navajo Mission. He drove to Escrito. The *belagana* at the mission there knew of Nakai but not his whereabouts. If he had scheduled a revival around there, they hadn't heard of it. Must be a mistake. Chee left, sensing that he wasn't alone in his disapproval of Slick Nakai. At Counselors Trading Post, where people tend to know what's happening on the north side of the Checkerboard Reservation, he hung around until he found someone who knew of a family not only fervently following the Jesus Road, but doing so as prescribed by the tenets of Nakai's sect. It was the family of Old

Lady Daisy Manygoats. The Manygoats outfit, unfortunately, lived way over by Coyote Canyon. Chee drove to Coyote Canyon, stopped at the chapter house, got directions down a road that was bad even by reservation standards, and found nobody at home at the Manygoats place except a boy named Darcy Ozzie. Yes, Darcy Ozzie knew about the Reverend Slick Nakai, had in fact gone to his recent revival over at Nageezi.

"They say he was going to preach over between White Rock and Tsaya, over there by the mountains," the boy said, indicating west in the Navajo fashion by a twist of his lips. "And then when he was finished there, he was going way over into Arizona to have a revival over there by Lower Greasewood. Over there south of the Hopi Reservation."

So Chee drove up the Chuska Valley toward Tsaya, with the Chuska Range rising blue to his left and autumn asters forming two lines of color along the opposite sides of the cracked old asphalt of U.S. 666, and snakeweed and chamisa coloring the slopes mottled tan-yellow-gold and the November sky dark blue overhead.

He had quit thinking of Slick Nakai about halfway between Nageezi and Coyote Canyon, having exhausted every possible scenario their meeting might produce. Then he considered Mary Landon. She loved him, he concluded. In her way. But there was love, and then there was love. She would not change her mind about living her life on the reservation. And she was right. Lacking some very basic change in Mary, she would not be happy raising their children here. He wanted Mary to neither change nor be unhappy. Which led him back to himself. She would marry him if he left the reservation. And he could do that. He'd had offers. He could go into federal law enforcement. Work somewhere where their children could go to school with white kids and be surrounded by white culture. Mary would be happy. Or would she? He could still be a Navajo in the sense of blood, but not in the sense of belief. He would be away from family and the Slow Talking Dineh, the brothers and sisters of his maternal clan. He would be outside of Dineh Bike'yah—that territory fenced in by the four sacred mountains within which the magic of the curing ceremonials had its compulsory effect. He would be an alien living in exile. Mary Landon would not enjoy life with that Jim Chee. He could not live with an unhappy Mary Landon. It was the conclusion he always eventually reached. It left him with a sense of anger and loss. That, in turn, moved his thoughts to something else.

He thought of Janet Pete, trying to work what little he knew of her character into the solution she would find to her own problem. Would she allow her lawyer to convert her into an Indian maiden? Not enough data to be sure, but he doubted if Janet Pete would ever buy that.

Who killed Nails and Etcitty? Find the motive. There lies the answer. But there could be a dozen motives and he had no basis for guessing. Leaphorn, obviously, believed Slick Nakai somehow fit into that puzzle. But then Leaphorn knew a lot more about this business than Chee. All Chee knew was that Nakai bought pots from Etcitty—or perhaps was given them. That Etcitty was one of Nakai's born-again Christians. That Leaphorn believed Nakai sold pots to the woman missing from Chaco Canyon. That was the focus of Chee's assignment. Leaphorn's voice on the telephone had sounded tired. "You want to stick with me a little longer on this Friedman-Bernal business?" he asked. "If you do, I can arrange it with Captain Largo."

Chee had hesitated, out of surprise. Leaphorn had identified the pause as indecision.

"I should remind you again that I'm quitting the department," Leaphorn had interjected. "I'm on terminal leave right now. I already told you that. I tell you now so if you're doing me a favor, remember there's no way I can return it."

Which, Chee had thought, was a nice way of

saying the reverse—I can't punish you for refusing.

"I'd like to stay on it," Chee had said. "I'd like to find out who killed those guys."

"That's not what we're working on," Leaphorn had said. "They're connected, I guess. They must be connected. But what I'm after is what happened to the woman missing from Chaco. The anthropologist."

"Okay," Chee had said. It seemed an odd focus. Two murders, apparently premeditated assassinations. And Leaphorn was devoting his leave time, and Chee's efforts, to a missing person case. Same case, probably, the way it looked now. But going at it totally backward. Well, Lieutenant Leaphorn was supposed to be smarter than Officer Chee. He had a reputation for doing things in weird ways. But he also had a reputation for guessing right.

At Tsaya, Chee found he'd missed Slick Nakai, but not by much. Nakai had canceled his planned revival there and headed north.

"Just canceled it?" Chee asked.

He was asking a plump girl of about eighteen who seemed to be in charge of the Tsaya Chapter—since she was the only one present in the chapter house.

"He sort of hurried in, and said who he was,

and said he had to cancel a tent meeting that was supposed to be for tonight," she said. "It's over there on the bulletin board." She nodded toward the notices posted by the entrance.

"*NOTICE!*" Nakai had scrawled at the top of a sheet of notepaper:

Due to an unexpected emergency Reverend Nakai is forced to cancel his revival for here. It will be rescheduled later if God wills it.

—Reverend Slick Nakai

"Well, shit!" said Jim Chee, aloud and in English, since Navajo lends itself poorly to such emotional expletives. He glanced at his watch. Almost four-thirty. Where the devil could Nakai have gone? He walked back to the desk where the girl was sitting. She had been watching him curiously.

"I need to find Nakai." Chee smiled at her, happy that he hadn't worn his uniform. A good many people her age looked upon Navajo Tribal Police as the adversary. "Did he say anything else? Like where he was going?"

"To me? Nothing. Just borrowed a piece of paper for his note. You one of his Christians?"

"No," Chee said. "Matter of fact, I'm a *hatathali*. I do the Blessing Way."

"Really?" the girl said.

Chee was embarrassed. "Just beginning," he said. "Just did it once." He didn't explain that the one time had been for a member of his own family. He fished out his billfold, extracted a business card, and handed it to her.

JIM CHEE

HATATHALI

SINGER OF THE BLESSING WAY

AVAILABLE FOR OTHER CEREMONIALS

FOR CONSULTATION CALL_____

(P.O. BOX 112, SHIPROCK, N.M.)

Since he had no telephone at his trailer, he'd left the number blank. His plan had been to list the Shiprock police station number, gambling that by the time Largo got wind of it and blew the whistle, he'd have a reputation and a following established. But the dispatcher had balked. "Besides, Jim," she'd argued, "what will the people think? They call for a singer to do a ceremonial and when the phone rings somebody says, 'Navajo Tribal Police.' "

"Give me some more," the girl said. "I'll stick one up on the board, too. Okay?"

"Sure," Chee said. "And give them to people. Especially if you hear of anybody sick."

She took the cards. "But what's a *hatathali* doing looking for a Christian preacher?"

"A minute ago, when I asked you if Nakai said anything about where he was headed, you said not to you. Did he tell somebody else?"

"He made a phone call," she said. "Asked if he could borrow the phone here"—she tapped the telephone on her desk—"and called somebody." She stopped, eyeing Chee doubtfully.

"And you overheard some of it?"

"I don't eavesdrop," she said.

" 'Course not," Chee said. "But the man's talking right there at your desk. How can you help it? Did he say where he was going?"

"No," she said. "He didn't say that."

Chee was smart enough to realize he was being teased. He smiled at her. "After a while you are going to tell me what he said," Chee said. "But not yet."

"I just might not tell you at all," she said, grinning a delighted grin.

"What if I tell you a scary story? That I'm not really a medicine man. I'm a cop and I'm looking for a missing woman, and Nakai is not really a preacher. He's a gangster, and he's already killed a couple of people, and I'm on his trail, and you are my only chance of catching him before he shoots everybody else."

She laughed. "That would fit right in with what he said on the phone. Very mysterious."

Chee managed to keep grinning. Just barely.
"Like what?"

She made herself comfortable. "Oh," she said.
"He said, did you hear what happened to so-and-
so? Then he listened. Then he said something
like, it made him nervous. And to be careful.
And then he said somebody-else-or-other was
who he worried about and the only way to warn
him was to go out to his hogan and find him. He
said he was going to cancel his revival here and
go up there. And then he listened a long time,
and then he said he didn't know how far. It was
over into Utah." She shrugged. "That's about it."

"About it isn't good enough."

"Well, that's all I remember."

Apparently it was. She was blank on both so-
and-so and somebody-else-or-other. Chee left,
thinking "over into Utah" was over into the
country Leaphorn wanted Nakai cross-examined
about—the source of Friedman-Bernal's pot ob-
session. He was also thinking that heading into
the Four Corners would take him past Shiprock.
Maybe he would take the night off, if he was
tired when he got there. Maybe he would run
Slick Nakai to earth tomorrow. But why had
Nakai changed his plans and headed for the
Utah border? Who knows? "So-and-so" was probably Etcitty. "Somebody-else-or-other" probably

another of Nakai's converts who stole pots on the side. To Chee, Nakai was seeming increasingly odd.

He was driving through the Bisti Badlands, headed north toward Farmington, when the five o'clock news began. A woman reporting from the Durango, Colorado, station on the letting of a contract for range improvement on the Ute Mountain Reservation, and a controversy over the environmental impact of an additional ski run at Purgatory, and a recall petition being circulated to unseat a councilman at Aztec, New Mexico. Chee reached up to change the channel. He'd get more New Mexico news from a Farmington station. "In other news of the Four Corners country," the woman said, "a prominent and sometimes controversial Southeast Utah rancher and political figure has been shot to death at his ranch near Bluff."

Chee stopped, hand on the dial.

"A spokesman for the Garfield County Sheriff's Office at Blanding said the victim has been identified as Harrison Houk, a former Utah state senator and one of southern Utah's biggest ranch operators. The body of Houk was found in his barn last night. The sheriff's office said he had been shot twice.

"Some twenty years ago, Houk's family was the victim of one of the Four Corners' worst tragedies. Houk's wife and a son and daughter were shot to death, apparently by a mentally disturbed younger son who then drowned himself in the San Juan.

"Across the line in Arizona, a suit has been filed in federal district court at . . ."

Chee clicked off the radio. He wanted to think. Houk was the man to whom Nakai had sold pots. Houk lived at Bluff, on the San Juan. Maybe Etcitty was Nakai's "so-and-so." More likely it would be Houk. Could Nakai have heard of Houk's murder en route to Tsaya? Probably, on an earlier newscast. That would explain the abrupt change in plans. Or maybe Houk was "somebody-else-or-other"—the man Nakai wanted to warn. Too late for that now. Either way, it seemed clear that Nakai would be headed to somewhere very close to Bluff, to where Houk, his customer for pots, had been killed.

Chee decided he would work overtime. If he could find the elusive Nakai tonight, he would.

It proved to be surprisingly easy. On the road north toward Bluff, far enough north of Mexican Water so he was sure he'd crossed the Arizona border into Utah, Chee saw Nakai's tent trailer. It was parked maybe a quarter-mile up an old oil field road that wanders off U.S. 191 into the rocky barrens south of Caso del Eco Mesa.

Chee made an abrupt left turn, parked by the

trailer, and inspected it. The tie-down ropes were in place, all four tires were aired, everything in perfect order. It had simply been unhooked and abandoned.

Chee jolted down the old road, past a silent oil pump, down into the bare stoniness of Gothic Creek, and out of that into a flatland of scattered sage and dwarf juniper. The road divided into two trails—access routes, Chee guessed, to the only two Navajo families who survived in these barrens. It was almost dark now, the western horizon a glowing, luminous copper. Which route to take? Far down the one that led straight ahead he saw Nakai's car.

He drove the five hundred yards toward it cautiously, feeling uneasy. He'd been joking with the girl at Tsaya when he cast Nakai in the role of gangster. But how did he know? He knew almost nothing. That Nakai had been preaching on the reservation for years. That he encouraged his converts to collect pots for him to sell to help finance his operation. Did he have a pistol? A criminal record? Leaphorn probably knew such things, but he hadn't confided in Chee. He slowed even more, nervous.

Nakai was sitting on the trunk of the massive old Cadillac, legs straight out, leaning against the rear window, watching him, looking utterly harmless. Chee parked behind the car, climbed out, stretched.

"*Ya te'eh,*" Nakai said. And then he recognized Chee, and looked surprised. "We meet again—but a long way from Nageezi."

"*Ya te,*" Chee said. "You are hard to find. I heard you were supposed to be"—he gestured southward—"first at Tsaya and then way down beyond the Hopi Country. Down at Lower Greasewood."

"Ran outta gas," Nakai said, ignoring the implied question. "This thing burns gas like a tank." He jumped down from the trunk, with the small man's natural agility. "Were you looking for me?"

"More or less," Chee said. "What brings you up here into Utah? So far from Lower Greasewood?"

"The Lord's business takes me many places," Nakai said.

"You planning a revival out here?"

"Sure," Nakai said. "When I can arrange it."

"But you left your tent," Chee said. And you're lying, he thought. Not enough people out here.

"I was on empty," Nakai said. "Thought I could save enough gas to get where I was going. Then come back and get it." He laughed. "Waited too long to unhook. Burned too much gasoline."

"You forget to look at your gauge?"

"It was already broke when I bought this

thing." Nakai laughed again. "Blessed are the poor," he said. "Didn't do no good to look at it. Before I got outta gas, I was outta money."

Chee didn't comment on that. He thought about how he could learn what Nakai was doing out here. Who he came to warn.

"Have a brother lives down there," Nakai explained. "Christian, so he's my brother in the Lord. And he's Paiute. My 'born to' clan. So he's a brother that way, too. I was going to walk. And then I saw you coming."

"So you just got here?"

"Five minutes, maybe. Look, could you give me a ride? Maybe eight miles or so. I could walk it, but I'm in a hurry."

Nakai was looking down the trail, westward. Chee studied his face. The copper light gave it the look of sculpture. Metal. But Nakai wasn't metal. He was worried. Chee could think of no clever way to get him to talk about what he was doing here.

"You found out Harrison Houk was killed," Chee said. "And you headed out here. Why?"

Nakai turned, his face shadowed now. "Who's Houk?"

"The man you sold pots to," Chee said. "Remember? You told Lieutenant Leaphorn about it."

"Okay," Nakai said. "I know about him."

"Etcitty dealt with you, and with Houk, and

with these pots, and he's dead. And now Houk. Both shot. And Nails, too, for that matter. Did you know him?"

"Just met him," Nakai said. "Twice, I think."

"Look," Chee said. "Leaphorn sent me to find you because of something else. He wants to locate this Eleanor Friedman-Bernal woman—find out what happened to her. He talked to you about her already. But now he wants more information. He wants to know what she said to you about looking for pots right out here in this part of the country. Along the San Juan. Up around Bluff. Around Mexican Hat."

"Just what I told him. She wanted those smooth polychrome pots. Those pinkish ones with the patterns and the wavy lines and the serration, or whatever you call it. Pots or the broken pieces. Didn't matter. And she told me she was particularly interested in anything that turned up around this part of the reservation." Nakai shrugged. "That was it."

Chee put his hands on hips and bent backward, eliminating a kink in his back. He'd spent ten hours in that pickup today. Maybe more. Too many. "If Joe Leaphorn were here," he said, "he'd say no, that wasn't quite it. She said more than that. You are trying to save time. Summarizing. Tell me everything she said. Let me do the summarizing."

Nakai looked thoughtful. An ugly little man, Chee decided, but smart.

"You're thinking that I am a cop, and that these pots came off the Navajo Reservation where they are *mucho, mucho* illegal. Felony stuff. You're thinking you are going to be careful about what you say." Chee slouched against the pickup door. "Forget it. We are doing one thing at a time and the one thing is finding this woman. Not figuring out who shot Etcitty. Not catching somebody for looting ruins on Navajo land. Just one single, simple thing. Just find Eleanor Friedman. Leaphorn seems to think she went looking for these pots. At least that's what I think he thinks. He thinks she told you where to find them. Therefore, I'd appreciate it, you'd win my gratitude and a ride to wherever you want to go, if you'll just tell me all of it. Whether or not you think it matters."

Nakai waited awhile, making sure Chee's outburst was finished.

"What matters isn't much," he said. "Let me remember a minute or two."

Behind Nakai the sunset had darkened from glowing pale copper to dark copper. Against that gaudy backdrop, two streaks of clouds were painted, blue-black and ragged. To the left, a three-quarter moon hung in the sky like a carved white rock.

"You want her words," Nakai said. "What she said, what he said, what she said. I don't remember that well. But I remember some impressions. One. She was thinking about very specific ruins. She'd been there. She knew what it looked like. Two. It was illegal. Better than that, it was on the Navajo Reservation. She good as said that. I remember I said something about it being illegal, and she said maybe it shouldn't be. I was a Navajo and it was Navajo land."

Nakai stopped. "How about the ride?"

"What else?"

"That's all I know, really. Did I say it was in a canyon? I'm sure it was. She said she'd been told about it. Didn't say who told her. Somebody she'd bought a pot from, I guess. Anyway, the way she described the place it had to be a canyon. Three ruins, she said. One down by the streambed in the talus, one on the shelf above it, and a third one out of sight in the cliff above the shelf. So that would have to be in a canyon. And that's all I know."

"Not the name of the canyon."

"She didn't know it. Said she didn't think it had one. Canyon *sin nombre*." Nakai laughed. "She didn't tell me much, really. Just that she was very, very interested in pots, or potsherds, even little fragments, but only if they had this pinkish glaze with the wavy light lines and the serration. Said she'd triple her price for them. That she wanted to know exactly where they came from. I wondered why she didn't go try to find the place herself. I guess she didn't want to risk getting caught at it."

"Leaphorn thinks she went. Or, I think he does."

"Now," Nakai said, "I earned my ride."

Chee took him to a hogan built on the slope of a wash that drained into Gothic Creek—using three-quarters of an hour to cover less than eight jarring miles. It was almost full dark when they pulled onto the slick rock surface that formed the hogan yard, but the moon was bright enough to show why the site had been picked. A growth of cottonwoods, tamarisks, and rabbitbrush at the lip of the wash showed where a spring flowed. It was probably the only live water within thirty miles, Chee guessed, and it wasn't lively enough to support a family in the dry season. A row of rusty water barrels on a wooden rack told him that. Chee parked, raced the pickup engine to make sure the hogan's occupants had noticed their arrival, and turned off the engine. A dim light, probably from a kerosene lamp, showed through the side window. The smell of sheep, a smell that always provoked nostalgia in Chee, drifted down from a brush compound behind the house.

"You have another little problem now," Chee said.

"What?"

"This brother of yours who lives here. He steals pots for you. You want to tell him about Etcitty, and Nails, and Houk. You want to tell him to be careful—that somebody's shooting pot hunters. But I'm a cop so you don't want me to hear it."

Nakai said nothing.

"No car. No truck. At least I don't see one. Or see any place to put one on this flat rock where I couldn't see it. So somebody who lives here has gone off with the truck."

Nakai said nothing. He drew in a breath and exhaled it.

"So if I just leave you here, as you'd intended, then you're stuck. No gas and no ride to where you can get some."

"One of his sons probably has the truck," Nakai said. "He probably keeps some gasoline here somewhere. At least a five-gallon can."

"In which case you walk that eight miles back to the Caddy with it," Chee said. "Or maybe he doesn't have any gas."

A blanket hanging over the hogan doorway swung aside. The shape of a man appeared, looking out at them.

"What do you have in mind?" Nakai said.

"You quit playing the game. I'm not going to

arrest anyone for stealing pots. But I gotta find out where they came from. That's all I care about. If you don't know where that is, this Paiute Clan man here does. Let him tell me. No more games."

The Paiute Clan man was called Amos Whistler. A skinny man with four of his lower front teeth missing. He knew where the pots had come from. "Way over there, toward the west. Toward Navajo Mountain," he said, indicating the direction. "Maybe thirty miles across the Nokaito Bench." But there were no roads, just broken country, sandstone cut by one wash after another. Whistler said he had heard about the ruins years ago from an uncle, who told him to stay out of the place because the ghosts were bad in there. But he had learned about Jesus, and he didn't believe in ghosts, so he packed in with a couple of horses, but it was tough going. An ordeal. He'd lost a horse. A good one.

Chee owned an excellent U.S. Geological Survey map of the Big Reservation, a book in which each page showed everything in a thirty-two-mile square. "What's the name of the canyon?"

"I don't know if it has a name," Amos Whistler said. "Around here they say its name is Canyon Where Watersprinkler Plays His Flute." It was a long name in Navajo, and Whistler looked embarrassed when he said it.

"Would you take me in there? Rent the horses and lead me in?"

"No," Amos Whistler said. "I don't go there no more."

"I'd hire you," Chee said. "Pay you for using your horses. Good money."

"No," Whistler said. "I'm a Christian now. I know about Jesus. I don't worry about Anasazi ghosts like I did when I was a pagan. Before I walked on the Jesus Road. But I won't go into that place."

"Good money," Chee said. "No problems with the law."

"I heard him in there," Whistler said. He took two steps away from Chee, toward the hogan door. "I heard the Watersprinkler playing his flute."

FOURTEEN

LEAPHORN MANAGED a forward seat by the window when he changed planes in Chicago. There was nothing to see—just the topside of solid cloud cover over the great flat, fertile American heartland. Leaphorn looked down at this gray mass and thought of the river of wet air flowing up from the Gulf of Mexico, and of cold rain, and bleak, featureless landscapes closed in by a sky no more than six feet above one's forehead. At least Emma had saved them from that by holding him on the reservation.

He was depressed. He had done what he had gone to do and achieved nothing useful. All he knew that he hadn't known before was that Etcitty had been too smart to sign a pot documentation admitting a violation of federal law. Leaphorn was fairly sure that the physical description of the site must be accurate. He could think of no reason for Etcitty to have made up such a complicated description. It seemed to flow from memory. An unsophisticated man following the form's instructions, describing reality with the single lie to avoid incrimination. That helped very little. The Utah–Arizona–New Mexico border country was a maze of washes, gulches, draws, and canyons. Thousands of them, and in their sheltered, sun-facing alcoves, literally scores of thousands of Anasazi sites. He'd seen an estimate of more than a hundred thousand such sites on the Colorado Plateau, built over a period of almost a thousand years. What Etcitty had given him was like a description of a house in a big city with no idea of its street address. He could narrow it down some. Probably in southern Utah or extreme northern Arizona. Probably north of Monument Valley. Probably east of Nokaito Mesa. Probably west of Montezuma Creek. That narrowed it to an area bigger than Connecticut, occupied by maybe five thousand humans. And all he had was a site description that might be as false as its location obviously was.

Perhaps Chee had done better. An odd young man, Chee. Smart, apparently. Alert. But slightly . . . slightly what? Bent? Not exactly. It wasn't just the business of trying to be a medicine man—a following utterly incongruous with police work. He was a romantic, Leaphorn decided. That was it. A man who followed dreams. The sort who would have joined that Paiute shaman who invented the ghost dance and the vision of white men withering away and the buffalo coming back to the plains. Maybe that wasn't fair. It was more that Chee seemed to think an island of 180,000 Navajos could live the old way in a white ocean. Perhaps 20,000 of them could, if they were happy on mutton, cactus, and piñon nuts. Not practical. Navajos had to compete in the real world. The Navajo Way didn't teach competition. Far from it.

But Chee, odd as he was, would find Slick Nakai. Another dreamer, Nakai. Leaphorn shifted in the narrow seat, trying vainly for comfort. Chee would find Nakai and Chee would get from Nakai about as much information as Leaphorn would have been able to extract.

Leaphorn found himself thinking of what he would say to Emma about Chee. He shook his head, picked up a *New Yorker*, and read. Dinner came. His seatmate examined it scornfully. To Leaphorn, who had been eating his own cooking, it tasted great. They were crossing the Texas panhandle now. Below, the clouds were thinning, breaking into patches. Ahead, the earth rose like a rocky island out of the ocean of humid air that blanketed the midlands. Leaphorn could see the broken mesas of eastern New Mexico. Beyond, on the western horizon, great cloud-castle thunderheads, unusual in autumn, rose into the stratosphere. Leaphorn felt something he hadn't felt since Emma's death. He felt a kind of joy.

Something like that mood was with him when he awoke the next morning in his bed at Window Rock—a feeling of being alive, and healthy, and interested. He was still weary. The flight from Albuquerque to Gallup in the little Aspen Airways Cessna, and the drive from Gallup, had finished what reserves he had left. But the depression was gone. He cooked bacon for breakfast and ate it with toast and jelly. While he was eating the telephone rang.

Jim Chee, he thought. Who else would be calling him?

It was Corporal Ellison Billy, who handled things that needed handling for Major Nez, who was more or less Leaphorn's boss.

"There's a Utah cop here looking for you," Billy said. "You available?"

Leaphorn was surprised. "What's he want? And what kind of cop?"

"Utah State Police. Criminal Investigation Division," Billy said. "He just said he wants to talk to you. About a homicide investigation. That's all

I know. Probably told the major more. You coming in?"

Homicide, he thought. The depression sagged down around him again. Someone had found Eleanor Friedman-Bernal's body. "Tell him ten minutes," he said, which was the time it took for him to drive from his house among the piñons on the high side of Window Rock to police headquarters beside the Fort Defiance Highway.

The desk had two messages for him. One from Jim Chee was short: "Found Nakai near Mexican Hat with a friend who says ruins is located in what the locals call Watersprinkler Canyon west of his place. I will stay reachable through the Shiprock dispatcher."

The other, from the Utah State Police, was shorter. It said: "Call Detective McGee re: Houk. Urgent."

"Houk?" Leaphorn said. "Any more details?"

"That's it," the dispatcher said. "Just call McGee about Houk. Urgent."

He put the message in his pocket.

The door to the major's office was open. Ronald Nez was standing behind his desk. A man wearing a blue windbreaker and a billed cap with the legend LIMBER ROPE on the crown sat against the wall. He got up when Leaphorn walked in, a tall man, middle-aged, with a thin, bony face.

Acne or some other scarring disease had left cheeks and forehead pocked with a hundred small craters. Nez introduced them. Carl McGee was the name. He had not waited for a call back.

"I'll get right to it," McGee said. "We got a homicide case, and he left you a note."

Leaphorn kept his face from showing his surprise. It wasn't Friedman-Bernal.

McGee waited for a response.

Leaphorn nodded.

"Harrison Houk," McGee said. "I imagine you know him?"

Leaphorn nodded again, his mind processing this. Who would kill Houk? Why? He could see an answer to the second question. And in general terms to the first one. The same person who had killed Etcitty, and Nails, and for the same reason. But what was that?

"What was the message?"

McGee looked at Major Nez, who looked back, expression neutral. Then at Leaphorn. This conversation was not going as McGee had intended. He extracted a leather folder from his hip pocket, took a business card from it, and handed it to Leaphorn.

BLANDING PUMPS
Well Drilling, Casing, Pulling

General Water System Maintenance

(We also fix your Septic Tanks)

The card was bent, dirty. Leaphorn guessed it had been damp. He turned it over.

The message there was scrawled in ballpoint ink.

It said:

Tell Leaphorn shes still alive up

Leaphorn handed it to Nez, without comment.

"I saw it," Nez said, and handed it back to McGee, who put it back in the folder, and the folder back in his pocket.

"What do you think?" he said. "You got any idea who the 'she' is?"

"A good idea," Leaphorn said. "But tell me about Houk. I saw him just the other day."

"Wednesday," McGee said. "To be exact." He looked at Leaphorn, expression quizzical. "That's what the woman who works for him told us. Navajo named Irene Musket."

"Wednesday sounds right," Leaphorn said. "Who killed Houk?"

McGee made a wry face. "This woman he wrote you about, maybe. Anyway, it looks like Houk quit trying to find a place to hide to tell you about her. Sounds like you two thought she was dead. Suddenly he sees her alive. He tries to tell you. She kills him."

Leaphorn was thinking that his terminal leave had five more days to run. Actually, only about four and two-thirds. He hadn't been in a mood to screw around like this for at least three months. Not since Emma got bad. He was in no mood for it today. In fact, he had never been tolerant of it. Nor for being polite to this *belagana*, who wanted to act as if Leaphorn was some sort of suspect. But he'd make one more effort to be polite.

"I've been away," he said. "Back east. Just got in last night. You're going to have to skip way back and tell me about it."

McGee told him. Irene Musket had come to work Friday morning and found a note on the screen door telling her that Houk was in the barn. She said she found his body in the barn and called the Garfield County Sheriff's Office, who notified Utah State Police. Both agencies investigated. Houk had been shot twice with a small-caliber weapon, in the center of the chest and in the lower back of the skull. There were signs that Houk had been rearranging bales of hay, apparently into a hiding place. Two empty .25 caliber cartridge casings were found in the hay near the body. The medical examiner said either of the bullets might have caused death. No witnesses. No physical evidence found in the barn except the shell casings. The housekeeper said she found the back screen door lock had been broken and Houk's office was in disarray. As far as she could tell, nothing had been stolen.

"But then, who knows?" McGee added. "Stuff could be gone from his office and she wouldn't know about it." He stopped, looking at Leaphorn.

"Where was the note?"

"In Houk's shorts," McGee said. "We didn't turn it up. The medical examiner found it when they undressed him."

Leaphorn found he was feeling a little better about McGee. It wasn't McGee's attitude. It was his own.

"I went Wednesday to see him about a woman named Eleanor Friedman-Bernal," Leaphorn said. He explained the situation. Who the woman was, her connection with Houk, what Houk had told him. "So I presume he was telling me she was still alive."

"You thought she was dead?" McGee asked.

"Missing two, three weeks. Leaves her clothes. Leaves a big dinner waiting to be cooked in her fridge. Misses important appointments. I don't know whether she's dead or not."

"Pretty fair bet she is," Nez said. "Or it was."

"You and Houk friends?" McGee asked.

"No," Leaphorn said. "I met him twice. Last Wednesday and about twenty years ago. One of his boys wiped out most of the family. I worked a little on that."

"I remember it. Hard one to forget." McGee was staring at him.

"I'm just as surprised as you are," Leaphorn said. "That he left me the note." He paused, thinking. "Do you know why he left the note in the screen door? About being in the barn?"

"Musket said she'd gone off and left some stuff—some squash—she was going to take home. He'd put it in the refrigerator and left the note. It said, 'squash in the icebox, I'm in the barn.' She figured he thought she'd come back for it."

Leaphorn was remembering the setting—the long, weedy drive, the porch, the barn well up the slope behind the house, a loading pen on one side of it, horse stalls on the other. From the barn, Houk would have heard a car coming. He might have seen it, watched its driver open the gate. He must have recognized death coming for him. McGee said he'd started preparing a hiding place—stacking bales with a gap behind them, to form a hidey-hole probably. And then he'd stopped to write the unfinished note. And put it in his shorts. Leaphorn imagined that. Houk, desperate, out of time, sticking the calling card under his belt line. The only possible reason would be to keep his killer from finding it. And that meant the killer would not have left it. And what did that mean? That the killer was Eleanor Friedman-Bernal, who would not want people to know she was alive? Or, certainly, that Houk knew she was alive.

"You have any theories yet?" he asked McGee.

"One or two," he said.

"Involving pot hunting?"

"Well, we know about Etcitty and Nails. They were hunting pots. Houk's been dealing with 'em for years and not particular where what he buys comes from," McGee said. "So, maybe somebody he cheated got tough about it. Houk screwed one person too many. He had a reputation for that. Or maybe it was this woman he was selling to." McGee got up stiffly, adjusted his hat. "Why else the note? He saw her coming. Back from the dead, so to speak. Knew she was after him. Figured she'd already bagged Nails and Etcitty. Started leaving you the note. Put it where she wouldn't find it and get off with it. I'd like you to tell me what you know about that woman."

"All right," Leaphorn said. "Couple of things I have to do and then I'll get with you."

He'd stayed away from his office since Emma's death and now it smelled of the dust that seeps gradually into everything in a desert climate. He sat in his chair, picked up the phone, and called Shiprock. Chee was in.

"This Watersprinkler Canyon," he asked. "Which side of the river?"

"South," Chee said. "Reservation side."

"No question of that?"

"None," Chee said. "Not if this Amos Whistler knew what he was talking about. Or where he was pointing."

"There isn't any Watersprinkler Canyon on my map. What do you think it is?"

"Probably Many Ruins," Chee said.

It was exactly what Leaphorn would have guessed. And getting into the north end of it was damn near impossible. It ran for its last forty miles through a roadless, jumbled stony wilderness.

"You knew Harrison Houk was shot?"

"Yes sir."

"You want to keep working on this?"

Hesitation. "Yes sir."

"Get on the telephone then. Call the police at Madison, Wisconsin. Find out if handguns are licensed there. They probably are. If they are, find out who does it and then find out exactly what kind of pistol was licensed to Eleanor Friedman-Bernal. It would have been . . ." He squeezed his eyes shut, recalling what Maxie Davis had told him about the woman's career. "Probably 1985 or '86."

"Okay."

"If she didn't license her gun in Madison, you're going to have to keep checking." He gave Chee other places he knew of where the woman had studied or taught, relying on his memory of his talk with Davis and guessing at the dates. "You may be spending all day on the phone," Leaphorn warned. "Tell 'em three homicides are involved. And then stay close to the phone where I can get you."

"Right."

That done, he sat a moment, thinking. He would go to Bluff and take a look at the barn where Harrison Houk had done the remarkable—written him a note while waiting for his killer. He wanted to see that place. The action jarred on him. Why would Houk care that much about a woman who was merely a customer? "Shes still alive up," the note had said. Up? Up to today? Up what? Up where? Up Watersprinkler Canyon? She had taken her sleeping bag. The boy had seen her loading a saddle. But back to Houk. Starting the note. At that point, almost certainly, Houk had been interrupted by the killer. Had run out of time. Had presumed the killer would destroy the note. Would not want the police to know that "she" was alive. So was "she" Eleanor hyphenated? Who else would care about the note? And yet Leaphorn had trouble putting into the picture the woman who marinated the beef and prepared the dinner so lovingly. He could not see her in that barn, firing her little pistol into the skull of an old man lying facedown in the hay. He shook his head. But that was sentiment, not logic.

Major Nez stood in his door, watching him. "Interesting case," Nez said.

"Yeah. Hard one to figure." Leaphorn motioned him in.

Nez simply leaned against the wall, holding a folded paper in his hand. He was getting fat, Leaphorn noticed. Nez had always been built like a barrel, but now his stomach sagged over his broad uniform belt.

"Doesn't sound like something you can get sorted out in less than a week," Nez said. He tapped the paper against the back of his hand, and it occurred to Leaphorn that it was his letter of resignation.

"Probably not," Leaphorn said.

Nez held out the letter. "You want this back? For now? You can always send it in again."

"I'm tired, Ron. Have been a long time, I guess. Just didn't know it."

"Tired of living," Nez said, nodding. "I get that way now and then. But it's hard to quit."

"Anyway, thanks," Leaphorn said. "You know where McGee went?"

Leaphorn found Detective McGee eating a late

breakfast at the Navajo Nation Inn and told him everything he knew about Eleanor Friedman-Bernal that seemed remotely pertinent. Then he drove back to his house, dug his pistol belt out of the bottom drawer of his dresser, took out the weapon, and dropped it into his jacket pocket. That done, he drove out of Window Rock, heading north.

FIFTEEN

THE YOUNG WOMAN to whom Chee's call was referred at the Madison Police Department had a little trouble believing in the Navajo Tribal Police. But after that was settled, things became most efficient. Yes, handguns were licensed. No, it would be easy to check the record. Just a moment. It was not much more than that.

The next voice was male. Eleanor Friedman-Bernal? Yes, she had been issued a license for a handgun. She had registered a .25 caliber automatic pistol.

Chee noted the details. The pistol was a brand he'd never heard of. Neither had the clerk in Madison. "Portuguese, I think," he said. "Or maybe it's Turkish, or Brazilian."

Step two went almost as quickly. He called the San Juan County Sheriff's Office and asked for

Undersheriff Robert Bates, who usually handled homicides. Bates was married to a Navajo, who happened to be "born to" the Kin yaa aanii—the Towering House People—which was linked in some way Chee had never understood to his grandfather's To' aheedlinii'—the Waters Flow Together Clan. That made Chee and Bates vaguely relatives. Just as important, they had worked together a time or two and liked each other. Bates was in.

"If you have the lab report back, I need to know about the bullets that killed Etcitty and Nails," Chee said.

"Why?" Bates asked. "I thought the FBI decided that killing wasn't on reservation land."

"Out on the Checkerboard, the FBI always decides that," Chee said. "We're just interested."

"Why?"

"Ah, hell, Robert," Chee said. "I don't know why. Joe Leaphorn is interested, and Largo has me working with him."

"What's going on with Leaphorn? We heard he had a nervous breakdown. Heard he quit."

"He did," Chee said. "But not yet."

"Well, it was a twenty-five-caliber pistol, automatic judging from the ejection marks on the empties. All the same weapon."

"You have a missing person's report on a woman who owns a twenty-five-caliber automatic pistol," Chee said. "Her name's Dr. Eleanor Friedman-Bernal. She worked out of Chaco Canyon. Anthropologist. Where Etcitty worked." He told Bates more of what he knew about the woman.

"I got her file right here on my desk," Bates said. "I just a minute ago got a call from a Utah State Policeman. They want us to do some checking up on her out at Chaco. Seems they had a fellow shot up at Bluff and he left a note to Leaphorn telling him this woman is still alive. You know about that?"

"Heard about the killing. Not about any note." He was thinking that a few years ago this weird roundabout communication would have surprised him. Now he expected it. He was remembering Leaphorn chewing him out for not passing along all the details. Well, there was no reason for Leaphorn not to have told him about this. Except that Leaphorn considered him merely an errand boy. Chee was offended.

"Tell me about it," he told Bates. "And don't leave anything out."

Bates told him what he'd been told. It didn't take long.

"So Utah State Police think Dr. Friedman showed up and offed Houk," Chee concluded. "Any theories about motive?"

"Big pot hunting conspiracy is what they seem

to think. They've had a federal crackdown up there on pot thieves last year. Bunch of arrests. Grand jury sitting in Salt Lake handing down indictments. So they're thinking pots," Bates said. "And why not? Big money in it the way prices are now. Hell, when we was kids and used to go out and dig 'em up around here, you were lucky to get five bucks. Listen," he added, "how you coming on being a medicine man?"

"No clients." It was not a subject Chee wanted to discuss. It was November, already into the "Season When Thunder Sleeps," the season for curing ceremonials, and he hadn't had a single contact. "You going to Chaco now?"

"Soon as I get off the telephone."

Chee gave him a quick rundown on the people he should talk to: Maxie Davis, the Lunas, Randall Elliot.

"They're worried about the woman. Friends of hers. Be sure and tell them about the note."

"Why, sure," Bates said. He sounded slightly offended that Chee had even mentioned it.

There was nothing to do then but stick close to the telephone and wait for Leaphorn's call from Bluff. He dug into his paperwork. A little before noon, the phone rang. Leaphorn, Chee thought.

It was Janet Pete. Her voice sounded odd. Was Chee doing anything for lunch?

"Nothing," Chee said. "You calling from Shiprock?"

"I drove up. Really just went for a drive. Ended up here." She sounded thoroughly down.

"Lunch then," he said. "Can you meet me at the Thunderbird Café?"

She could. And did.

They took a booth by the window. And talked about the weather. A gusty wind was rattling the pane and chasing dust and leaves and now a section of the *Navajo Times* down the highway outside.

"End of autumn, I guess," Chee said. "You watch Channel Seven. Howard Morgan says we're going to get the first blast of winter."

"I hate winter," Janet Pete said. She hugged herself and shivered. "Dismal winter."

"The counselor has the blues," Chee said. "Anything I can do to cheer you up? I'll call Morgan and see if he can postpone it."

"Or call it off altogether."

"Right."

"Or there's Italy."

"Which is warm, I hear," Chee said, and then he saw she was serious.

"You hear from your Successful Attorney?"

"He flew all the way to Chicago, to Albuquerque, to Gallup. I met him at Gallup."

Not knowing what to say, Chee said: "Not exactly meeting him halfway." It sounded flippant. Chee didn't feel flippant. He cleared his throat. "Has he changed? Time does that with people. So I'm told."

"Yes," Janet Pete said. But she shook her head. "But no. Not really. My mother told me a long time ago: 'Don't ever expect a man to change. What you see is what you live with.'"

"I guess so," Chee said. She looked tired, and full of sadness. He reached out and took her hand in his. It was cold. "Trouble is, I guess you love him anyway."

"I don't know," Janet Pete said. "I just . . ." But the sympathy was too much for her. Her voice choked. She looked down, fumbling in her purse.

Chee handed her his napkin. She held it to her face.

"Rough life," Chee said. "Love is supposed to make us happy, and sometimes it makes us miserable."

Through the napkin he heard Janet sniff.

He patted her hand. "This sounds like a cliché, or whatever it is, but I know how you feel. I really do."

"I know," Janet said.

"But you know, I've decided. I'm giving up. You can't go on forever." As he heard himself saying that, he was amazed. When did he decide that? He hadn't realized it. He felt a surge of relief. And of loss. Why can't men cry? he wondered. Why is that not allowed?

"He wants me to go to Italy with him. He's going to Rome. Taking over their legal affairs for Europe. And Africa. And the Middle East."

"He speak Italian?" As he said it, it seemed an incredibly stupid question. Totally beside the point here.

"French," she said. "And some Italian. And he's perfecting it. A tutor."

"How about you?" he said. Why couldn't he think of something less inane. He would be asking her next about her passport. And packing. And airfares. That wasn't what she wanted to talk about. She wanted to talk about love.

"No," she said.

"What did he say? Does he understand now that you want to be a lawyer? That you want to practice it?"

The napkin was in her lap now. Her eyes dry. But they showed she'd been crying. And her face was strained.

"He said I could practice in Italy. Not with his company. It has a nepotism rule. But he could line something up for me after I got the required Italian license."

"He could line something up. For you."

She sighed. "Yeah. That's the way he put it.

And I guess he could. At a certain level in law, the big firms feed on one another. There would be Italian firms doing feed-out work. The word would go into the good-old-boy network. Tit for tat. I guess once I learned Italian I would be offered a job."

Chee nodded. "I'd think so," he said.

Lunch came. Mutton stew and fry bread for Chee. Janet was having a bowl of soup.

They sat looking at the food.

"You should eat something," said Chee, who had totally lost his appetite. He took a spoonful of the stew, a bite of fry bread. "Eat," he ordered.

Janet Pete took a spoonful of soup.

"Made a decision yet?"

She shook her head. "I don't know."

"You know yourself better than anyone," he said. "What's going to make you happy?"

She shook her head again. "I think I'm happy when I'm with him. Like dinner last night. But I don't know."

Chee was thinking about the dinner and how it had ended, and what happened then. Had she gone to his room with him? Had she spent the night there? Probably. The thought hurt. It hurt a lot. That surprised him.

"I shouldn't let things like this drag on," she said. "I should decide."

"We let ours drag on. Mary and I. And I guess she decided."

He had released her hand when lunch arrived. Now she reached over and put hers on his. "I have your napkin," she said. "Slightly damp but still"—she looked at it, a rumpled square of pale blue paper—"usable in case of emergency."

He realized instantly that this was her bid to change the subject. He took the napkin, dropped it in his lap.

"Have you realized how lucky you are to have been brought to the only café in Shiprock with napkins?"

"Noted and appreciated," she said. Her smile seemed almost natural. "And how are things going with you?"

"I told you about the Backhoe Bandit. And Etcitty?"

She nodded. "That must have been gruesome. How about finding the woman?"

"How much did I tell you about that?"

She reminded him.

He told her about Houk, about the note left for Leaphorn, about Eleanor Friedman-Bernal's pistol and how it was the same caliber used in the killings, about Leaphorn's obsessive interest in finding the Utah site to which Friedman's long-lost potter seemed to have moved.

"You know you have to file for a permit to dig sites like that on the reservation. We have an office in Window Rock that deals with it," Janet Pete said. "Did you check that?"

"Leaphorn might have," Chee said. "But apparently she was trying to find out where the stuff was coming from. You'd have to know that before you could file."

"I guess so. But I think they're all numbered. Maybe she would just guess at it."

Chee grinned and shook his head. "Back when I was an anthropology student, I remember Professor Campbell, or somebody, telling us there were forty thousand sites listed with New Mexico Laboratory of Anthropology numbers. That's in New Mexico alone. And another hundred thousand or so on other registries."

"I didn't mean just pick a number at random," she said, slightly irked. "She could describe the general location."

Chee was suddenly interested. "Maybe Leaphorn already looked into it," he said. He was remembering that probably he would be hearing from Leaphorn soon. He'd left word with the switchboard to relay the call here. "But would it take long to check?"

"I could call," she said, looking thoughtful. "I know the man who runs it. Helped him with the regulations. I think, to dig on the reservation,

I think you have to apply to the Park Service and the Navajo Cultural Preservation Office both. I think you have to name a repository for whatever you recover, and get the archive system approved. And maybe . . ."

Chee was thinking how great it would be if, when Leaphorn called, he could tell him the map coordinates of the site he was looking for. His face must have showed his impatience. Janet stopped midsentence. "What?" she said.

"Let's go back to the station and call," he said.

The call from Leaphorn was waiting when they walked in. Chee gave him what he'd learned from the Madison police and from Bates at the San Juan County Sheriff's Office. "They're expecting a report from the Utah State Police," Chee added. "Bates said he would call when he gets it."

"I've got it," Leaphorn said. "It was twenty-five-caliber, too."

"Do you know if Friedman applied for a permit to dig that site you're looking for?"

Long silence. "I should have thought of that," Leaphorn said finally. "I doubt if she did. The red tape takes years and it's a double filing. Park Service clearance plus tribal clearance, and all sorts of checking and screwing around gets involved. But I should have checked it."

"I'll take care of it," Chee said.

The man to call, Janet Pete said, was T. J.

Pedwell. Chee reached him just back from lunch. Had he had any applications from Dr. Eleanor Friedman-Bernal to dig on a reserved Anasazi site on the reservation?

"Sure," Pedwell said. "Two or three. On Checkerboard land around Chaco Canyon. She's that ceramics specialist working over there."

"How about over on the north side of the reservation? Up in Utah."

"I don't think so," Pedwell said. "I could check on it. Wouldn't know the site number, would you?"

" 'Fraid not," Chee said. "But it might be somewhere near the north end of Many Ruins Canyon."

"I know that place," Pedwell said. "Helped with the Antiquities survey all up through that part of the country."

"You know the canyon the local people call Watersprinkler?"

"It's really Many Ruins," Pedwell said. "It's full of pictographs and petroglyphs of Kokopelli. That's the one the Navajos call the Watersprinkler *yei*."

"I have a description of the site, and it sounds unusual," Chee said. He told Pedwell what Amos Whistler had told him.

"Yeah," Pedwell said. "Sounds familiar. Let me check my files. I have photos of most of them."

Chee heard the telephone click against something. He waited and waited. Sighed. Leaned a hip against the desk.

"Trouble?" Janet Pete asked.

Pedwell's voice was in his ear before he could respond.

"Found it," Pedwell said. "It's N.R. 723. Anasazi. Circa 1280–1310. And there's two other sites right there with it. Probably connected."

"Great!" Chee said. "How do you get there?"

"Well, it ain't going to be easy. I remember that. We packed into some of them on horseback. Others we floated down the San Juan and walked up the canyon. This one I think we floated. Let's see. Notes say it's five point seven miles up from the mouth of the canyon."

"Dr. Friedman. She apply to dig that one?"

"Not her," Pedwell said. "Another of those people out at Chaco did. Dr. Randall Elliot. They working together?"

"I don't think so," Chee said. "Does the application say he was collecting St. John's Polychrome pots?"

"Lemme look." Papers rustled. "Doesn't sound like pots. Says he is studying Anasazi migrations." Mumbling sounds of Pedwell reading to himself. "Says his interest is tracing genetic patterns." More mumbling. "Studying bones. Skull thickness. Six-fingeredness. Aberrant jaw formation."

More mumbling. "I don't think it has anything to do with ceramics," Pedwell said, finally. "He's looking at the skeletons. Or will be if your famous Navajo bureaucracy, of which I am a part, ever gets this processed. Six-fingeredness. Lot of that among the Anasazi, but hard to study, because hands don't survive intact after a thousand years. But it sounds like he's found some family patterns. Too many fingers. An extra tooth in the right side of the lower jaw. A second hole where those nerves and blood vessels go through the back of the jaw, and something or other about the fibula. Physical anthropology isn't my area."

"But he hasn't gotten his permit yet?"

"Wait a minute. I guess we weren't so slow on this one. Here's a carbon of a letter to Elliot from the Park Service." Paper rustled. "Turn-down," Pedwell said. "More documentation needed of previous work in this field. That do it?"

"Thanks a lot," Chee said.

Janet Pete was watching him.

"Sounds like you scored," she said.

"I'll fill you in," he said.

"On the way back to my car." She looked embarrassed. "I'm normally the usual stolid, dull lawyer," she said. "This morning I just ran off in hysterics and left everything undone. People coming in to see me. People waiting for me to finish things. I feel awful."

He walked to the car with her, opened the door.

"I'm glad you called on me," he said. "You honored me."

"Oh, Jim!" she said, and hugged him around the chest with such strength that he caught his breath. She stood, holding him like that, pressed against him. He sensed she was about to cry again. He didn't want that to happen.

He put his hand on her hair and stroked it.

"I don't know what you'll decide about your Successful Attorney," he said. "But if you decide against him, maybe you and I could see if we could fall in love. You know, both Navajos and all that."

It was the wrong thing to say. She was crying as she drove away.

Chee stood there, watching her motor pool sedan speed toward the U.S. 666 junction and the route to Window Rock. He didn't want to think about this. It was confusing. And it hurt. Instead he thought of a question he should have asked Pedwell. Had Randall Elliot also filed an application to dig in that now-despoiled site where Etcitty and Nails had died?

He walked back into the station, remembering those jawbones so carefully set aside amid the chaos.

SIXTEEN

TO LEAPHORN, the saddle had seemed a promising possibility. She had borrowed it from a biologist named Arnold, who lived in Bluff. Other trails led to Bluff. The site of the polychrome pots seemed to be somewhere west of the town, in roadless country where a horse would be necessary. She would go to Arnold's place. If he could loan her a saddle, he could probably loan her a horse. From Arnold he would learn where Eleanor Friedman-Bernal had headed. The first step was finding Arnold, which shouldn't be difficult.

It wasn't. The Recapture Lodge had been Bluff's center of hospitality for as long as Leaphorn could remember. The man at the reception desk loaned Leaphorn his telephone to call Chee. Chee confirmed what Leaphorn had feared. Whether or not Dr. Friedman was killing pot hunters, her pistol was. The man at the desk also knew Arnold.

"Bo Arnold," he said. "Scientists around here are mostly anthropologists or geologists, but Dr. Arnold is a lichen man. Botanist. Go up to where the highway bends left, and take the right toward Montezuma Creek. It's the little redbrick house with lilac bushes on both sides of the gate. Except I think Bo let the lilacs die. He drives a Jeep. If he's home, you'll see it there."

The lilacs were indeed almost dead, and a dusty early-model Jeep was parked in the weeds beside the little house. Leaphorn parked beside it and stepped out of his pickup into a gust of chilly, dusty wind. The front door opened just as he walked up the porch steps. A lanky man in jeans and faded red shirt emerged. "Yessir," he said. "Good morning." He was grinning broadly, an array of white teeth in a face of weathered brown leather.

"Good morning," Leaphorn said. "I'm looking for Dr. Arnold."

"Yessir," the man said. "That's me." He stuck out a hand, which Leaphorn shook. He showed Arnold his identification.

"I'm looking for Dr. Eleanor Friedman-Bernal," Leaphorn said.

"Me too," Arnold said enthusiastically. "That

biddy got off with my kayak and didn't bring it back."

"Oh," Leaphorn said. "When?"

"When I was gone," Arnold said, still grinning. "Caught me away from home, and off she goes with it."

"I want to hear all about that," Leaphorn said.

Arnold held the door wide, welcomed Leaphorn in with a sweep of his hand. Inside the front door was a room crowded with tables, each table crowded with rocks of all sizes and shapes—their only common denominator being lichens. They were covered with these odd plants in every shade from white through black. Arnold led Leaphorn past them, down a narrow hall.

"No place to sit in there," he said. "That's where I work. Here's where I live."

Where Arnold lived was a small bedroom. Every flat surface, including the narrow single bed, was covered with boards on which flat glass dishes were lined. The dishes had something in them that Leaphorn assumed must be lichens. "Let me make you a place," Arnold said, and cleared off chairs for each of them.

"Why you looking for Ellie?" he asked. "She been looting ruins?" And he laughed.

"Does she do that?"

"She's an anthropologist," Arnold said, his chuckle reduced again to a grin. "You translate the word from academic into English and that's what it means: ruins looter, one who robs graves, preferably old ones. Well-educated person who steals artifact in dignified manner." Arnold, overcome by the wit of this, laughed. "Somebody else does it, they call 'em vandals. That's the word for the competition. Somebody gets there first, gets off with the stuff before the archaeologists can grab it, they call 'em Thieves of Time." His vision of such hypocrisy left him in high good humor, as did the thought of his missing kayak.

"Tell me about that," Leaphorn said. "How do you know she took it?"

"She left a full, signed confession," Arnold said, fumbling in a box from which assorted scraps of papers overflowed. He extracted a small sheet of lined yellow notepaper and handed it to Leaphorn.

Here's your saddle, a year older but no worse for wear. (I sold that damned horse.) To keep you caring about me, I am now borrowing your kayak. If you don't get back before I do, ignore the last part of this note because I will put the kayak right back in the garage where I got it and you'll never know it was gone.

Don't let any lichens grow on you!

Love,
Ellie

Leaphorn handed it back to him. "When did she leave it?"

"I just know when I found it. I'd been up there on Lime Ridge collecting specimens for a week or so and when I got back, the saddle was on the floor in the workroom up front with this note pinned on it. Looked in the garage, and the kayak was gone."

"When?" Leaphorn repeated.

"Oh," Arnold said. "Let's see. Almost a month ago."

Leaphorn told him the date Eleanor Friedman-Bernal had made her early-morning departure from Chaco Canyon. "That sound right?"

"I think I got back on a Monday or Tuesday. Three or four days after that."

"So the saddle might have been sitting there three or four days?"

"Could have been." Arnold laughed again. "Don't have a cleaning lady coming in. Guess you noticed that."

"How did she get in?"

"Key's over there under the flower box," Arnold said. "She knew where. Been here before. Go all the way back to the University of Wisconsin." Abruptly Arnold's amusement evaporated. His bony, sun-beaten face became somber. "She's really missing? People worried about her? She didn't just walk off for a few days of humanity?"

"I think it's serious," Leaphorn said. "Almost a month. And she left too much behind. Where would she go in your kayak?"

Arnold shook his head. "Just one place to go. Downstream. I use it to play around with. Like a toy. But she'd have been going down the river. Plenty of sites along the river until you get into the deep canyon where there's nothing to live on. And then there's hundreds of ruins up the side canyons." There was no humor at all left in Arnold's face. He looked at least his age, which Leaphorn guessed at forty. He looked worn and worried.

"Ceramics. That's what Ellie would be looking for. Potsherds." He paused, stared at Leaphorn. "I guess you know we had a man killed here just the other day. Man named Houk. The son of a bitch was a notorious pot dealer. Somebody shot him. Any connection?"

"Who knows?" Leaphorn said. "Maybe so. You have any more specific idea where she took your kayak?"

"Nothing more than I said. She borrowed it

before and went down into the canyons. Just poking around in the ruins looking at the potsherds. I'd guess she did it again."

"Any idea how far down?"

"She'd ask me to pick her up the next evening at the landing upstream from the bridge at Mexican Hat. Only place to get off the river for miles. So it would have to be between Sand Island and Hat."

Her car too could be found between Sand Island and Mexican Hat, Leaphorn was sure. She would have to have hauled the kayak within dragging distance of the river. But there was no reason now to look for the car.

"That narrows it down quite a bit," Leaphorn said, thinking Ellie's trips were into the area Etcitty had described in his falsified documentation, the area Amos Whistler had pointed to in his talk with Chee. He would find a boat and go looking for Arnold's kayak. Maybe, when he found it, he would find Eleanor Friedman, and what Harrison Houk meant in that unfinished note. ". . . shes still alive up." But first he wanted a look at that barn.

Irene Musket came to the door at Harrison Houk's old house. She recognized him instantly and let him in. She was a handsome woman, as Leaphorn remembered, but today she looked years older, and tired. She told him about finding the note, about finding the body. She confirmed that she had found absolutely nothing missing from the house. She told him nothing he didn't already know. Then she walked with him up the long slope toward the barn.

"It happened right in here," she said. "Right in that horse stall there. The third one."

Leaphorn looked back. From the barn you could see the driveway, and the old gate with its warning bell. Only the front porch was obscured. Houk might well have seen his killer coming for him.

Irene Musket stood at the barn door. Kept out, perhaps, by her fear of the *chindi* Harrison Houk had left behind him and the ghost sickness it would cause her. Or perhaps by the sorrow that looking at the spot where Houk had died would bring to her.

Leaphorn's career had made him immune to the *chindi* of the dead, immune through indifference to all but one of them. He walked out of the wind and into the dimness.

The floor of the third horse stall had been swept clean of the old alfalfa and prairie-hay straw that littered the rest of the place. That debris now formed a pile in one corner, where the Utah crime lab crew had dumped it after sorting through it. Leaphorn stood on the dirt packed by a hundred years of hooves and wondered what he had expected to find. He walked across the barn floor, inspected the piles of alfalfa bales. It did, indeed, seem that Houk might have been rearranging them to form a hiding place. That touched him oddly, but taught him nothing. Nothing except that Houk, the hard man, the scoundrel, had set aside a chance to hide to make time to leave him a message. "Tell Leaphorn shes still alive up"—up the canyon? That seemed likely. Up which canyon? But why would Houk have put his own life at greater risk to help a woman who must have been nothing more than one of his many customers? It seemed out of character. Not the Houk he knew about. That Houk's only weakness seemed to have been a schizophrenic son, now long dead.

Outside the barn the wind shifted direction slightly and howled through the cracks, raising a small flurry of straw and dust on the packed floor and bringing autumn smells to compete with the ancient urine. He was wasting his time. He walked back toward where Irene Musket was standing, checking the stalls as he passed. In the last one, a black nylon kayak was leaning against the wall.

Bo Arnold's kayak. Leaphorn stared at it. How could it have gotten here? And why?

It was inflated, standing on one pointed end in the stall corner. He walked in for a closer look. Of course it wasn't Arnold's kayak. He had described his as dark brown, with what he called "white racing stripes."

Leaphorn knelt beside it, inspecting it. It seemed remarkably clean for this dusty barn. He felt inside, between the rubber-coated nylon of its bottom and the inflated tubes that formed its walls, hoping to find something telltale left behind. His fingers encountered paper. He pulled it out. The crumpled, water-stained wrapper from a Mr. Goodbar. He ran his fingers down toward the bow.

Water.

Leaphorn pulled out his hand and examined his wet fingers. Whatever water had been left in the kayak had drained down into this crevice. How long could it have been there? How long would evaporation take in this no-humidity climate?

He walked to the door.

"The inflated kayak in there. You know when it was used?"

"I think four days ago," Irene Musket said.

"By Mr. Houk?"

She nodded.

"His arthritis didn't bother him?"

"His arthritis hurt all the time," she said. "It didn't keep him from that boat." She sounded as if this represented an argument lost, an old hurt.

"Where did he go? Do you know?"

She made a vague gesture. "Just down the river."

"Do you know how far?"

"Not very far. He would have me pick him up down there near Mexican Hat."

"He did this a lot?"

"Every full moon."

"He went down at night? Late?"

"Sometimes he would watch the ten o'clock news and then we would go down to Sand Island. We'd make sure nobody was there. Then we'd put it in." The wind whipped dust around Mrs. Musket's ankles and blew up her long skirt. She held it down, pressed back against the barn door. "We would put it in, and then the next morning, I would drive the pickup down to that landing place upstream from Mexican Hat and I'd wait for him there. And then . . ." She paused, swallowed. Stood a moment, silently. Leaphorn noticed her eyes were wet, and looked away. Hard as he was, Harrison Houk had left someone to grieve for him.

"Then we would drive back to the house together," she concluded.

Leaphorn waited awhile. When he had given

her enough time, he asked: "Did he tell you what he did when he went down the river?"

The silence lasted so long that Leaphorn wondered if his question had been lost in the wind. He glanced at her.

"He didn't tell me," she said.

Leaphorn thought about the answer.

"But you know," he said.

"I think so," she said. "One time he told me not to guess. And he said, 'If you guess anyway, then don't ever tell anybody!'"

"Do you know who killed him?"

"I don't," she said. "I wish they would have killed me, instead."

"I think we will find the one who did it," Leaphorn said. "I really do."

"He was a good man. People talked about how mean he was. He was good to good people and just mean to the mean ones. I guess they killed him for that."

Leaphorn touched her arm. "Would you help me put the kayak in? And then tomorrow, drive my truck down to Mexican Hat and pick me up?"

"All right," Irene Musket said.

"First I have to make a telephone call. Can I use your telephone?"

He called Jim Chee from Houk's house. It was after six. Chee had gone home for the day. No telephone, of course. Typical of Chee. He left Houk's number for a call back.

They slid the kayak into the back of his truck, with its double-bladed paddle and Houk's worn orange jacket, tied it down, and drove south to Sand Island launch site. Bureau of Land Management signs there warned that the river was closed for the season, that a license was required, that the San Juan catfish was on the extinction list and taking it was prohibited.

With the kayak in the water, Leaphorn stood beside it, feet in the cold water, doing a last-minute inventory of possibilities. He wrote Jim Chee's name and the Shiprock police station number on one of his cards and gave it to her.

"If I don't meet you by noon tomorrow down at Mexican Hat, I hope you will call this man for me. Tell him what you told me about Mr. Houk and this kayak. And that I took it down the river."

She took it.

He climbed into the kayak.

"You know how to run that thing?"

"Years ago I did. I think I'll remember."

"Well, put on the life jacket and buckle it. It's easy to turn over."

"Right," Leaphorn said. He did it.

"And here," she said. She handed him a heavy canteen with a carrying strap and a plastic bread sack. "I got something for you to eat out of the kitchen," she said.

"Well, thanks," Leaphorn said, touched.

"Be careful."

"I can swim."

"I didn't mean the river," Mrs. Musket said.

SEVENTEEN

TRAILERS ARE POOR PLACES to sleep on those nights when seasons are changing on the Colorado Plateau. All night Jim Chee's narrow bed quivered as the gusts shook the thin walls of his home. He slept poorly, wrestling with the problem of Elliot's application while he was awake, dreaming of jawbones when he dozed. He rose early, made coffee, and found four Twinkies abandoned in his otherwise empty bread box to round out his breakfast. It was his day off, and time to buy groceries, do the laundry, check three overdue books back into the Farmington library. He'd refilled his water reservoir, but his butane supply was low. And he needed to pick up a tire he'd had repaired. And, come to think of it, drop by the bank and see about the $18.50 difference between his checkbook balance and their records.

Instead he looked in his notebook and found the number Dr. Pedwell had given him for the Laboratory of Anthropology in Santa Fe. "That would have an MLA number," Pedwell had told him when he'd asked if Elliot had also applied to excavate the site where Etcitty and Nails had been killed. "It's in New Mexico, and apparently on public land. If it's on a Navajo section, we record it. If it's not, Laboratory of Anthropology handles it."

"Sounds confusing," Chee had said.

"Oh, it is," Pedwell had agreed. "It's even more confusing than that." And he'd started explaining other facets of the numbering system, the Chaco numbers, the Mesa Verde, until Chee had changed the subject. Now he realized he should have asked for a name at Santa Fe.

He made the call from the station, drawing a surprised look from the desk clerk, who knew he was off. And it took three transfers before he connected with the woman who had access to the information he needed. She had a sweet, distinct middle-aged voice.

"It's easier if you know the MLA number," she said. "Otherwise I have to check through the applicant files."

And so he waited.

"Dr. Elliot has eleven applications on file. You want all of them?"

"I guess so," Chee said, not knowing exactly what to expect.

"MLA 14,751. MLA 19,311. MLA—"

"Just a moment," Chee said. "Do they have site locations? What county they're in. Like that?"

"On our map, yes."

"The one I'm interested in would be in San Juan County, New Mexico."

"Just a minute," she said. The minute passed. "Two of them. MLA 19,311 and MLA 19,327."

"Could you pin the location down any more?"

"I can give you the legal description. Range, township, and section." She read them off.

"Was he issued the permits?"

"Turned down," she said. "They're saving those sites to be dug sometime in the future when they have better technology. It's hard to get permission to dig them now."

"Thanks a lot," Chee said. "It's exactly what I need."

And it was. When he checked the legal description on the U.S. Geological Survey map in Captain Largo's office, MLA 19,327 proved to share range, township, and section with the oil well pump beyond which he'd found the U-Haul truck.

He had less luck trying to call Chaco Canyon. The phone was suffering some sort of satellite relay problem that produced both fade-out and echo. Randall Elliot was out of reach at one of the down-canyon ruins. Maxie Davis was somewhere. Luna was doing something, unintelligible to Chee, at Pueblo Bonito.

Chee glanced at his watch. He calculated the distance to Chaco. About a hundred miles. He remembered the condition of that last twenty-five miles of dirt. He groaned. Why was he doing this on his day off? But he knew why. Much as Leaphorn irritated him, he wanted the man to pat him on the head. To say, "Good job, kid." Might as well admit it. Also he might as well admit another fact. He was excited now. That grotesque line of lower jaws suddenly seemed to mean something. Perhaps something important.

The strange weather slowed him a little, rocking his truck when he stretched the limit on the fast pavement of N.M. 44 across the sagebrush flats of Blanco Plateau. End of autumn, he thought. Winter coming out of the west. Behind him over Colorado's La Plata range, the sky was dark, and when he left the pavement at Blanco Trading Post, he had a direct side wind to deal with—and the tiring business of steering against it as he fought chugholes and ruts. And tumbleweeds and blowing sand chased him across the parking lot at the Chaco visitors' center.

The woman he'd talked to was at the desk, looking trim in her park ranger uniform and glad to have Chee break the boredom of a day, and a season, that brought few visitors. She showed him on the Chaco map how to get to Kin Kletso, the site where Randall Elliot would be working today, "if he can work in this wind." Where Maxie Davis was seemed a mystery, "but maybe she'll be working with Randall." Luna had driven into Gallup and wouldn't be back until tonight.

Chee went back to his truck, leaning into the wind, squinching his eyes against the dust. At Kin Kletso, he found a Park Service truck parked and an employee sitting in the shelter of one of the walls.

"Looking for Dr. Randall Elliot," Chee said. "Did I miss him?"

"A mile," the man said. "He didn't show up today."

"You know where . . ."

The man waved a dismissive wave. "No idea," he said. "He's independent as a hog on ice."

Maybe he was home. Chee drove to the temporary housing. Nothing in the parking area. He knocked at the door marked Elliot. Knocked again. Walked around the building to the back. Randall Elliot hadn't pulled the drapes across his sliding-glass patio door. Chee peered into what must be the living room. Elliot seemed to have converted it into a work area. Sawhorses supported planks on which cardboard cartons were lined. Those that Chee could see into seemed to contain bones. Skulls, ribs, jawbones. Chee pressed his forehead against the cool glass, shading his eyes with both hands, straining to see. Against the wall, boxes were lined. Books on shelves against the kitchen partition. No sign of Elliot.

Chee glanced down at the lock that held the door. Simple enough. He looked around him. No one visible. He dug out his penknife, opened the proper blade, slipped the catch.

Once inside he closed the drapes and turned on the light. He hurried through a quick search of the bedroom, kitchen, and bath, touching hardly anything and using his handkerchief to avoid leaving prints. This made him nervous. Worse, it made him feel dirty and ashamed.

But back in the living room he lingered over the boxes of bones. They seemed to be arranged in groups, tagged by site. Chee checked the tags, looking for either N.R. 723 or MLA 19,327. On the makeshift table by the kitchen door he found the N.R. number.

The tag was tied through the eye socket of a skull, number on one side, notes on the other. They seemed to be in some sort of personal shorthand, with numbers in millimeters. Bone thickness, Chee guessed, but the rest of it meant nothing to him.

The N.R. 723 box contained four lower jaws,

one apparently from a child, one broken. He examined them. Each contained an extra molar, or a trace of one, on the right side. Each had two of the small holes low in the bones through which Elliot's petition had stated nerves and blood vessels grow.

Chee put the jaws back in the box exactly as he had found them, wiped his fingers on his pants legs, and sat down to sort out the significance of this. It seemed clear enough. Elliot's genetic tracking had led him to the same site as had Eleanor Friedman-Bernal's pottery chase. No. That didn't state it accurately. In their mutual fishing expeditions, both had struck pay dirt in the same ruins. Perhaps, Chee thought, one of the jawbones belonged to the potter.

He thought about site MLA 19,327, the lined jawbones, the missing plastic sack from the box of thirty. Thinking about that, he made another search of the apartment.

He found a black plastic sack in the bottom of a wastebasket in the kitchen. He carefully set aside the table scraps and wadded papers that had buried it and put it on the counter beside the sink. The top was tied in a knot. Chee untied it and examined the plastic. SUPERTUFF was printed around the top. The missing sack.

Inside it were seven human mandibles, two of them child-sized, two broken. Chee counted teeth. Each had seventeen—one more than standard—and in each the superfluous molar was second from the back and out of line.

He put the sack back in the wastebasket, recovered it with waste, and picked up the telephone.

No, the woman at the visitors' center said, Elliot hadn't reported in. Nor had Luna or Maxie Davis.

"Can you get me Mrs. Luna?"

"Now that's easy," she said.

Mrs. Luna answered on the third ring and remembered Chee instantly. How was he? How was Mr. Leaphorn? "But this isn't what you called about."

"No," Chee said. "I came out to talk to Randall Elliot but he's away somewhere. I remembered you said he went to Washington last month. You said his travel agent called and you took the message. Do you remember the name of the agency?"

"Bolack's," Mrs. Luna said. "I think just about everybody out here uses Bolack's."

Chee called Bolack Travel in Farmington.

"Navajo Tribal Police," he told the man who answered. "We need to confirm the dates of an airline ticket. Don't know the airline, but the tickets were issued by your agency to Randall Elliot, address at Chaco Canyon."

"You know about when? This year? This month? Yesterday?"

"Probably late last month," Chee said.

"Randall Elliot," the man said. "Randall Elliot. Let's see." Chee heard the clacking sound of a computer keyboard. Silence. More clacking. More silence.

"That's funny," the man said. "We issued them, but he didn't pick them up. It was an October eleven departure, with an October sixteen return. Mesa from Farmington to Albuquerque, American from Albuquerque to Washington. You just need the dates?"

"The tickets weren't picked up? You're certain?"

"I sure am. Makes a lot of work for nothing."

Chee called Mrs. Luna again. Listening to the ring, he felt a sense of urgency. Randall Elliot wasn't in Washington that morning Eleanor Friedman-Bernal drove away to oblivion. He didn't go. But he pretended to go. He arranged it so that everyone in this gossipy place would think he was in Washington. Why? So they wouldn't be curious about where he'd actually gone. And where was that? Chee thought he knew. He hoped he was wrong.

"Hello," Mrs. Luna said.

"Chee again," he said. "Another question. Did a deputy sheriff come out here yesterday to talk to people?"

"He did. About a month late, I'd say."

"Did he tell you about the note left for Lieutenant Leaphorn? The one that sounded like Dr. Friedman might still be alive."

"Is alive," Mrs. Luna said. "He said the note said, 'Tell Leaphorn she is still alive.'"

"Does everybody here know about that? Does Elliot?"

"Of course. Because everybody was beginning to have their doubts. You know, that's a long time to just disappear unless something bad has happened."

"You sure about Elliot?"

"He was right here when he told Bob and me."

"Well, thanks a lot," Chee said.

The wind had fallen now into something near a calm. Which was lucky for Chee. He drove back to Blanco Trading Post much faster than the rutted dirt roadbed made wise, and then much faster than the law allowed on N.M. 44 to Farmington. He was worried. He had told Undersheriff Bates to tell the people at Chaco about Houk's note. He should not have done that. But maybe these suspicions were groundless. He thought of a way he could check—a call he should have made before he left Chaco.

He pulled into the grocery store at Bloomfield and ran to the pay phone, then ran back to his truck for the supply of quarters he kept in the glove box. He called the Farmington airport, identified himself, asked the woman who answered who there rented helicopters. He jotted down the two names she gave him, and their numbers. The line was busy at Aero Services. He dialed Flight Contractors. A man who identified himself as Sanchez answered. Yes, they had rented a copter that morning to Randall Elliot.

"Pretty sorry weather for flying, even in a copter," Sanchez said. "But he's got the credentials and the experience. Flew for the navy in Nam."

"Did he say where he was going?"

"He's an anthropologist," Sanchez said. "We been renting to him for two, three years now. Said he was going down over the White Horse Lake country hunting one of them Indian ruins. If you're going to fly in this kind of weather, that's a good place to fly. Just grass and snakeweed down that way."

It was also just about exactly the opposite direction from where Elliot was really flying, Chee thought. Southeast instead of northwest.

"When did he leave?"

"I'd say maybe three hours ago. Maybe a little longer."

"Do you have another one to rent? With a pilot."

"Have the chopper," Sanchez said. "Have to see about the pilot. When's it for?"

Chee made some instant calculations. "Thirty minutes," he said.

"I doubt it by then," Sanchez said. "I'll try."

It took Chee a little less than that, at considerable risk of a speeding ticket. Sanchez had found a pilot, but the pilot hadn't arrived.

"He's the substitute pilot for the air ambulance service," Sanchez said. "Man named Ed King. He didn't care much for this weather, but then the wind's been dying."

In fact the wind had moderated to a steady breeze. It seemed to be dying away as the weather front that brought it moved southeast. But now the sky to the north and west was a solid dark overcast.

While they waited for King, he'd see if he could get hold of Leaphorn. If he couldn't, he'd leave word for him. Tell him about finding the missing wastebasket liner hidden in Elliot's kitchen with the bones in it, and about Elliot's rejected applications to dig those sites. He'd tell Leaphorn that Elliot hadn't taken the flight to Washington the weekend that Friedman-Bernal disappeared. That provoked another thought.

"Mr. Sanchez. Could you check and see if Dr. Elliot took out a helicopter on, let's see, the thirteenth of October?"

Sanchez looked as doubtful as he had when

Chee had said he should bill the copter rental to the Navajo Tribal Police. The look had hardened, and Chee had finally presented his MasterCard and waited while Sanchez checked his credit balance. It seemed to have reached the minimum guarantee. ("Now," said Sanchez, cheerful again, "if it's okay with the tribal auditors you can get your money back.")

"I don't know that I'm supposed to be telling all this stuff," Sanchez said. "Randall's a regular customer of ours. It might get back to him."

"It's police business," Chee said. "Part of a criminal investigation."

"About what?" Sanchez looked stubborn.

"Those two men shot out in the Checkerboard. Nails and Etcitty."

"Oh," Sanchez said. "I'll check."

"While you do, I'll call my office."

Benally was in charge of the shift. No, Benally knew no way to get in touch with Leaphorn.

"Matter of fact, you have a message from him. Woman named Irene Musket called from Mexican Hat. She said Leaphorn headed down the San Juan—" Benally paused, chuckling. "You know," he said, "this sounds just like the screwy stuff you get mixed up in, Jim. Anyway, she said Leaphorn took off down the San Juan yesterday evening in a boat, looking for a boat this anthropologist you're looking for took. She was supposed to pick him up this morning at Mexican Hat, and call you if he didn't show up. Well, he didn't show up."

And just then the door opened behind Chee, letting in the cold breeze.

"Somebody here want a chopper ride?"

A burly, bald-headed man with a great yellow mustache was standing holding it open, looking at Chee. "You the daredevil who wants to fly out into this weather? I'm the daredevil here to take you."

EIGHTEEN

FINDING THE KAYAK Eleanor Friedman-Bernal had borrowed seemed simple enough to Leaphorn. She could have gone only downriver. The cliffs that walled in the San Juan between Bluff and Mexican Hat limited takeout places to a few sandy benches and the mouths of perhaps a score of washes and canyons. Since Leaphorn's reason and instincts told him her target ruin was on the reservation side of the river, his hunting grounds were further limited. And the description he had been given of the woman suggested she wouldn't be strong enough to pull the heavy rubber kayak very far out of the water. Therefore, finding it, even in the gathering darkness with only a flashlight, would be easy. Finding the woman would be the tough part.

Leaphorn had calculated without the wind. It

treated Houk's little craft like a sail, pushing against its sides and forcing Leaphorn into a constant struggle to keep it in the current. About four miles below the Bluff bridge, he let the kayak drift into a sandbar on the north side of the river, as much to stretch cramping muscles and give himself a rest as in any hope of finding something. On the cliffs here he found an array of petroglyphs cut through the black desert varnish into the sandstone. He studied a row of square-shouldered figures with chevron-like stripes above their heads and little arcs suggesting sound waves issuing from their mouths. If they hadn't predated the time his own people had invaded this stone wilderness, he would have thought they represented the Navajo *yei* called Talking God. Just above them was the figure of a bird— an unambiguous representation of the snowy egret. Above that, Kokopelli played his flute, bent so far forward that it pointed at the earth. The ground here was littered with shards of pottery but Leaphorn found no sign of the kayak. He hadn't expected to.

Relaunched, he paddled the kayak back into the current. Twilight now, and he found himself relaxing. Someone had said that "the rush of the river soothes the mind." It did seem to, in contrast to the sound of wind, which always made him tense. But the wind was moderating now.

He heard the call of a bird behind him, and a coyote somewhere on the Utah side, and the distant voice of rapids from the darkness ahead.

He checked two possible landing points on the reservation side, and spent more time than he'd planned looking at the mouths of Butler Wash and Comb Creek on the Utah side. When he pushed off again, it was into the light of the rising moon—a little past full. Leaphorn heard an abrupt flurry of sound. A snowy egret had been startled from its roosting place. It flew away from him into the moonlight, a graceful white shape moving against the black cliff, solitary, disappearing into the darkness where the river bent.

Egrets, he thought, were like snow geese and wolves and those other creatures—like Leaphorn himself—that mated only once and for life. That would explain its presence here. It was living out its loneliness in this empty place. Leaphorn's kayak slid out of the darkness under the cliff and into a moonlit eddy. His shadow streaked out from that of the kayak, making a strange elongated shape. It reminded him of the bird, and he waved the paddle to magnify the effect. As he rested with his arms relaxed, he became the stick figure of the *yei* Black God as Navajo shamans represented him in the dry painting of the Night Chant. Bent over the paddle, pulling his weight against the water, he was Kokopelli, with his hunched back full of sorrows. He was thinking that, as the current swept him around the cliff into the dark. Here, with all black except the stars directly overhead, the shout of the river drowned out everything.

As the San Juan drops toward its rendezvous with the mighty Colorado, its rapids are relatively mild. It is the goal of those who run rivers for joy to nose their tough little kayaks into the throats of these cataracts for the thrill of being buried under the white water. It was Leaphorn's goal to skirt the bedlam and keep dry. Even so, he emerged soaked from the waist down and well splashed elsewhere. The river here had cut through the Comb Ridge anticline—what millions of years of erosion had left of the Monument Upwarp. Here, eons ago, the earth's crust had bulged outward in a massive bubble of bending stone layers. Leaphorn drifted past slanting layers of stone which, even in this dim light, gave the eerie impression of sliding toward the center of the earth.

Beyond the anticline, he used his flashlight to check another sandy bench and the mouth of two washes. Then, around another bend and through another rapids, he guided the kayak into the eddy where Many Ruins Wash drained a huge expanse of the Navajo Reservation into the San Juan. If he had a specific destination when he left Sand Island, this was it.

Leaphorn had long since stopped trying to keep dry. He waded knee-deep through the eddy, pulled the kayak well ashore, and sat on the sand beside it, catching his breath. He was weary. He was wet. He was cold. Abruptly, he was very, very cold. He found himself shaking and unable to control the motion. His hands shook. So did his legs. His teeth chattered. Hypothermia. Leaphorn had suffered it before. It frightened him then and it frightened him now.

He pushed himself to his feet, staggered down the sand, the flashlight beam jittering erratically ahead of him. He found a place where a flash flood had left a tangle of twigs. He fumbled the lip balm tube in which he kept kitchen matches out of his jacket, managed to get his shaking fingers to open it, managed to stuff desiccated grass under a pile of twigs, managed on the third match to get the fire going. He added driftwood, fanned the fire into a blaze with his hat, and stood beside it, panting and shaking.

In his panic he had made the fire in the wrong place. Now, with his jeans steaming and some warmth returning to his blood, he looked around for a better place. He built this new fire where two walls of stone formed a sand-floored pocket, collecting enough heavy driftwood to keep it going until morning. Then he dried his clothing thoroughly.

This was where he'd expected to find the kayak. Up this canyon somewhere he expected to find the site that had drawn Eleanor Friedman-Bernal. When the river delayed him, he'd decided to wait for daylight to hunt the kayak. But now he couldn't wait. Tired as he was, he picked up the flashlight and walked back to the water.

She had hidden it carefully, dragging it with more strength than he credited her with far up under the tangled branches of a cluster of tamarisks. He searched, expecting to find nothing, and finding only a little nylon packet jammed under the center tube. It held a red nylon poncho. Leaphorn kept it. Back at the fire, he kicked himself a loosened place in the sand, spread the poncho as a ground cloth and lay down to sleep, leaving his boots close enough to the flames to complete the drying process.

The flames attracted flying insects. The insects attracted the bats. Leaphorn watched them fluttering at the margin of the darkness, darting to make their kill, flashing away. Emma had disliked bats. Emma had admired lizards, had battled roaches endlessly, had given names to the various spiders that lived around their house and—all too often—in it. Emma would have enjoyed this trip. He had always planned to take her, but there was never time, until now, when time no longer mattered. Emma would have been

intensely interested in the affair of Eleanor
Friedman-Bernal, would have felt a rapport with
her. Would have asked him, if he'd forgotten to
report, what progress was being made. Would
have had advice for him. Well, tomorrow he would
find that woman. A sort of gift, it would be.

He shifted himself into the sand. A chunk of
driftwood fell, sending a shower of sparks up toward the stars. Leaphorn slept.

The cold awakened him. The fire had burned
to dim embers, the moon was down, and the sky
over him was an incredible dazzle of stars humans can see only when high altitude, clear, dry
air, and an absence of ground light combine. Below these black thousand-foot cliffs, it was like
looking into space from the bottom of a well.
Leaphorn rebuilt the fire and dozed off again,
listening to the night sounds. Two coyotes were
on their nocturnal hunt now somewhere up the
canyon and he could hear another pair very distant across the river. He heard a saw-whet owl
high in the cliffs, a cry as shrill as metal rubbing
metal. Just as he fell into sleep he heard the
sound of a flute. Or perhaps it was just part of his
dream.

When he awoke again, he was shivering with
cold. It was late dawn, with the coldest air of
night settled into this canyon slot. He got up,
flinching against the stiffness, restarted the fire,

drank from his canteen, and looked for the first time into the sack of food Irene Musket had sent with him—a great chunk of fry bread and a coil of boiled Polish sausage. He was hungry, but he would wait. He might need it much more later.

Despite their age, he found a fair set of Eleanor Friedman-Bernal's tracks pressed into the hard sand under the tamarisks—where the hanging vegetation had protected them from the moving air. Then he methodically searched the rest of this junction of canyons. He wanted to confirm that this was the place Houk had come, and he did. In fact, Houk seemed to have come here often. Probably it was his monthly destination. Someone, presumably Houk, had repeatedly slid a kayak up the sloping sand at the extreme upper end of the bench and left it under a broken-off cottonwood. From there a narrow trail took an unlikely course about five hundred yards through the brush, through the little dunes of blown sand, and down into the bottom of Many Ruins. It stopped at a little cul-de-sac of boulders.

Leaphorn spent a half-hour in that much-used spot, partly because he could find no sign that Houk had gone beyond it. This sheltered place seemed to be where Houk's moonlit journeys ended. Again, he was looking for confirmation of what he was now sure must be true. This damp and protected place held footprints well, and

Houk's were everywhere. Many were fresh, evidence of the final visit before his murder. On these Leaphorn focused his attention, narrowing it finally to two prints. Both had been pressed upon by something heavy and partly erased. A soft, edgeless pressure. But not a moccasin. Something odd about it. Finally, looking at both prints from every possible angle, Leaphorn realized what caused the strange lines. Fur. But they weren't animal tracks. When patched together in Leaphorn's mind, the pressed places had the shape of a man's foot.

With nothing else to learn, Leaphorn started up-canyon. While he walked he considered what he was now almost certain were the facts. Brigham Houk probably had not drowned. Somehow he had managed to get across the river. Brigham Houk, the boy who had slaughtered his mother, his brother, and his sister, was somewhere in this canyon. Had been here almost twenty years, living away from people as he had longed to live. Houk had found the boy after the hue and cry of murder died away, had sustained him secretly all these years with whatever this born hunter had needed to stay alive. Nothing else seemed to explain Houk's note. Nothing else Leaphorn could think of would have motivated the man to stop an admittedly futile effort to build a hiding place to write a note. Houk didn't want this mad son of his abandoned here. He wanted him found by the same policeman who had once shown some awareness of the boy's humanity. He wanted him cared for, and he'd given up whatever minuscule chance he'd had of living to write his note. The writing had been tiny, Leaphorn remembered, and started at one end of the card. What would Houk have said had time allowed? Would he have explained about Brigham? He'd never know.

About two miles up the twisting canyon Leaphorn found the only sign of modern human occupancy. The bare poles of an old sweat bath stood on the broad shelf above the canyon floor. The ashes under it suggested it hadn't been used for years. If the canyon had ever been grazed, it hadn't been recently. He found no tracks of horses, sheep, or goats. The only hoofprints he found were mule deer, and there seemed to be plenty of rabbits, porcupines, and small rodents. He noticed three game trails leading to a deep spring-fed pothole at the canyon bottom. Four miles up, he stopped in a shady place and ate a small piece of the bread and a couple of inches of the sausage. There was heavy cloud cover over the northwest sky now. It was colder and yesterday's wind was back again now with a vengeance. It blew cross-canyon, forming powerful eddies of air that swirled this way here, and that way there.

It made the odd sounds wind makes when it pours through stony crevices. It sent whirlwinds of fallen leaves sweeping around Leaphorn's legs. It blotted out all other sound.

The wind made walking difficult, and the crooked, erratic nature of the canyon bottom made estimating distance—even for one as experienced as Leaphorn—little more than guesswork. Double guesswork, he thought. He had to guess how much of this climbing over tumbled boulders and detouring around brush would have added to the five and a half miles Etcitty had estimated. It would be less than that, he was sure, and he'd been looking for the landmarks Etcitty had mentioned since about mile three. Just ahead, where the canyon bottom made a sharp bend, he saw a crevice in the cliff walled in with stones—an Anasazi storeroom. On the cliff below it, half obscured by tall brush, he saw pictographs. He climbed the soft earth to the floor of the bench and pushed his way through the heavy growth of nettles for a closer look.

The dominant shape was one of those broad-shouldered, pin-headed figures that anthropologists believe represented Anasazi shamans. It looked, as Etcitty had described it, "like a big baseball umpire holding up a pink chest protector." Leaphorn recrossed the canyon bottom and climbed the shelf on the other side. He saw what he had come to find.

Near its beginnings in the Chuska Mountains, Many Ruins Canyon is cut deep and narrow through the Chinle sandstone formation of that plateau. There its cliffs rise sheer and vertical almost a thousand feet above a narrow, sandy bottom. It is much shallower by the time it emerges into Chinle Valley and becomes a mere drainage wash as it meanders northward toward Utah through the Greasewood Flats. But the cut deepens again in its passage through the Nokaito Bench to the San Juan. Here the crazy mishmash geology of the earth's crust had given Many Ruins a different shape. One climbed out of it on a series of steps. First the low, sometimes earthen cliffs that crowded its narrow streambed, then a broken sandstone shelf hundreds of yards wide, then more cliffs, rising to another shelf, and still more cliffs rising to the flat top of Nokaito Mesa.

In the spring when the snowpack melts a hundred miles away in the Chuska Mountains, Many Ruins carries a steady stream. In the late-summer thunderstorm season it rises and falls between a trickle and booming flash floods, which send boulders tumbling like marbles down its bottom. In late autumn it dries. The life that occupied it finds water then only in spring-fed potholes.

From where he stood on the sandstone shelf above such a pothole, Leaphorn could see the second of the ruins Etcitty had described. Two ruins, in fact.

Part of the wall of one was visible in an alcove in the second level of cliffs above him. Another, reduced to little more than a brushy hump, had been built along the base of the cliff not two hundred yards from the alcove.

All this day he had fought down his sense of excitement and urgency. He had a long ways to go and he went at a careful walk. Now he trotted across the sandstone bench.

He stopped when the alcove came in full view. Like those invariably picked as building sites by the Anasazi, it faced the low winter sun, with enough overhang to shade it in the summer. A cluster of brushy vegetation grew under it, telling him it was also the site of seep. He walked toward it, more slowly now. He didn't consider Brigham Houk particularly dangerous. Houk had called him schizophrenic—unpredictable but not likely to be a threat to a stranger. Still, he had killed once in an insane rage. Leaphorn unsnapped the flap that held his pistol in its holster.

Eons of water running down the inner face of the alcove had worn a depression several feet into the sandstone below it. Water stains indicated this held a pool about four feet deep in wetter seasons. Now only a foot or two was left—still fed by a tiny trickle from a mossy crevice in the cliff, and now green with algae. It was also the home of scores of tiny leopard frogs, which hopped away from Leaphorn's feet.

Only some of them hopped.

Leaphorn squatted, grunted with surprise. He studied the small scattered frog bodies, some already shriveled, some newly dead, each with a leg secured by a yucca thread to a tiny peg cut from a twig. He stood, trying to make sense of this. The pegs followed a series of faint concentric circles drawn around the pothole, the outside one perhaps four feet from the water. Some sort of game, Leaphorn guessed. He tried to understand the mind that would be amused by it. He failed. Brigham Houk was insane, probably dangerous.

He considered. Brigham Houk almost certainly would already know he was here.

Leaphorn made a megaphone of his hands. "Eleanor," he shouted. "Ellie. Ellie." Then he listened.

Nothing. Outside the alcove, the wind made whimpering sounds.

He tried again. Again, nothing.

The Anasazi had built their structure on a stone shelf above the pool. About a dozen small rooms once, Leaphorn estimated, with part of it at two levels. He skirted around the pool, climbed over the tumbled walls, peered into the still-intact rooms. Nothing. He walked back to the pool, puzzled. Where to look next?

At the edge of the alcove, a worn set of footholds had been cut into the sandstone—a climbway leading to the shelf above the alcove. Perhaps that led to another site. He walked out of the alcove around the cliff to the brushy hump. Immediately he saw it had been plundered. A ditch had been dug along the outside wall. Bones were scattered everywhere. The digging had been recent—hardly any rain since the earth was disturbed. Leaphorn inspected it. Was this why Eleanor Friedman-Bernal had slipped away from Chaco, slipped down the San Juan? To search this site for her polychrome pots? So it would seem. And what had happened then? What had interrupted her? He checked in the disturbed earth for shards and collected a handful. They might be the sort that interested her. He couldn't be sure. He looked down in the trench. Jutting from the earth was part of a pot. And another. In the bottom were a half-dozen shards, two of them large. Why had she left them there? Then he noticed an oddity. Among the bones littering the trench he saw no skulls. On the earth outside more than a dozen were scattered. None had jawbones. Natural, probably. The mandible would be attached only by muscle and gristle, which wouldn't survive an eight-hundred-year burial. Then where were the missing mandibles? He saw five of them together beside the trench, as if discarded there. It reminded him of the jawbones lined so neatly at the dig site where Etcitty and Nails had died.

But where was the woman who had dug the trench? He went back to the pool and inspected the footholds. Then he started climbing, thinking as he did that he was far too old for this. Fifty feet up the cliff, he was aware of two facts. These Anasazi footholds were in regular current use, and he was a damn fool to have attempted the climb. He clung to the stone, reaching blindly for the next handhold, wondering how many remained. Finally the slope eased. He looked up. He had done it. His head was almost even with the top. He pulled himself up, his upper body over the edge.

Standing there, watching him, was a man. He wore a beard cut straight across, a nylon jacket so new it still had the creases of its folds, a pair of tattered jeans, and moccasins that seemed to have been sewn together from deer hide.

"Mr. Leaphorn," the man said. "Papa said you coming."

NINETEEN

As Harrison Houk's message to him had promised, Dr. Eleanor Friedman-Bernal was still alive. She lay dozing under a gray wool blanket and a covering of sewn-together rabbit skins. She looked very, very ill.

"Can she talk?" he asked Brigham.

"A little," he said. "Sometimes."

It occurred to Leaphorn that Brigham Houk might have been describing himself. He talked very little and sometimes not at all. What you'd expect, Leaphorn thought, after twenty years of no one to talk to except once every full moon.

"How bad is it? Her injuries I mean?"

"Knee's hurt," he said. "Arm broken. Place in her side. Place in her hip."

And probably all infected, Leaphorn thought. Thin as her face was, it was flushed.

"You found her and brought her here?"

Brigham nodded. Like his father, he was a small man, tightly built, with short arms and legs and a thick, strong torso.

"Do you know what happened to her?"

"The devil came and hurt her," Brigham said in an odd, flat voice. "He hit her. She ran away. He chased. She fell down. He pushed her off. She fell into the canyon. Broke everything."

Brigham had made a bed for her by digging a coffin-shaped pit in the sand that had drifted into a room of the sheltered ruin. He'd filled it with a two- or three-foot layer of leaves. Open as it was to the air, it had the sickroom smell of urine and decay.

"Tell me about this," Leaphorn said.

Brigham was standing at what had been the entry door to the little room—now a narrow gap into a roofless space. Behind him the sky was dark. The wind, which had fallen during the afternoon, was blowing again now. It blew steadily out of the northwest. Winter, Leaphorn thought. He kept his eyes locked with Brigham's. The young man's eyes were the same odd blue-gray as his father's. Had the same intensity about them. Leaphorn looked into them, searching for insanity. Looking for it, he found it.

"This devil came," Brigham said, speaking very slowly. "He dug up the bones, and sat on the ground there looking at them. One after another he would look at them. He would measure them with a tool he had. He was looking for the souls of people who never had been prayed for. He would suck the souls out of the skulls and then he would throw them away. Or some of them he would take away in his sack. And then one day the last time the moon was full—" He paused and his somber bearded face converted into an expression of delight. "When the moon is full, that's when Papa comes and talks to me, and brings me what I need." The smile drifted away. "A little after that, this woman came." He nodded at Friedman-Bernal. "I didn't see her come and I think maybe the angel Moroni brought her because I didn't see her come and I see everything in this place. Moroni left her to fight with that devil. She had come to the old cliff house down below here where I keep my frogs. I didn't know she was there. I was playing my flute and I frightened her and she ran away. But the next day, she came to where the devil was digging up the bones. I saw them talking."

Brigham's mobile face became fierce. His eyes seemed to glitter with the anger. "He knocked her down, and he was on top of her, fighting with her. He got up and was searching through her pack, and she jumped up and ran over to the edge where the cliff drops down to the streambed and then she fell down. That devil, he went over and pushed her over with his foot." Brigham stopped, his face wet with tears.

"He just left her there, where she fell?"

Brigham nodded.

"You kept her alive," Leaphorn said. "But now I think she is starting to die. We have to get her out of here. To a hospital where doctors can give her medicine."

Brigham stared at him. "Papa said I could trust you." The statement was reproachful.

"If we don't get her out, she dies," Leaphorn said.

"Papa will bring medicine. The next time the moon is full he will come with it."

"Too long," Leaphorn said. "Look at her."

Brigham looked. "She's asleep," he said, softly.

"She has fever. Feel her face. How hot. She has infections. She has to have help."

Brigham touched Eleanor Friedman-Bernal's cheek with the tips of his fingers. He jerked them away, looking frightened. Leaphorn thought of the shriveled bodies of the frogs and tried to square that image with this tenderness. How do you square insanity?

"We need to make something to carry her on," Leaphorn said. "If you can find two poles long enough, we can tie the blanket between them and carry her on that."

"No," Brigham Houk said. "When I try to move her, to clean her after she does number one or number two, she screams. It hurts too bad."

"No choice," Leaphorn said. "We have to do it."

"It's terrible," Brigham said. "She screams. I can't stand that, so I had to leave her dirty." He looked at Leaphorn for understanding. Houk had apparently given him a haircut and trimmed his beard on the last visit. The old man was no barber. He had simply left the hair about an inch long everywhere, and whacked the beard off a half-inch under Brigham's chin.

"It was better to leave her dirty," Leaphorn said. "You did right. Now, can you find me two poles?"

Brigham nodded. "Just a minute. I have poles. It's close." He disappeared, making no sound at all.

Here is how it must have been when man lived as predator, Leaphorn thought. He developed the animal skills, and starved with his children when the skill failed him. How had Brigham hunted? Traps, probably, and a bow to kill larger game. Perhaps his father had brought him a gun—but someone might have heard gunshots. He listened to the sound of Eleanor Friedman's shallow breathing, and over that, the wind sounds. Suddenly he heard a thumping. Steady at first, then louder. He leaped to his feet. A helicopter. But before he could get into the open there was only the wind. He stared into the grayness, frustrated. He had found her. He must get her out of here alive. The risk lay in carrying such a fragile load over such rough terrain. It would be difficult. It might be impossible. A helicopter would save her. Why hadn't Houk done more to get her out? No time, Leaphorn guessed. His son had told him of this injured woman, but perhaps not how near she was to death. Houk would have wanted a way to save the woman without giving up this mad son to life (or perhaps death) in a prison for the criminally insane. Even Houk needed time to solve such a puzzle. He was too crippled to bring her out himself. If he did, she would talk of the man who had nursed her, and Brigham would be found— an insane triple murderer in the eyes of the law. The only solution Leaphorn saw would be to find Brigham another hideaway. That would take time, and the killer had allowed Houk no time.

The woman stirred, moaned. He and Brigham would have to carry her to the canyon bottom, then five miles down to the river. They could tie the kayaks together, put her litter on one of them, and float her to Mexican Hat. Five or six hours at least, and then an ambulance would come for her. Or the copter would come from Farmington if the weather allowed. It hadn't been too bad for whatever had just flown over.

He walked out under the dark sky. He smelled ozone. Snow was near. Then he saw Randall Elliot walking toward him.

Elliot raised his hand. "I saw you from up there," he said, pointing past Leaphorn to the rim of the mesa. "Came down to see if you needed help."

"Sure," Leaphorn said. "Lots of help."

Elliot stopped a few feet away. "You find her?"

Leaphorn nodded toward the ruin, remembering Elliot was a copter pilot.

"How is she?"

"Not good," Leaphorn said.

"But alive at least?"

"In a coma," Leaphorn said. "She can't talk." He wanted Elliot to know that immediately. "I doubt if she'll live."

"My God," Elliot said. "What happened to her?"

"I think she fell," Leaphorn said. "A long ways. That's what it looks like."

Elliot was frowning. "She's in there?" he said. "How did she get here?"

"A man lives out here. A hermit. He found her and he's been trying to keep her alive."

"I'll be damned," Elliot said. He moved past Leaphorn. "In here?"

Leaphorn followed. They stood, Elliot staring at Friedman-Bernal, Leaphorn watching Elliot.

He wanted to handle this just exactly right. Only Elliot could fly the helicopter.

"A hermit found her?" he said softly, posing the question to himself. He shook his head. "Where is he?"

"He went to get a couple of poles. We're going to make a litter. Carry her down to the San Juan. Her kayak's there, and mine. Float her down to Mexican Hat and get help."

Elliot was looking at her again, studying her. "I have a helicopter up on the mesa. We can carry her up there. Much quicker."

"Great," Leaphorn said. "Lucky you found us."

"Really, it was stupid," Elliot said. "I should have remembered about this place. She'd told me once she'd found the polychrome pattern she was chasing on potsherds in here. Back when she was helping inventory these sites. I knew she'd planned to come back." He turned away from the woman. His eyes locked with Leaphorn's.

"As a matter of fact, she said some things that made me think she had come here earlier. She didn't exactly say it, but I think she did some illegal digging in here. I think she found what she was looking for, and she came back to get some more."

"I think you're right," Leaphorn said. "She dug up that ruins on the shelf down below here. Dug up a bunch of graves."

"And got careless," Elliot added, looking at her.

Leaphorn nodded. Where was Brigham? He'd said just a minute. Leaphorn walked out of the ruin, looking along the talus slope under the cliff. Two poles leaned against the wall not ten feet away. Brigham had returned and seen his devil, and gone away. The poles were fir, apparently, and weathered. Driftwood, Leaphorn guessed, carried down Many Ruins all the way from the mountains by one of its flash floods. On the ground beside them was a loop of rawhide rope. He hurried back into the room with them.

"A very skittish man," Leaphorn said. "He left the poles and disappeared again."

"Oh," Elliot said. He looked skeptical.

They doubled the blanket, made lacing holes, and tied it securely to the poles.

"Be very careful," Leaphorn said. "Knee probably broken. Broken arm, all sorts of internal injuries."

"I used to collect the wounded," Elliot said, without looking up. "I'm good at this."

And Elliot seemed to be careful. Even so, Eleanor Friedman-Bernal uttered a strangled moan. Then she was unconscious again.

"I think she fainted," Elliot said. "Do you really think she's dying?"

"I do," Leaphorn said. "I'm giving you the

heavy end because you're younger and stronger and not so exhausted."

"Fair," Elliot said. He picked up the end of the poles at the woman's head.

"You know the way back to your copter, so you lead the way."

They carried Eleanor Friedman-Bernal carefully down the talus, then toward a long rock slide which sloped down from the rim. Beyond the slide—probably the cause of it—was a deep erosion cut which carried runoff water down from the top. Elliot turned toward the cut.

"Rest a minute," Leaphorn said. "Put her down on this slab."

He was fairly sure now what Elliot planned. Somewhere between here and the helicopter, wherever that was, something fatal had to happen to Eleanor Friedman-Bernal. Elliot simply could not risk having her arrive at a hospital alive. Ideally, something fatal would also happen to Leaphorn. If Elliot was smart, he would wait until they had climbed a hundred feet or so up the cut. Then he would push the litter backward, tumbling Friedman-Bernal and Leaphorn down the jumble of boulders. Then he would climb back down and do whatever was needed, if anything, to finish them off. A bang of the head on a rock would do it and leave nothing to arouse the suspicion of a medical examiner. Figuring that out had been easy enough. Knowing what to do about it was another matter. He could think of nothing. Shooting Elliot was shooting the copter pilot. Pointing a gun at him to force him to fly them out wasn't practical. Elliot would know Leaphorn wouldn't shoot him once they were airborne. He'd be able to make the helicopter do tricks that Leaphorn couldn't handle. And he probably had the little pistol. And yet, once they started that steep climb, Elliot had simply to drop his end of the litter and Leaphorn would be helpless.

"Is this the only way up?" Leaphorn asked.

"Only one I could see," Elliot said. "It's not as bad as it looks. We can take it slow."

"I'll wait here with the lady," Leaphorn said. "You fly the copter down here, land it somewhere where we don't have to make the climb." You could land a copter on this shelf if you had to, Leaphorn guessed. You'd have to be good, but someone who'd flown evacuations in Vietnam would be very good.

Elliot seemed to consider. "That's a thought," he said.

He reached into his jacket, extracted a small blue automatic pistol, and pointed it at Leaphorn's throat. "Unbuckle your belt," he said.

Leaphorn unbuckled it.

"Pull it out."

Leaphorn pulled it out. His holster fell to the ground.

"Now kick the gun over here to me."

Leaphorn did.

"You make it tough," Elliot said.

"Not tough enough."

Elliot laughed.

"You'd rather not have a bullet hole in me," Leaphorn said. "Or her either."

"That's right," Elliot said. "But I don't have any choice now. You seem to have figured it out."

"I figured you were going to get us far enough up the rocks to make it count and then tumble us down."

Elliot nodded.

"I'm not sure of your motive for all this. Killing so many people."

"Maxie told you that day," Elliot said. The good humor was suddenly gone, replaced by bitter anger. "What the hell can a rich kid do to impress anyone?"

"Impress Maxie," Leaphorn said. "A truly beautiful young woman." And he was thinking, maybe I'm like you. I don't want this to go wrong now because of Emma. Emma put little value on finding people to punish them. But this would really have impressed her. You love a woman, you want to impress her. The male instinct. Hero finds lost woman. The life saved. He didn't want it to go wrong now. But it had. In a very little while, wherever and whenever it was most convenient, Randall Elliot would kill Eleanor Friedman-Bernal and Joe Leaphorn. He could think of nothing to prevent it. Except maybe Brigham Houk.

Brigham must be somewhere near. It had taken him only minutes to get the poles and return. He had seen his devil, recognized him, and slipped away. Brigham Houk was a hunter. Brigham Houk was also insane, and afraid of this devil. What would he do? Leaphorn thought he knew.

"We'll leave her here for now and we'll walk over there," Elliot said, pointing with the pistol toward the edge of the shelf. It was exactly the direction Leaphorn wanted to go. It was the only way that led to convenient shelter. It must be the way Brigham had gone.

"It's going to look funny if too many people fall off things," Leaphorn said. "Two is too many."

"I know," Elliot said. "Do you have a better idea?"

"Maybe," Leaphorn said. "Tell me your motive for all this."

"I think you guessed," Elliot said.

"I guess Maxie," Leaphorn said. "You want her. But she's a self-made, class-conscious woman with a lot of bad memories of being put down by the upper class. On top of that, she's a tough one, a little mean. She resents you, and everybody like you, because it's all handed to you. So I think you're going to do something that has nothing to do with being born to the upper, upper, upper class. Something that neither Maxie nor anybody else can ignore. From what you told me at Chaco it's something to do with tracing what happened to these Anasazi by tracking genetic flaws."

"How about that," Elliot said. "You're not as dumb as you try to act."

"You found the flaw you were hunting in the bones here, and over at the site on the Checkerboard, too, I guess. You were digging here illegally, and our friend here came in and caught you at it."

Elliot held up his empty hand. "So I tried to kill her and screwed it up."

"Curious about something," Leaphorn said. "Were you the one who called in the complaint about Eleanor being a pot hunter?"

"Sure," Elliot said. "You figured why?"

"Not really," Leaphorn said. Where the devil was Brigham Houk? Maybe he'd run. Leaphorn doubted it. His father wouldn't have run. But then his father wasn't schizophrenic.

"You can't get a permit to dig," Elliot said. "Not in your lifetime. These asshole bureaucrats are always saving it for the future. Well, if a site is being vandalized, that puts it in a different category. Not so tough then, after it's already been messed up. I was going to follow up later with some hints about where to find digs Eleanor was stealing from. They'd find her body, so they'd have their Thief of Time. They wouldn't have to be looking for one and maybe suspecting me. And then I'd get my dig permit." He laughed. "Roundabout way, but I've seen it work."

"You were getting your bones anyway," Leaphorn said. "Buying some, digging some up yourself."

"Wrong category, friend," Elliot said. "Those are unofficial bones. Not 'in site.' I was finding 'em unofficially, so I'd know where to find 'em officially when I got my permit. You understand that?" Elliot peered at him, grinning. He was enjoying this. "When I get my permit to excavate, I come back and the bones I find then are registered in place. Photographed. Documented." He grinned again. "Same bones, maybe, but now they're official."

"How about Etcitty," Leaphorn asked, "and Nails?" Over Elliot's shoulder, Leaphorn had seen Brigham Houk. He saw Houk because the man wanted Leaphorn to see him. He was behind a fallen sandstone slab, screened by brush. He held something that might have been a curved staff and he motioned Leaphorn toward him.

"That was a mistake," Elliot said.

"Killing them?"

Elliot laughed. "That was correcting the mistake. Nails was too careless. And too greedy. Once the silly bastards stole that backhoe they were sure to get caught." He glanced at Leaphorn. "And Nails was sure to tell you guys everything he knew."

"Which would have been bad for your reputation," Leaphorn said.

"Disastrous," Elliot said. He waved the pistol. "But hurry it up. I want to get out of here."

"If you're working on what I think," Leaphorn said, "there's something I want to show you. Something Friedman-Bernal found. You're interested in jaw deformities. Something like that?"

"Well, a little like that," Elliot said. "You understand how the human chromosome works? Fetus inherits twenty-three from its mother, twenty-three from its father. Genetic characteristics handed down in the genes. Once in a while polyploidy occurs in the genetic crossover points. Someone gets multiple chromosomes, and you get a characteristic change. Inheritable. But you need more than one to do a trace which has any real meaning. At Chaco, in some of the early Chaco burials, I found three that were passed along. A surplus molar in the left mandible. And that went along with a thickening of the frontal bone over the left eye socket, plus—" Elliot stopped. "You understanding this?"

"Genetics wasn't my favorite course. Too much math," Leaphorn said. What the devil was Brigham Houk doing? Was he still behind that slab up ahead?

"Exactly," Elliot said, pleased by this. "It's one percent digging and ninety-nine percent working out statistical models for your computer. Anyway, the third thing, which sort of mathematically proves the passalong genes, is that hole in the mandible through which the blood and nerve tissue passes. At Chaco, from about 650 A.D. until they turned out the lights, this family had two holes in the left mandible and the usual one in the right. Plus those other characteristics. And out here, I'm still finding it among these exiles. Can you see why it's important?"

"And fascinating," Leaphorn said. "Dr. Friedman must have known what you were looking for. She saved a lot of jawbones." He was almost to the great sandstone slab. "I'll show you."

"I doubt if she found anything I overlooked," Elliot said. He followed Leaphorn, keeping the pistol level. "But this is the way we were going anyway."

They were passing the sandstone now. Leaphorn tensed. If nothing happened here, he would have to try something else. It wouldn't work, but he wouldn't simply stand still to be shot.

"Right over here," Leaphorn said.

"I think you're just—"

The sentence ended with a grunt, a great exhalation of breath. Leaphorn turned. Elliot was leaning slightly forward, the pistol hanging at his side. About six inches of arrow shaft and the feathered tip protruded from his jacket.

Leaphorn reached for him, heard the whistle and thump of the second arrow. It went through Elliot's neck. The pistol clattered on the stone. Elliot collapsed.

Leaphorn retrieved the pistol. He squatted beside the man, turned him on his back. His eyes were open but he seemed to be in shock. Blood trickled from the corner of his mouth.

There was snow in the wind now, little dry flakes that skittered along the surface like white dust. Leaphorn tested the arrow. It was the sort of bow hunters buy in sporting goods stores and it was lodged solidly through Elliot's neck. Pulling it out would just make things worse. If they could be worse. Elliot was dying. Leaphorn stood, looking for Brigham Houk. Houk was standing beside the slab now, holding a great ugly bow of metal, wood, and plastic, looking upward. From somewhere Leaphorn heard the clatter of a helicopter. Brigham Houk had heard it earlier. He stood very close to cover, ready to vanish.

The helicopter emerged over the rim of the mesa almost directly overhead. Leaphorn waved, saw an answering wave. The copter circled and disappeared over the mesa again.

Leaphorn checked Elliot's pulse. He didn't seem to have one. He looked for Brigham Houk, who seemed never to have existed. He walked over to the litter where Dr. Eleanor Friedman-Bernal lay. She opened her eyes, looked at him without recognition, closed them again. He tucked the rabbit fur cloak around her, careful to apply no pressure. Now it was snowing harder, still blowing like dust. He walked back to Elliot. No pulse now. He opened his jacket and shirt and felt for a heartbeat. Nothing. The man was no longer breathing. Randall Elliot, graduate of Exeter, of Princeton, of Harvard, winner of the Navy Cross, was dead by arrow shot. Leaphorn gripped him under the arms and pulled him into the cover of the slab where Brigham Houk had hidden. Elliot was heavy, and Leaphorn was exhausted. By pulling hard and doing some twisting, he extracted the arrows. He wiped the blood off as well as he could on Elliot's jacket. Then he picked up a rock, hammered them into pieces, and put the pieces in his hip pocket. That done, he found dead brush, broke it off, and made an inefficient effort to cover the body. But it didn't matter. The coyotes would find Randall Elliot anyway.

Then he heard the clatter of someone scrambling down the cut. It proved to be Officer Chee, looking harassed and disheveled.

It took some effort for Leaphorn not to show he was impressed. He pointed to the litter. "We need to get Dr. Friedman to the hospital in a hurry," he said. "Can you get that thing down here to load her?"

"Sure," Chee said. He started back toward the cut at a run.

"Just a second," Leaphorn said.

Chee stopped.

"What did you see?"

Chee raised his eyebrows. "I saw you standing beside a man slumped down on the ground. I guess it was Elliot. And I saw the litter over there. And maybe I saw another man. Something jumping out of sight back there just as we came over the top."

"Why did you think it was Elliot?"

Chee looked surprised. "The helicopter he rented is parked up there. I figured when he heard she was still alive he'd have to come out here and kill her before you got here."

Leaphorn again was impressed. This time he

made a little less effort to conceal it. "Do you know how Elliot knew she was alive?"

Chee made a wry face. "I more or less told him."

"And then made the connection?"

"Then I found out he had filed for permission to dig this site, and the site where he killed Etcitty. Turned down on both of them. I went out there to talk to him and found—you remember the box of plastic wastebasket liners at the Checkerboard site. One missing from it. Well, it was hidden in Elliot's kitchen. Had jawbones in it."

Leaphorn didn't ask how Chee had gotten into Elliot's kitchen.

"Go ahead, then, and get the copter down here. And don't say anything."

Chee looked at him.

"I mean don't say anything at all. I'll fill you in when we get a chance."

Chee trotted toward the cut.

"Thank you," Leaphorn said. He wasn't sure if Chee heard that.

It was snowing hard by the time they had the litter loaded and the copter lifted off the shelf. Leaphorn was jammed against the side. He looked down on a stone landscape cut into vertical blocks by time and now blurred by snow. He looked quickly away. He could ride the big jets, barely. Something in his inner ear made anything less stable certain nausea. He closed his eyes, swallowed. This was the first snow. They would come when the weather cleared to recover the copter and look for Elliot. But they wouldn't look hard because it was so obviously hopeless. Snow would have covered everything. After the thaw, they would come again. Then they would find the bones, scattered like the Anasazi skeletons he looted. There would be no sign of the arrow wounds then. Cause of death unknown, the coroner would write. Victim eaten by predators.

He glanced back. Chee was jammed in the compartment beside the litter, his hand on Dr. Eleanor Friedman-Bernal's arm. She seemed to be awake. I will ask him what curing ceremony he would recommend, Leaphorn thought, and knew at once that his fatigue was making him silly. Instead he said nothing. He thought of the circumstances, of how proud Emma would be of him tonight if she could be home to hear about this woman brought safely to the hospital. He thought about Brigham Houk. In just about twenty-four more days, the moon would be full again. Brigham would be waiting at the mouth of Many Ruins Canyon, but Papa wouldn't come.

I will go, Leaphorn thought. Someone has to tell him. And that meant that he would have to postpone his plan to leave the reservation, probably a long postponement. Solving the problem of what to do about Brigham Houk would take more than one trip down the river. And if he had to stick around, he might as well withdraw that letter. As Captain Nez had said, he could always write it again.

Jim Chee noticed Leaphorn was watching him.

"You all right?" Chee asked.

"I've felt better," Leaphorn said. And then he had another thought. He considered it. Why not? "I hear you're a medicine man. I heard you are a singer of the Blessing Way. Is that right?"

Chee looked slightly stubborn. "Yes sir," he said.

"I would like to ask you to sing one for me," Leaphorn said.

TONY HILLERMAN was a former president of the Mystery Writers of America and received the Edgar and Grand Master Awards. His other honors include the Center for the American Indian's Ambassador Award, the Spur Award for Best Western Novel and the Navajo Tribal Council Special Friend of the Dineh award. He lived with his wife in Albuquerque, New Mexico.

www.tonyhillermanbooks.com

BOOKS BY TONY HILLERMAN

THE BLESSING WAY
Available in Paperback, Mass Market, and eBook

DANCE HALL OF THE DEAD
Available in Paperback, Mass Market, and eBook

LISTENING WOMAN
Available in Paperback, Mass Market, and eBook

PEOPLE OF DARKNESS
Available in Paperback, Mass Market, and eBook

THE GHOSTWAY
Available in Paperback, Mass Market and eBook

SKINWALKERS
Available in Paperback, Mass Market and eBook

A THIEF OF TIME
Available in Paperback, Mass Market and eBook

TALKING GOD
Available in Mass Market, eBook, and Digital Audio

COYOTE WAITS
Available in Mass Market and eBook

SACRED CLOWNS
Available in Paperback, Mass Market, eBook, and Digital Audio

THE FALLEN MAN
Available in Mass Market, eBook, and Digital Audio

THE FIRST EAGLE
Available in Mass Market and eBook

HUNTING BADGER
Available in Mass Market, eBook, and Audiobook CD

THE WAILING WIND
Available in Mass Market, eBook, and Audiobook CD

THE SINISTER PIG
Available in Mass Market and eBook

SKELETON MAN
Available in Mass Market and eBook

THE SHAPE SHIFTER
Available in Mass Market, eBook, Audiobook CD, and Large Print

THE BEST OF THE WEST
Available in Paperback

SELDOM DISAPPOINTED
Available in Paperback and eBook

BOOKS BY ANNE HILLERMAN

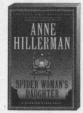

SPIDER WOMAN'S DAUGHTER
A Leaphorn, Chee & Manuelito Novel
Available in Paperback, eBook, Mass Market, Large Print, and Digital Audio

"Chip off the literary block—there are a lot of things Tony taught his daughter, Anne, and one of them was how to tell a good story. *Spider Woman's Daughter* is a proud addition to the legacy, capturing the beauty and breath of the Southwest as only a Hillerman can."
—Craig Johnson, author of the Walt Longmire Mysteries

ROCK WITH WINGS
A Leaphorn, Chee & Manuelito Novel
Available in Paperback, eBook, Mass Market, Large Print, and Digital Audio

"Hillerman uses the southwestern setting as effectively as her late father did while skillfully combining Native American lore with present-day social issues."
—*Publishers Weekly*

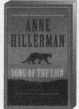

SONG OF THE LION
A Leaphorn, Chee & Manuelito Novel
Available in Paperback, eBook, Mass Market, Large Print, and Digital Audio

"Hillerman seamlessly blends tribal lore and custom into a well-directed plot, continuing in the spirit of her late father, Tony, by keeping his characters (like Chee) in the mix, but still establishing Manuelito as the main player in what has become a fine legacy series."
—*Booklist*

CAVE OF BONES
A Leaphorn, Chee & Manuelito Novel
Available in Hardcover, Mass Market, eBook, Large Print, and Digital Audio

"This fictional universe now belongs firmly in the hands of Anne Hillerman."
—*New York Journal of Books*

TONY HILLERMAN'S LANDSCAPE
On the Road with Chee and Leaphorn
Available in Hardcover and eBook

Narrated by his daughter, Anne Hillerman, with original photos from Don Strel, *Tony Hillerman's Landscape* is a timely showcase of a hauntingly beautiful region that captured one man's imagination for a lifetime, and is a daughter's loving tribute to her father.

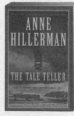

THE TALE TELLER
A Leaphorn, Chee & Manuelito Novel
Available in Hardcover, Mass Market, eBook, Large Print, and Digital Audio

"A natural hit with Hillerman's many fans; [The Tale Teller] is also a good choice for readers who are interested in fiction touching on today's social issues."
—*Booklist*